Tattered Loyalties

A Talon Pack Novel

CARRIE ANN RYAN

Author Highlights

Praise for Carrie Ann Ryan....

"Carrie Ann Ryan knows how to pull your heartstrings and make your pulse pound! Her wonderful Redwood Pack series will draw you in and keep you reading long into the night. I can't wait to see what comes next with the new generation, the Talons. Keep them coming, Carrie Ann!" –Lara Adrian, New York Times bestselling author of CRAVE THE NIGHT

"Carrie Ann Ryan never fails to draw readers in with passion, raw sensuality, and characters that pop off the page. Any book by Carrie Ann is an absolute treat." – New York Times Bestselling Author J. Kenner

"With snarky humor, sizzling love scenes, and brilliant, imaginative worldbuilding, The Dante's Circle series reads as if Carrie Ann Ryan peeked at my personal wish list!" – NYT Bestselling Author, Larissa Ione

"Carrie Ann Ryan writes sexy shifters in a world full of passionate happily-ever-afters." – *New York Times* Bestselling Author Vivian Arend

"Carrie Ann's books are sexy with characters you can't help but love from page one. They are heat and heart blended to perfection." *New York Times* Bestselling Author Jayne Rylon

Carrie Ann Ryan's books are wickedly funny and deliciously hot, with plenty of twists to keep you guessing. They'll keep you up all night!" USA Today Bestselling Author Cari Quinn

"Once again, Carrie Ann Ryan knocks the Dante's Circle series out of the park. The queen of hot, sexy, enthralling paranormal romance, Carrie Ann is an

author not to miss!" *New York Times* bestselling
Author Marie Harte
Praise for the Redwood Pack Series...

"You will not be disappointed in the Redwood Pack."
Books-n-Kisses
"I was so completely immersed in this story that I felt
what the characters felt. BLOWN AWAY." *Delphina's
Book Reviews.*
"I love all the wolves in the Redwood Pack and eagerly
anticipate all the brothers' stories." *The Book Vixen*
"Shifter romances are a dime a dozen, but good ones
aren't as plentiful as one would think. This is one of
the goods one." *Book Binge*
"With the hints of things to come for the Redwoods, I
can't wait to read the next book!" *Scorching Book
Reviews*
"Ryan outdid herself on this book." *The Romance
Reviews*

Praise for the Dante's Circle Series...

"This author better write the next books quickly or I
will Occupy Her Lawn until she releases more! Pure
romance enjoyment here. Now go put this on your
TBR pile—shoo!" *The Book Vixen*
"I, for one, will definitely be following the series to see
what happens to the seven." *Cocktails & Books*
"The world of Dante's Circle series is enthralling and
with each book gets deeper and deeper as does Carrie
Ann's writing." Literal Addiction

Praise for the Montgomery Ink Series...

"Shea and Shep are so cute together and really offset
each other in a brilliant way. " *Literal Addiction*

"This was a very quick and spicy read. I really enjoyed reading about Sassy, Rafe & Ian. I really hope there will be more of these three in the future." *Books n Kisses*

Praise for the Holiday, Montana Series...

"Charmed Spirits was a solid first book in this new series and I'm looking forward to seeing where it goes." *RR@H Novel Thoughts & Book Thoughts*
"If you're looking for a light book full of magic, love and hot little scenes on various objects, then this book is for you! You'll soon find that tables are no longer for eating meals of the food variety ... Bon appétit!" *Under the Covers*
"The book was well written and had the perfect setting the steamy bits where really really hot and the story one of sweet romance. Well done Carrie" *Bitten by Love Reviews*

Dedication

To Kennedy. Thank you darling for pushing me.

Author's Note

Thank you all for picking up Tattered Loyalties! I do hope you enjoy Gideon and Brie's story. In case you didn't know, this book is also set in the same world as The Redwood Pack series. It's set thirty years after the end of Fighting Fate (Book 7) and has a few familiar faces. However if you're new to the series, then welcome! You do not need to read the other series to jump into this one. Thank you so much for reading!

TATTERED LOYALTIES

When the great war between the Redwoods and the Centrals occurred three decades ago, the Talon Pack risked their lives for the side of good. After tragedy struck, Gideon Brentwood became the Alpha of the Talons. But the Pack's stability is threatened, and he's forced to take mate—only the one fate puts in his path is the woman he shouldn't want.

Though the daughter of the Redwood Pack's Beta, Brie Jamenson has known peace for most of her life. When she finds the man who could be her mate, she's shocked to discover Gideon is the Alpha wolf of the Talon Pack. As a submissive, her strength lies in her heart, not her claws. But if her new Pack disagrees or disapproves of fate's choice, the consequences could be fatal.

As the worlds Brie and Gideon have always known begin to shift, they must face their challenges together in order to help their Pack and seal their bond. But when the Pack is threatened from the inside, Gideon doesn't know who he can trust and Brie's life could be forfeit in the crossfire. It will take the strength of an Alpha and the courage of his mate to realize where true loyalties lie.

CHAPTER ONE

He really needed to kill this bastard.

Gideon Brentwood rolled his neck, enjoying the slight crack that came when he stretched it just right. He had enough tension in his shoulders to make him feel as though the world rested on his shoulders. He didn't feel like killing today, although the prospect of the fight slid through his veins and pumped adrenaline into his system.

His wolf craved the fight, the dominance.

The man just wanted this to end so he could get on with his day.

He was so freaking tired of doing this over and over again. They never seemed to learn.

The lone wolf in front of him had tried to lay claim to the Talon land and had challenged Gideon's role as Alpha.

Stupid wolf.

The moon goddess gave him his title, but he had been fighting to keep it every day since.

The slice on his chest burned, but he shrugged it off. He was the Alpha, and this lone wolf couldn't hurt him if Gideon put his head in the game. The fact that his head *wasn't* in the game told him how tired he was of all the challenges.

He smelled the rotten odor coming from his opponent and heard his labored breathing. The wolf had been rangy and dying before he'd set his first paw on Talon land, and Gideon would be forced to end his life if the intruder didn't back down. Goddess, he hated his duty, hated this role he'd been forced to take, but if he didn't do it, who else would?

His cousin Mitchell and his brother Ryder stood back, their gazes on the fight. They wouldn't be jumping in and helping unless the lone wolf pulled a trick or dark magic out of the air. He didn't need them there and this wasn't their fight, but his wolf appreciated their presence anyway.

The taste of blood was seconds away, and he knew, without a doubt, that he could either kill or maim the intruder—challenge or no, this wolf *was* a coward—in front of him.

The first possibility weighed heavily on his mind. The second would be par for the course.

"Yield," Gideon growled, low, deadly.

The wolf yipped at him but didn't lower his head fully, nor did he meet Gideon's eyes or challenge him in that respect. Gideon wasn't sure the wolf had enough energy to do so in the first place.

He let out a breath. "If you don't yield, I'm going to have to kill you. You get that, right? You're not strong enough to beat me, and I can't let a wolf who challenges me go without punishment. You know our ways. If you yield, I won't have to kill you." It was a technicality, but one he'd greedily use if he needed to.

He was tired of the death, the pain, and the loss of the little parts of his soul that were stripped away with each kill, each *justified* death. He'd killed the one man who should have protected him, and now he had to deal with the day-to-day responsibilities and consequences that came from that one decision.

It haunted him with each breath, each step he took, even though thirty years had passed since he killed the wolf who'd tried to kill them all.

Now Gideon was once again faced with a decision that might ultimately take the last piece of his soul away. It wasn't as if he truly needed it. He was Alpha. He could function and rule without those facets of his psyche he'd once relied on and had thought were the most important parts of him.

Through absolute necessity, he had become a man who would not hesitate to kill and would make any sacrifice in order to keep his people safe.

The wolf in front of him growled again, and Gideon sighed.

There would be no retribution this day. No healing and forgiveness. He would do what he had to do in order to protect his family and his Pack.

He'd deal with the consequences later.

He always did.

The lone wolf leaped at him, and Gideon rolled out of the way, coming to his feet in a swift movement. He didn't need to shift fully into his wolf form. One: That would take too long. He might be the Alpha and able to shift faster than any of his other wolves, but that didn't mean he had the time to spare right then. Two: He was dominant enough that he could partially shift his hands into claws and keep them there without losing control like so many other wolves did.

He let his wolf come to the surface, fully aware it was begging for a fight. In the twilight hour, he could see the glow from the rim of gold around his irises, reflected on the fur of his opponent. Gideon's eyes only lit up when he was ready to fight or fuck. And since it had been way too fucking long since he'd had a woman, he knew the fighting was the reason. He needed this to end soon though, or his pent up aggression from the lack of the former would roll over and he'd be screwed. He couldn't waste any more time on this lone wolf, sad as it was.

The wolf struck again, this time swiping along Gideon's side. Two lucky shots from the bastard. He was going to win—that was never in doubt. The question was how much he'd get hurt in the process. Now he just had to see how long he'd need to draw the process out. At this point, he was merely tiring out the bastard. Yeah, the lone wolf was getting a few hits in, but that was because Gideon was off his game.

Though that would be one way to do it, he didn't want to prolong the fight. It wasn't fair to the wolf to make him suffer any more than he had already. He didn't know this wolf, didn't know why he was without a Pack and trying to fight the Talons. It didn't matter. Gideon would protect what was his no matter what.

He growled softly then bent at the knees, letting the wolf think he had the advantage. The lone wolf pounced again, his large, menacing teeth bared. Gideon struck the other wolf with his claws around the neck, piercing its flesh. It let out a small whine then went limp when Gideon twisted.

The wolf had been as good as dead before he stepped on Talon land.

Gideon *knew* this.

It didn't make the kill any easier.

"That was the second lone wolf in as many months," Mitchell, his cousin and Beta, remarked casually as he made his way to Gideon's side. Mitchell and his brother, Max, had been raised with Gideon and his brothers, so he was practically a brother.

"I don't like how close he got to hurting you," Ryder, his Heir and brother, said softly. Ryder always

4

spoke softly, unless there was something that needed to be growled, though Gideon wasn't sure why. It was just the way his brother worked.

Gideon looked down at the two gashes on his side and chest and shrugged. "They'll heal well enough. He didn't get too deep."

"I don't know why you let him get that close to begin with," Mitchell snapped. His brother squatted down near the lone wolf's body and let out a sigh. "Why the hell did he challenge you? It makes no sense. From the smell of him, he clearly wasn't healthy or strong enough to fight even our weaker dominants. Why fight our Alpha?"

Gideon raised his hand to run it over his face then paused. Shit, he still had blood on his hands—literally and figuratively. He needed to go home and shower to try to wash away some of this piss-poor day.

Piss-poor decade it seemed like.

"I don't know, Mitchell," Gideon finally answered. "Could be lots of things. Maybe he wanted to go out fighting an Alpha. Maybe his wolf took over and had to challenge. Maybe someone made him do it. I just don't fucking know anymore."

Ryder knelt down by the body and let out a breath. "I'll bury him. I don't like the fact that we don't know who he is or if he has family somewhere. He might be lone, but that doesn't mean he's alone."

That made a twisted sort of sense. Just because a wolf didn't have a Pack didn't mean he didn't live with a family. Packs were there to protect, nourish, and comfort. The bonds made between members, as well as the Alpha and the other members of the hierarchy, helped not only control the wolf inside but also formed a unit that spoke of something more than friendship and family.

Sometimes wolves were born outside of the den or left over the years for one reason or another—banished or not—and ended up Packless. Gideon wasn't too fond of the numbers being so vague, but the world was shifting faster than he could blink. It wouldn't be long before they couldn't hide their existence anymore, and the fact that there were wolves out there not under the protection and rule of an Alpha worried him.

A lot worried him these days.

"I'll help you bury him," Gideon finally said to Ryder. "I took his life. I'll help lay him to rest."

Mitchell and Ryder gave him long looks then nodded. It didn't matter if they said he couldn't help. He was Alpha, and this was his responsibility in more ways than one.

They dug the hole deep enough that no critters could find the body and said a prayer to the moon goddess. The wolf might have challenged Gideon, but that didn't mean he deserved eternal damnation. Gideon wasn't conceited enough to think he had the right to judge.

"I'm going to go get cleaned up," he said once they finished their work.

Mitchell pulled out his phone. "I'll make sure Walker is there for you when you show up."

Gideon closed his eyes and let out a curse. "I don't need the Healer. I'm fine. Don't make him waste his powers and energy on these superficial cuts."

Ryder raised a brow. "Walker's your brother, our brother, so yeah, he's going want to make sure you're okay. Plus, the Redwoods are coming to the den for our meeting. You forget that? You don't want to smell of blood and weakness in front of another Alpha and his Pack. It doesn't matter that Kade and the rest of them are our friends. They aren't Talons."

Gideon looked up at the sky and prayed for just a moment's rest. Was that really too much to ask for?

"Did you forget about the meeting?" Mitchell asked from behind him.

Gideon sighed. "No." *Yes.* "Let's get this over with so I can go make nice with the others," he growled.

"I thought Kade was your friend," Ryder added as they made their way through the forest to the center of the den. His brother kept looking over his shoulder, as if he was afraid Gideon was going to keel over any minute. He might be the eldest brother, but he wasn't weak. Ryder, though, tended to worry about those close to him more than he cared about himself. Luckily, his brother was also a wolf and turned away from Gideon in time to make sure he didn't trip on their way through the den.

The Talon Pack den was located in central Oregon with their territory reaching into northern California. Most of the Packs across the United States were far older than the country itself, so their boundaries had to do with landmarks rather than arbitrary lines. They shared a neutral territory with the Redwoods, who lived in western Oregon. Thanks to the humans' national initiatives, the wolves' forests had been untouched and safe from human eyes for centuries. The den might have been surrounded by wards infused with wolf and witch magic so humans were repelled from the area, but without the trees and the ability to hide from prying eyes, they wouldn't be as safe as they were.

Or at least as safe as they used to be.

That was one reason they were meeting with Kade and the other Redwoods in their den today. It used to be that only the right people knew about the fact that shifters existed. Now, though, far too many people knew and some were...*searching*. Human patrols were

7

getting too close to their den as well as the Redwoods' den, and no amount of magic would save them if technology found them. The majority of the population might not know about shifters, but those who did and weren't on the wolves' side, were on a hunt. Those military and even civilian patrols hid themselves as well, so normal humans remained unaware of a potential war on and within their borders.

As it was, too many of the wrong people knew about the existence of wolves. The military had long since known about them and had even used them as soldiers when they could. Some higher-ups in the government knew about them, but not everyone. If certain factions ever found out...well, Gideon didn't want to think about that. He knew he would be forced to face it eventually—sooner rather than later if the feeling in his gut was any indication—but he wasn't sure how his people were going to remain safe once the secret was out.

In the thirty years since the Central war had ended and the Redwoods and Talons had formed a treaty, they had been forced to learn to rely on each other through thick or thin. The fact that they were running out of land and methods to conceal their existence meant they would have to rely on each other once again.

Gideon wasn't sure if they would ever be ready to come out to the humans, but at some point, they might not have a choice in the matter.

Cameras and satellites were far too precise and could track them with the click of a button. Magic went only so far, and he was afraid they'd strained their powers enough as it was.

If they were going to come out to human society, they were going to have to do it their way.

That is, if they could decide on what that way was.

After all, there were more than just the two Packs in the United States and far more than that all over the world. In the past fifteen years since they'd formed the Northwest Council, they'd done their best to open the lines of communication in ways that no one had ever thought possible, and with their Voice of the Wolves, Parker Jamenson, they were at least trying to maintain peace within their own dens.

For some reason, Gideon didn't think the next battle he fought would be claw against claw. No, the next would be far worse.

He shook his head, trying to clear his thoughts. He didn't have time to think about the end of the world, *his* world, right then. He pressed his hand against the keypad to unlock his home then walked through the door. He needed to wash off the blood of decisions that were beyond his control. He was in the middle of a world that didn't make sense—one where rites and rituals of the past warred with the technology and unknowns of his present.

He was almost afraid to see what his future would be.

"Took you long enough to get here," Walker remarked from his spot in Gideon's kitchen.

Gideon snorted then peeled off his shirt, ignoring the aches and pains. The fabric stuck to his cuts and dried blood, but he was healing well.

Walker clucked his tongue like a mother hen then rubbed his hands together. "I *will* Heal these wounds so you're in top form when there are other wolves about. I don't want to hear any lip from you."

Gideon raised a brow. "You're the one being lippy. Remember, I'm the Alpha. And, hello, I'm the eldest brother. You're the baby."

Walker snorted then pressed his hands to Gideon's wounds. At the sharp warmth, he sucked in a breath then released it slowly.

"We're over a hundred years old, Gideon. At some point, being younger or older shouldn't matter. And, I'll have you know, Brandon is younger than me. So there."

Gideon smiled at the familiar remark. "You're like five minutes older than Brandon, and Kameron is another five minutes older than you."

Walker rolled his eyes then narrowed them as he examined Gideon's skin. "You're Healed but don't go getting sliced up for a couple of days. There's only so much skin I can knit together at a time."

Gideon nodded his thanks then headed back to his shower. He was starting to itch from the blood and mud coating his body, and that wasn't a pleasant feeling. He probably should have been used to it considering how many times he'd been covered in it over his life, but he also hoped he never did.

"Any idea what we're going to talk about?" Walker asked as he leaned against the bathroom door.

Gideon shrugged out of his clothes then stepped into his shower letting the hot water pound down his back. His muscles ached from the fight and the tension of the unknown.

He closed his eyes and spoke loudly over the hum of the water. Walker probably would have been able to hear him with his sensitive hearing, but he didn't want his brother to have to strain. "We're going to talk about plans to come out to the public. Or, at least, plans to make plans. Then we're going to make sure our underground tunnels are in shape since the connection between the two packs is relatively new."

No one knew what would happen once the humans found out about the existence of shifters and demons. They'd been planning for years, though, on the eventual outcome of protecting themselves from people who didn't understand and feared what they didn't know. It wasn't like underground tunnels were the perfect way to save his people, but it was only one of their many steps. They needed to be able to hide their most precious and those unable to protect themselves quickly in case the wards went down. They also had other procedures in place, but he needed to talk to Kade to ensure that as much as they could do was being done.

He let out a breath and quickly soaped up, knowing he was running late. Between the lone wolves trying to find a way to stay alive, his Pack watching him more than usual for some reason, and this meeting, he needed a damned weekend off.

He was the Alpha, however, so he knew that would never happen. Alphas didn't get weekends. Or vacations. Or sleep apparently.

He shut off the water and got out so he could get ready for the meeting. Walker had left him alone, thankfully, and he quickly pulled on a long-sleeved cotton shirt and jeans. With any other Alpha, he'd put on something a little more formal, but this was Kade and his family—Gideon could go with a little comfort and be okay.

When he walked out to his living room to pull on his boots, he sighed. He knew they were there, of course, but his wolf wasn't in the mood to deal with his entire family in one room.

"I suppose just meeting me at chambers would have been too much for all of you?"

"You love us, brother dearest," Brynn, his sister and the lone Brentwood female, teased from her perch on the edge of the couch.

Gideon pinched the bridge of his nose. "No, seriously. Why are you all here?"

"Because you need us," Brandon, his youngest brother and the Talon Omega, said from the couch.

"Do I really need you here?" he asked, knowing he was fighting a lost cause.

"Of course," Max, his cousin, answered. "We're all going to the meeting anyway. Why not go together?"

"We're one big happy family," Mitchell said dryly.

"What they aren't saying is that we're worried about you," Kameron, his brother and Enforcer, added in.

Gideon growled while Ryder closed his eyes and cursed.

"Really, Kameron?" Ryder put in. "I thought we had a plan."

Gideon stiffened. "A plan? Why the hell would you need a plan to deal with me? Why are you *here*?"

Brynn stood up and walked toward him. She brushed her long, dark brown hair—the same color as the rest of the Brentwoods—behind her shoulders and blinked up at him with the Brentwood blue eyes.

"You're our brother, and you're hurting," she whispered. They were all wolves so they could hear her clearly. "You had to kill a lone wolf who threatened the border and wouldn't back down. Now you're having to make decisions that, as we see it, won't have an easy outcome. So, Gideon, brother mine, brother ours, we're here for you. Even if we annoy you to no end. We're here."

Gideon narrowed his eyes, even as his heart warmed at her words. Yeah, his siblings and cousins were there for him, but some things were meant for only the Alpha. If he had a mate, he'd be able to lean on her just a little, but since the goddess hadn't blessed him, he didn't have that option.

At this point, he wasn't sure he ever would.

On that depressing thought, he led his family out of his home and headed toward the meeting room. He wanted to get this over with. It wasn't as though they were going to get anything done anyway. They couldn't. Not with the rest of the Packs in the US keeping silent. Parker, the Voice of the Wolves, was on a mission at the moment searching for the other Packs and trying to convince them to talk to Gideon and Kade, but Gideon didn't hold out high hopes. Parker was a Redwood, and though he'd been adopted into the Redwood family, he was the biological son of a mass murderer. Corbin had been the Alpha of the Centrals and had almost destroyed their world.

Some wolves just couldn't see past that, and Gideon was worried that might hurt their chances of finding a way to make all of the Packs work together. However, he could work on only one problem at a time—even if it felt like he was working on a hundred at once most days.

They made their way as a group to the other side of the den where the Redwoods would be entering the woods. They had to go past the sentries at the wards to be let through, but most of them had done it before. Actually, on second thought, Gideon wasn't sure who Kade was bringing.

The Redwoods were in the middle of a shift in hierarchy. The younger Jamensons were taking over for their parents slowly but surely. That meant that Kade could be bringing any number of his powerhouse to the table. It didn't really matter since Gideon had met most of them and liked those he'd met. Not that he'd tell them that. No, he was still the grumpy, badass Alpha to the outside world.

It worked for him.

Kade came up first, a small smile on his face. With so many people and coming into a different den, the ceremony of walking to a meeting was a little ridiculous, and both of them knew it. It had to be done though.

Kade had brought his mate, Melanie, as well as both sets of Betas, Omegas, and Healers with him. He'd left the Enforcers at home to protect the den with countless other wolves apparently. Interesting, but it made sense. As the younger generation came into their powers, they were learning from the older generation. It would be interesting to see how the whole lot of them reacted in the future when the older generation, Kade's brothers, had to step down fully.

He'd also brought his Heir, his son Finn, with him, which made sense, as well as another wolf. A younger woman who, from the look of her, was a Jamenson, but Gideon wasn't sure he'd ever met her. Her long chestnut brown hair flowed over her shoulders, blowing slightly in the wind. She wasn't small. No, she was at least of average height, but where most of the wolves in front of her were all muscle and strength, her body held curves and a softness he didn't see in most wolves.

Odd, he thought he'd met most, if not all, of the Jamensons. He wondered how this one had slipped by him.

Her cheekbones angled high, and her plump lips thinned into a line when she looked at him. She tilted her head and blinked up at him with bright green eyes, and he froze, his wolf howling.

Shocked, he almost took a step back, and it was only because of his strength as Alpha that he didn't.

Mate.

That scent, that pull on his wolf.

Mate.

14

"Gideon, Brentwoods," Kade said, his voice deep, "I think you've met most of us before. Probably not Brie, though. Brie, these are the Brentwoods. Brentwoods, this is Jasper and Willow's daughter, my niece, Brie."

She smiled softly, but her eyes were on only him, not on the rest of the Pack or her family. In fact, he was looking only at her, not at Kade or the others.

Holy shit.

He'd just found his mate, and she was a fucking Redwood.

And from the way her wolf reached out to his seeking protection yet wanting to comfort as well, she was a submissive as well.

A Talon Alpha and a Redwood submissive?

Yeah, fate royally sucked.

CHAPTER TWO

No matter how many times she'd thought of this moment, nothing like this had ever crossed Brie Jamenson's mind. When she was a little girl and pictured finding her mate, she thought it would be all sparkles and happiness. Then she'd heard the story of how her parents had been mated and her image of mating had changed a bit. The start of their mating hadn't been so romantic. It had been more of a way to save each other's lives, but they loved each other more with each passing day.

When she was seventeen, she'd seen the shadow of a man and the long lines of his body. He'd been turned away from her as she stared out the window with her cousin Gina. She'd even commented on how hot his butt was. She'd never seen his face, but she'd known who he was.

Her mate.

The one wolf in the entire world that could complete her in every cheesy and romantic way possible. He'd be her protector—she'd be his as well—even if she protected in a different way. They'd grow together as one, learning about each other slowly yet combusting all the same. When she saw the back of him, she'd been on pins and needles to find out his identity and start her journey as a mated wolf. It hadn't mattered that she was young, she thought, because her mate would let her grow and be whoever she wanted to be. That's what mates did. After all, she had her parents and uncles and aunts to show her how wonderful mating could be. She wouldn't accept anything less. Before she figured out who he was, she'd had images of white dresses and flowers in her hair. He'd run his hands through her hair and then get down on one knee, before taking her as his to complete the mating ceremony.

Then her cousin Gina had told her exactly who that man was.

Gideon Brentwood.

The Alpha of the Talon Pack.

The exact wrong person for a girl like her.

Luckily she'd never told a soul about the wolf that could have been hers when she grew older. Gina never suspected—at least Brie hoped not. It wasn't like she had the same mating urge the others in the den had when they found their mates. Those wolves hadn't been able to hold themselves back and had pounced in the best ways possible. They'd been growly, on edge, and in need of the other person. Some people had found themselves in compromising positions, but Brie would never find herself there.

Apparently, she'd been too young to truly feel that. She knew deep down that the Alpha would have been the one to entwine with her soul and stand by her side until the end of eternity.

Too bad that would never happen.

She wasn't like the other wolves around her. She wasn't dominant and didn't hold a position in the hierarchy. While her cousins were all slowly coming into their powers and bonds, she had been left behind. It wasn't as if she ever thought she'd become something more than she was though.

She was strong.

She was fierce.

She was also a submissive. Meaning her wolf didn't want to fight if it didn't have to. There were other ways to find ranking within the den and other ways to show strength. She used her nurturing instincts and the strength of her heart to love completely, but she wasn't even a maternal wolf who had the inner strength necessary to protect the pups of the Pack.

She was just Brie.

There wasn't anything wrong with her—she *knew* that. Yet she was the exact wrong person for an Alpha of a Pack. The Alpha needed a mate by his side who would fight tooth and claw to protect the Pack. She might have the skills to do that because she'd forced herself to learn at a young age, but her wolf wasn't as strong as the others. She was smaller, softer, and needed to protect in other ways.

While dominants needed to protect, submissives needed to soothe and care. That's where her strength lay, and it would never be good enough for an Alpha.

So she'd spent the better part of fifteen years hiding from the Alpha of the Talon Pack and ensuring they never had to meet. Many things could have happened when and if Gideon ever saw her, and Brie hadn't wanted to face either the mating urge or risk the pain of rejection when he found her lacking.

And he would find her lacking.

It wouldn't be his fault. His wolf and Pack deserved more than a submissive wolf. It wouldn't be smart to have a submissive in the role of Alpha female. She'd never heard of it, and honestly, she didn't think she could do it. It wasn't that she was afraid of failing. It was that she was afraid of hurting others because of her own selfishness in wanting a mate at all.

So instead of facing what could happen, she'd done her best to never let it occur in the first place. Fifteen years of her wolf aching and not wanting another wolf hadn't been easy, and she knew her mother and others had felt something was wrong, but it was the best for everyone. At first she hadn't been old enough for Gideon, and then it had gotten easier to stay away.

Or at least that's what she told herself.

This night, though, she had no choice. Her uncle Kade, the Redwood Alpha, had wanted her by his side when they went into the Talon den to talk about what they could do for their future. The world was changing, and the wolves needed to change with it. He wanted a submissive to calm down the dominants in case things got too intense. The Omegas would be able to release some of the tension by taking those heightened emotions and siphoning them through their Pack bonds, but even those wolves were far more dominant than she. Her presence could soothe egos and wolves simultaneously.

That's what her uncle hoped.

He might have thought differently if she'd ever shared with him the true reason she never ventured onto Talon land. She *should* have told them she couldn't come and even the reason *why*. Yet she hadn't been able to hold herself back from this meeting. Maybe she *was* weak.

Now she stood by her family outside her den and in front of the Talons...in front of Gideon.

She'd seen pictures of him over the years of course. She hadn't been able to stop herself. Her family had met with him numerous times, and her cousin Gina

19

had mated a former Talon wolf, Quinn, so she'd been able to observe through their eyes the role of the Talon Alpha. But none of that prepared her for the shock of seeing him in person.

Her wolf howled, pushing at her with more determination than she'd imagined was possible.

He was big. Way big. She'd grown up with large men, so she shouldn't have been surprised at his size, but the touch-starved woman within took note. He had to be a few inches over six feet. With his wide shoulders and chest, he had a look about him that spoke of power and strength. That wide chest tapered down to a slender waist and hips, but his thighs were wide, all muscle, and looked strong as hell. She forced her gaze up even as she blushed, knowing what her gaze had *also* trailed over.

Since her parents, uncles, aunts, and cousins were standing near her, she refused to acknowledge anything *else* she might have seen. While his body looked fierce as hell and spoke of his dominance, it was his face—his eyes in particular—that told her he was an Alpha. It was as though the wolf was *always* near the surface. Her uncle was slightly different, but that might have been because he had her Aunt Melanie to keep him steady. The gold rim around Gideon's eyes told her of a strength she'd never seen before.

A strength she was sure she'd never see again once she left.

His black hair had been pulled back so it was away from his face, enhancing his sharp features. He wasn't beautiful, but he was handsome in a brutal sort of way. A way that seemed to make her wolf *very* pleased. She met his gaze and sucked in a breath. She was a submissive and shouldn't have been able to meet his gaze at all, yet her wolf pushed her enough to make it happen. It was as if her wolf *knew* that the man in front of her would never hurt her. That was a lie though; he could. He could hurt her heart, her soul, her dreams—but her wolf didn't understand that. Her body nearly trembled under the power, and at the same time, she wanted to bare her throat, crawl up his body and never let go.

Those vivid green eyes didn't blink. Instead, he looked right at her.

Could he tell? Did he know that she'd been chosen by the moon goddess for him?

Oh, goddess. What had she been thinking? She shouldn't have come with her family, even if her uncle had ordered her to. There was always a way out of these things. There were other submissive members of the den who could have accompanied the Redwoods to the Talon den.

Kade might have wanted it to be comprised of as much family as possible because he could trust them implicitly, but there could have been another way.

Instead, she'd risked it all because she'd wanted to see Gideon. She'd held back for so long that she'd been weak.

And now she'd have to deal with the consequences.

"Brie," Kade said.

She blinked and pulled her gaze from Gideon, her heart hammering in her ears. What had her uncle said? What had she missed when she'd been staring at the Alpha like some schoolgirl who'd found her first crush?

Only she wasn't a girl, and this wasn't a crush. This was an eon's worth of connection and promise in a single look. Yet that promise would come to nothing because it couldn't. If she uttered a single word that pushed her toward what she couldn't have, she'd be lost.

"What?" she asked, her voice breathless. Oh yes, that was going to make everyone think she was okay. Now they probably thought she was either going crazy, or worse, frightened of all the dominant wolves around her. Unlike some of the submissives in the Pack, she was never truly scared of those with stronger wolves. It was more of a strong embrace of power that surrounded her when they were near. Her wolf knew that they would be protected and fought for as well as the fact that they could also do some good with their own power. Her wolf would then want to ensure that the stronger wolves around her were okay and soothed. A dominant wolf couldn't truly succeed in protecting if they didn't protect their own hearts and wolves as well.

That's what a submissive was for.

"I was just introducing you," Kade said, his eyes narrowed. She knew he wanted to ask if she was all right, but that might show weakness or some other power play in front of the Talons.

Great. Her first shot at helping the Pack in a political arena and she was losing it because of the man she shouldn't want.

Way to go, Brie.

"Thanks," she said softly then turned toward the Talons. She made sure her gaze stayed below all of the others. She was the lowest ranked of the bunch, although in reality, submissives weren't ranked the same way as dominants. There were stronger dominants and weaker ones, and the same applied for submissives. She was one of the higher ranked submissives because of the way she could care for a higher ranked wolf. That didn't mean, however, that she wanted to meet all of their gazes and force a challenge. The ways of the Packs and wolves were complicated, and even though she'd grown up submersed in it, she still got confused sometimes.

Submissives were part of a Pack to be cherished and loved, not beaten down like some Packs thought. The Talons were like the Redwoods in the fact that they, as far as she knew, treated their submissives with respect. Unlike the Centrals—the Pack that had fought her own thirty years go and lost—the Talons weren't rotting from within. That hadn't always been the case, but that was before her time, and she hadn't wanted to ask too much about them. If she did, the others might have surmised her obsession with a certain Alpha.

No, it wasn't an obsession.

It couldn't be an obsession if she never met him.

Only she'd just met him, so who knew what would happen?

You're stronger than this.

The Talons each nodded at her, and she nodded back. Once they were out of the open area and in the meeting place, maybe they would be less formal. Only then, she'd be in a closed room with Gideon, and she wasn't sure how she'd react.

For that matter, she wasn't sure how *he'd* react. He hadn't said anything. He hadn't jumped across the space between them and picked her up in his arms, swinging her around with a smile on his face because he'd found his mate.

None of those childhood fantasies had come true.

Now Brie knew she'd been right in hiding.

No good would come from meeting her mate. She'd learn to deal as she always had and eventually, in another century or two, she'd find another mate more suited to her. The moon goddess made mistakes all the time.

Well, she'd heard of it only once, and that was with her Aunt Lexi years before she'd met Brie's Uncle North. It could happen again.

The moon goddess was wrong.

Brie wouldn't be with Gideon, and that was just something they'd all have to deal with.

"Glad you could be here," Gideon said, his voice low, tempting.

Darn it. She needed to keep strong and not fall into the vice that was his voice. If she wasn't careful, she'd make an even bigger fool of herself and hurt the purpose of this meeting.

"Let's move to the meeting room so we can get going," Gideon continued.

"Sounds good to me," Kade agreed then stepped forward, holding out his arm.

Gideon did the same, and the two of them did that man-hug, back-thumping thing. She never truly understood it since she liked hugs in general, but whatever the guys needed to do to show that they were friendly, even though they were from two different Packs, was okay with her.

She took a deep breath then followed the rest of them as they made their way to the meeting place. Gideon gave her one last look then turned away as if nothing had happened between them. For all she knew, nothing had happened. He hadn't acknowledged her beyond that look. It could have been that he stared at her because she was a submissive and he didn't know why she was there in the first place. Maybe he didn't feel her as his mate at all.

An odd pang echoed in her chest, and she rubbed the spot over her heart. It was silly to be emotional over this. She'd known for fifteen years she would never be enough for the Talon Alpha, so why was she worrying about it now?

Maybe because I'd never seen him in person.

She ignored her inner thoughts and pushed on, raising her chin without looking confrontational. It was a skill she'd learned growing up. She'd been a tomboy at heart, climbing on trees and digging in the dirt along with her cousin Finn and the others. She might not have been aggressive when she shifted, but she also wasn't the girly-girl her mother might have wanted at first. Of course, Willow had dug right into the dirt with her, so really, it never mattered that Brie had grown up with dirt on her nose instead of a sparkly tiara on her head.

"What's up with you?" Finn asked, his voice low.

Brie turned to look at him and shook her head. Finn was Kade's son and Heir to the Pack. In reality, he shouldn't have been the Heir yet, but when their grandparents had died in the Central war, everything shifted far earlier than it should have. In fact, Finn had been their Heir since before he started school. Everything changed that day, although Brie had been too young to remember the full extent of it.

Now she and Finn were in their thirties, relatively young for wolves but adults nevertheless. He looked just like his dad, but Brie could see glimpses of Melanie in him when he laughed. She was grateful for that since he didn't laugh often. Something had happened to him before he'd become Heir—he was just two at the time—that had damaged him far more than gaining the bonds of the Heir at a young age had.

Not that they ever talked about it, but since her wolf begged her to, she tried to soothe him when she could. He was her best friend and roommate—even if they were growing farther apart as they grew older.

"I'm fine," she finally answered.

He raised a brow. "You're lying. Something happened when we met up with the Talons, and now you're all in your head. If you don't want to talk about it here, that's fine, but we *will* talk about it when we get back to the den."

She let out a small growl, low enough that only Finn would be able to hear, but from the look on his face, she'd surprised him. She didn't growl in human form often—she didn't need to—but when she did, others knew that she wasn't going to back down.

"I'm fine, Finn. Keep your mind on the task at hand and not what's going on in my head. Got it?"

He frowned then nodded, turning his attention back to their path. She relaxed and studied their surroundings. Unlike the rest of her family, she'd never stepped foot on Talon ground, so she wanted to soak in as much as she could. With the way they had to constantly conceal who they were from others, she didn't get out as much as she should have.

They were walking along the outside of the more populated areas. This way, they didn't encroach on the Talon pups and families but were still shown a measure of respect since the Redwoods were considered friends and allies.

By the time they entered the nondescript building for the meeting, Brie's nerves were frayed. The wolves around her were starting to get amped up, not only because of the proximity of dominant wolves, but also because they were going to discuss the tunnels beneath their feet. Brie's wolf wanted to hug and rub up against each of them, letting them know that things would be okay and taking a deep breath could solve many problems.

It was just that she wasn't sure she should. She'd never been in a situation with so many other wolves that weren't of her Pack. Yes, Kade had wanted her there, but now she needed to figure out what to do and *when* to do it.

Her mother took that decision out of her hands and tugged her close. Willow was probably the least dominant wolf in the room besides her, and Brie was so thankful she was there. Brie leaned into her mother's hold and took a deep breath. Cinnamon. Her mom always smelled of cinnamon—something that made Brie's dad, Jasper, growl and tug her mom to their bedroom often.

So not going to think about that.

The others began to sit down, talking to each other in low tones. She wasn't there to help make decisions. If they asked her opinion, she'd give it, but too many cooks in the kitchen ended up with a broken plate or two. She was there to ensure the wolves were as calm as she could make them.

With that thought in mind, she hugged her mom back then went to each of her family members, hugging them or placing her hand on their arms and backs, showing her support. As she watched the tension slide out of their shoulders, she knew she was doing the right thing. Her uncle Maddox, the former Omega grinned at her, as did her cousin Drake, the current Omega. They would deal with the heightened emotions, as would the Talon Omega, if things got testy, but as long as her wolves knew she was there, then she was doing a good job.

A few of them sat, but others needed to stand because their wolves needed to pace. Shifter meetings were slightly different than human ones.

"The wards are extending underground through the tunnels, which means we should be able to have our wards brush up against one another's soon so they can connect in times of emergency."

Brie lost her focus at the sound of Gideon's voice and tripped over her Uncle Kade's foot. She held her arms up to break her fall, but strong arms caught her and brought her to a solid chest.

She inhaled a forest and spice scent that sent her wolf into a shuddering howl.

Gideon.

This was Gideon.

She was in Gideon's arms.

And she needed to run away before she made a fool of herself.

"You okay?" he asked, his voice that low growl that caused shivers in all the right places.

No, those were the *wrong* places.

This was the wrong wolf. The wrong place. The wrong time.

She pulled away and nodded. "Lost my footing," she replied softly then stepped back so she was at Finn's side. Finn wrapped his arm around her shoulders, but she didn't lean into him.

Gideon gave her a look she couldn't decipher then turned back to Kade, continuing his conversation as if he'd never held her, never seen her.

Well, that settled that.

There would be no mating.

What kind of Alpha would want a submissive wolf by his side? Especially a submissive wolf from a different Pack?

She took a deep breath and pulled away from Finn. She'd get over this. She did when she was seventeen, and she would do so it again.

Gideon Brentwood was not for her.

Her loyalties were to the Redwoods, to her family.

Not to a fate that lay in tatters thanks to a bond she would never have.

She would cope.

She had no other choice.

CHAPTER THREE

Gideon couldn't get her scent off his mind. That sweet and sugar scent that sent his wolf into hyperdrive and made him want to bend that pretty little Redwood Pack princess over the table and fuck her until they were both spent, sweaty, and mated.

Fuck.

It had been two days since he'd last seen her, since he'd held her in his arms when she tripped, and yet he couldn't push her from his mind.

Fuck. Again.

He was the goddamn Alpha of the Talon Pack. He'd been through war, torture, mutiny, and goddess knew what else. He was over a hundred years old and had seen humanity and his kind at their worst.

Yet he couldn't stop thinking about a girl as though he was a teenage boy on the cusp of manhood. His dick was in a perpetual state of hardness because he couldn't get Brie out of his mind.

He couldn't get the feeling of her body pressed against his out of his mind.

And he hadn't even had a full conversation with her. Hadn't even truly met her beyond the quick introductions. He pushed her from his mind as far as he was able in order to focus on the tasks at hand. There were more important things in the world than what his dick wanted and what his wolf thought they needed.

Because there was no way his wolf could be right.

Fate wouldn't be so cruel as to finally bless him with a mate he didn't want.

Considering how much he'd seen of fate in his life, though, he shouldn't have been surprised that he'd found a potential mate in a too-young wolf from another Pack.

A *submissive* wolf at that.

There was no way a submissive wolf could be his mate.

It wasn't that he couldn't protect her and didn't value the submissives in his Pack as a whole. It was the fact that, as his mate, the Alpha female would have to be as strong, if not stronger in some respects, than he. She had to stand by his side and fight for their Pack's safety and help him make the tough decisions that marred his soul daily.

There was no way a submissive could handle that kind of power.

There was no way he'd *force* a submissive to deal with that darkness.

So he'd do what he had to and not see her again. He'd somehow managed not to meet her once over the years, so it hadn't been a problem. He'd get over this mating urge and find a way to move on. Maybe in another hundred years, fate would provide him another potential mate, one more suitable.

And one who didn't make him feel like an ass.

It was for Brie's own good.

31

She hadn't come to him or even spoken of it when they met, so she must have seen the logic in not mating with him as well. At least, he hoped she'd recognized that they were potential mates. From the way her body reacted in his arms and the look of...not fear but something close to it, he had a feeling she'd known just as he had. Of course, her family had surrounded her the entire time they'd been in the same room, and it would have been fucking awkward for everyone if they'd discussed it then. He wasn't about to let *that* logic trip him up. The sooner he pushed her away and ignored the bond his wolf craved, the better for both of them.

Even if it hurt like hell to think about it.

The image of her bright green eyes filled his mind, and he cursed.

She wasn't going to be easy to forget, and he hadn't even gotten to know her. Thank the goddess he hadn't, though, because he knew it would have been near impossible to push her away at that point.

He was doing the right thing.

And as long as he kept telling himself that, he'd be okay.

His cock ached since he couldn't get her out of his head, but he ignored it like he was ignoring everything else. Instead of dealing with it, he'd work out to burn off some adrenaline, then wait for Brynn to show up so they could watch a movie before they met with the elders that night. He tried to spend time with each of his siblings, and Brynn was his favorite—not that he'd tell her or the others that. Unlike the Jamensons, the lone daughter in the Brentwood family wasn't the youngest. They all might have treated her as though she was, but she fought back and was stronger for it.

Gideon sighed then stripped off his shirt so he could get a workout in. That would help him burn off

32

some of the adrenaline in his system so he could face the day. The way his thoughts kept drifting to Brie and those plump lips of hers, it seemed he'd be doing a lot of extra workouts in the future.

He gripped the bar at the top of his doorway and started doing pull-ups. About three hundred or so would help him start to feel the burn. Being a wolf—an Alpha wolf at that—helped with the endurance. When he got to about a hundred, someone knocked at the front door. He set his feet on the ground and inhaled.

Well hell.

This could either help him out or be really shitty timing.

He strode to the door, wiping his chest down with his shirt, and opened the door. "Iona."

The high-ranking female grinned at him, her eyes bright and glued to his naked chest. Gideon didn't have a girlfriend or anyone he had a real commitment to. It was hard as wolves to date and be serious when they weren't potential mates. Once a wolf found their potential, it was hard as hell to *want* to stay with the other person. Their wolves would push them toward the one who was perfect for them according to fate, rather than the one the human had chosen. Sometimes it worked out with the original person and mating bonds formed over time without fate intervening, but it wasn't easy.

Iona wasn't a wolf he'd ever mate or love. In fact, he knew Iona wanted him only for his cock, so he didn't feel bad that he didn't want her for more.

Right then, though, he wasn't sure he wanted her in his bed today.

Maybe not ever again.

And the fact that he knew it was because of a certain green-eyed wolf made him wary.

"Gideon," she purred then ran her finger down his chest. Once, that would have set his wolf on edge and he'd have pulled her inside. Iona was hella good in bed and usually could help his wolf calm down if he worked them both into a sweaty mess. Today, though, he wanted nothing to do with her. Her touch made his skin crawl.

He gripped her hand and stilled her before she could go any lower. He liked Iona. She was a good person, a fantastic fighter, great in bed, and didn't take what they had too seriously.

Yet he didn't want her in his bed anymore.

Not since he'd seen Brie.

Just the idea of having Iona beneath him made his wolf growl and his cock deflate.

Iona frowned and looked down at his crotch. "What's wrong?" she asked, taking her hand back. She tilted her head and inhaled. "You were all revved up when I opened the door. I scented it. Now you're cold as ice. What's up your ass?" She pushed at his chest and growled.

Gideon lifted one lip in a snarl, letting some of his power push out toward her. *This* was why he was careful who he slept with inside the Pack. Just because someone shared his bed occasionally didn't give them the right to jump beyond their place in the hierarchy. She wasn't his mate and Alpha wolf, and she wasn't even the most dominant female in the Pack. He hoped she wasn't getting ideas because he sure as hell wasn't in the mood to deal with it.

Her eyes widened and then lowered before she bared her throat. "I meant no disrespect, Alpha."

"I hope not," he said, his voice low. "I'm meeting Brynn soon, and then I have a meeting with the elders. What I do beyond that is none of your business. Not anymore." He held back a flinch. Fuck. He wasn't saying the right words, and he was being an asshole.

She raised her head then narrowed her eyes. "I don't know what's going on, but I'll be back once you figure out what you want."

It won't be you.

Thankfully, because he knew better than to be a complete asshole to a woman, he didn't say that.

"We're done, Iona. What we had was good, but it's time to move on."

"Excuse me? You don't just get to decide when it's time to break up. You might be my Alpha, but that doesn't give you the right to make my choices."

Gideon closed his eyes and prayed for patience—for himself and for her. "First, we're not together. We never were. We *both* made that clear long ago. In fact, you were the one who first said you wanted to roam in order to find your mate. Second, if I don't want you in my bed anymore, then it's my choice. We both have to want it for it to work, and I don't want it anymore. So don't think that you can dictate to me because, if you wanted me out, I'd be out. *That* is what we had. Nothing more. Nothing less. Don't try to act like I'm your mate because we both know that was never a possibility."

No, his mate was Brie, and he was sure not going to let that happen either.

Not when his Pack would eat her alive.

Iona raised her chin, but because she didn't meet his gaze directly, he didn't call her on it. "We'll see."

She stormed away, and he let out a breath. He was going to have to watch her to make sure she didn't fuck up things for the Pack, but that was his fault. He was the one who'd wanted to fuck her, so now he had to deal with the outcome of them not seeing to each other's needs anymore.

35

For the time being, the only person seeing to his needs was himself. His hand was going to get a fucking workout it seemed.

"You sure have a way with the ladies, big brother," Brynn teased as she made her way to his side.

Gideon closed his eyes yet again and prayed for patience. Of course his sister would be there to witness him being an asshole. Why wouldn't fate provide her, and thereby the rest of the Brentwoods, entertainment?

"Did you have to watch everything?" he growled, moving to the side to let her in the house. "Can't some things be private?"

Brynn snorted then headed to the kitchen. She pulled out a couple beers and handed him one. "Really? Privacy? Hello, big brother, you were on the fucking porch having your conversation with Iona. It's not like you were in your secret room whispering. No, you were outside where the whole world could hear you lay down the law." She held up her hand to quiet him. "I'm not saying what you did was wrong because, come on, she's not your mate. If it's not working for either one of you, then it's stupid to keep screwing. You might have done it a little less harshly, but we both know Iona, and sweet and kind doesn't work with her. Other than writing in a big marker on her forehead that you're through with her, I'm not sure how else you could have gone about it."

Gideon laughed, despite himself. "A marker?"

Brynn shrugged, her eyes sparkling. "I don't like her since she's always been a bitch to me. She doesn't like that I'm more dominant than she is and that I have better boobs. She always tries to pick fights with me but loses when I actually let her nip at my heels. You have poor taste in bed partners, but whatever. It's not my bed."

Gideon just shook his head then went back to his room to pull on another shirt. It looked as though he wouldn't be finishing his workout until after the elder meeting. That sucked considering he probably could have gotten rid of the extra aggression in his system *before* he met with some of the elders. Sure, a few were nice and not as batshit crazy as others, but there was at least one—Shannon—who hated him.

She'd been an elder during his father's reign and had loved the brutal way Joseph had ruled his Pack. She liked the whippings, beheadings, and other cruel punishments and had even helped sentence some of the wolves who had risen against Joseph's rule. Gideon and his brothers, cousins, and Brynn had done their best to save those they could, but there was only so much they could do in a flawed system.

The power might have been in the Alpha's hands, but it was the role of a good Alpha to ensure that power didn't become corrupt. Joseph had succumbed to the temptation of absolute power and cruelty, and the Pack had suffered for it.

Shannon was a symbol of a past that Gideon was *still* fighting to overcome. As much as he wanted to banish her from the Pack, so she wouldn't interfere with his rule, he couldn't. The elders were there for a reason. They didn't interfere with the Alpha, but they *were* there to see that the laws of their people were being followed. When the Alpha and the elders worked together—like Gideon did with another elder named Xavier—things worked smoothly. When one was trying to oust the other, then things got complicated fast.

Gideon didn't know the underlying reason for this meeting today. He knew only that the elders had requested his presence. Request, though, was putting it lightly. As long as he didn't have a war or more pressing matters like trying to survive, he didn't really have a choice in the matter. Refusing to see them would be an act of disrespect, and if he showed such disrespect to the elders, then it was setting a bad precedent for the entire Pack. It was a tricky path to walk, and he hated it. However, as the Alpha, he didn't have a choice.

Maybe if he had a mate, things would have been and would be easier. He could rely on her for things like this and find a balance. But he didn't have a mate. The only one fate had given him was so ill-suited for him that it wasn't even a choice. His wolf pushed at him with the thought of her, and he held back a growl. He couldn't let her fill is mind and soul, not when so much rode on his control. Like he'd done before, he pushed Brie from his mind and tried to focus on the matters at hand.

There were only a few short hours of relaxation remaining before he had to assume the role of political Alpha, using his voice instead of claws to make his point. As with human politicians, he wasn't his own person—not that he'd ever been.

"So, what movie are we watching?" Brynn asked from the living room. She'd already popped popcorn and was munching down.

He had to grin at her. Brynn had seen her share of pain and heartache and, as a result, wasn't the softest person to get to know, but when things counted, she was one of the sweetest. He wasn't sure why the goddess hadn't blessed her with any of the powers that came from the Pack since she was blood, but there had to be a reason. She was destined for great things. It just didn't happen to be as a Beta, Omega, or Healer. Hell, she'd make a fucking good Alpha—but he'd never tell her that.

"Why are you looking at me like that? Do I have something on my face?" She scrunched her eyes, and he snorted.

"Just thinking. Ignore me. As for the movie, something with fighting that we can make fun of works. I like watching to see if they actually have the moves down or if it's too Hollywood."

She smiled then hit play on the remote. "Good. Because I already picked it out."

He rolled his eyes then sat down next to her, and stole the bowl of popcorn. He should have known she'd pick the movie. He might be Alpha of the Pack, and this might be his house, but Brynn owned the remote. It was just the way things worked.

They watched the movie and compared notes, yelling when the bad guy did something completely stupid so the hero could win. It never worked that way in real life. The villain didn't make a mistake, and the hero didn't magically find a way to use that mistake to win. The only way for the hero to win was to find a way to break the villain down, to find that weakness. In the process, the hero's weakness might prove too much, and the villain could win. It took more than a promise and luck to win. It took sacrifice and the idea that maybe the hero wasn't so heroic, but maybe just a little less dark than the bad guy.

Gideon let out a breath then turned off the TV once the credits started to roll.

This was a difficult time for the Pack. Instead of being able to fully move forward and find a way to protect his Pack from what could be coming, Gideon still had to straddle the line between his past and his present. He didn't like thinking about his father and how he'd succeeded his father as Alpha. He knew he had to think of the future and plan accordingly—hence the tunnels between dens and the meetings with the

Redwoods—he couldn't engage to the full extent of his power. The past wouldn't go away, no matter what he did, and now the elders wanted to speak to him, which reinforced the fact that he could never leave that past behind.

There had to be a resolution of the past, present and future before he and his Pack could move forward.

He was exhausted merely thinking about it.

"You ready to head out?" Brynn asked.

He stood and stretched. "Yeah. We meeting Mitchell and Ryder there?" The elders had asked his Heir and Beta to join them. Brynn would be going as the most dominant female of the Pack. Usually, in these cases, the Alpha would bring his mate, but seeing how he didn't have one, Brynn had to fill that role.

Just another reason Bric wouldn't work for him. He wouldn't want to force her into that kind of position.

Hell, he needed to stop thinking of her. It wasn't helping anyone, and it was only making him angrier at the cards he'd been dealt.

"That's what they said," Brynn answered as she led them out of his home. "You know what this meeting is about?"

"No clue. I hate when they do this. For all I know, they just want to see how the meeting with the Redwoods went, but if they really cared, they could have sent Xavier to come with me. I don't mind if he comes to those kind of meetings."

"Yeah, and Shannon knows that. She'd rather have you come and lay prostrate at her feet than actually use common sense and have one of them act like they're part of the Pack, rather than on the periphery."

"Don't start, Brynn. I'm not in the mood to deal with your logic." His wolf rumbled, pacing. Neither of them wanted to deal with what they had to do and he knew for a fact his wolf would rather be with a certain green-eyed wolf, but that wasn't about to happen.

Ever.

"By logic you mean logic that makes sense rather than whatever they say, but sure. Let's just get this over with."

"Sounds good to me."

They made their way to the other side of the den where the elders kept their residences. They were far older than any of the wolves in the Pack and liked to be off to themselves. All of them were either unmated or had lost their mates years before, so they had essentially cut themselves off when they got to an age when it was too hard to look into the future while the past filled their minds.

Gideon knew of one Redwood elder who had found a mate years after she'd given up on having a future, but that was a rare occurrence. The Talon elders were old and set in their ways.

Especially Shannon.

Mitchell and Ryder were already in the center of the elder area, standing on the outside of the rock circle where they all would eventually sit. Neither of them looked happy to be there, and Gideon couldn't blame them.

"You're not going to believe who else got invited," Mitchell said softly when Gideon and Brynn walked up.

Gideon frowned. "Who?" He didn't need an answer though. He saw and scented her as soon as he said it. "Why the *fuck* is Iona here?"

41

"Want me to knock her down a peg?" Brynn asked. "I promise not to maim her pretty face." She paused. "Much."

"We're in the elder area, Brynn," Ryder said softly. "Try not to kill anyone in front of them. It gets them all riled up."

Gideon ground his teeth together. "I don't like the look of this. Iona isn't part of the upper circle, so why the hell would the elders invite her?"

"She's here because we asked her to be," Shannon snapped as she walked toward them. She looked to be in her thirties, just like the rest of them, but her eyes spoke of centuries of memories. "Sit down, and we'll get to it."

Gideon growled. "I'm here because you asked, but you don't get to order me around."

"Respect your elders," Shannon growled back.

"Shannon, take a step back," Xavier said smoothly from her side. "Everyone, please take a seat if you will. Then we can start the discussion." The older male wolf gave Gideon a look he couldn't decipher then sat.

Since Xavier sat first, Gideon gave his family a nod. Mitchell, Brynn, and Ryder sat down at the same time as Iona. Gideon raised his chin then waited for Shannon to sit. As much as the woman wanted to fight, she didn't. She sat down first, her wolf much less dominant than his, and then he sat down. He didn't like power games, but he had to play them with this wolf in particular.

"Why have you called us here?" Gideon asked, tired. Normally, he might have tried to be a little more tactful, but he had a bad feeling about this meeting. Add in the fact that Iona was here when she'd never been part of meetings with the elders before, as far as he knew, and it just didn't sit right with him.

"It's come to our attention that you've been leading our Pack for three decades now without a mate."

Gideon froze at Shannon's words.

What. The. Fuck.

He held up his hand as his family started to speak. They were here for him, but since this was apparently *about* him, he'd be the one to speak for now.

"That is correct, though I don't know why it's suddenly now a surprise. I've yet to bond with a mate." He was careful not to say *find* his mate for that would be a lie, and he knew the others might scent the lie on him. He might have been able to hide it under normal circumstances, but his wolf was on edge from meeting Brie and now this summons. He didn't want to risk it.

Shannon raised one side of her mouth in a smile. "While it was okay for you to go mateless for so long as an Heir under Joseph's rule, you've been alone during these times for an exceedingly long wait. We've been...patient waiting for the moon goddess to bless you. I know after the Central war there was a time of unrest when *no* Talon was mating, but that is not the case anymore. Yet you've not found your mate. That is unacceptable."

The hair on the back of his neck rose. "Excuse me?"

"You heard me correctly, Gideon Brentwood. The lack of Alpha female is hurting our Pack. It has left a hole your own sister has been forced to fill, though she is not the right wolf to do so. It is...perverse to even think of doing so for as long as you have. The Pack is on edge, and your unwillingness to mate is only harming them."

"You've got to be fucking kidding me. I don't choose my mate. Fate does." *Lie.* "Where the hell do you get off telling me that I need to mate to protect the Pack? I've done just fine for the past thirty years. You can't just *provide* me a mate because you're unhappy with the way I rule."

Something like triumph filled Shannon's eyes, and Gideon held back a curse.

"That's what you're planning on doing, isn't it?" Ryder said. "You're planning on invoking the Mating Clause."

Gideon stood up, his hands fisting so he wouldn't let his claws out. "The Mating Clause?" He'd heard of the damn thing, but it had never crossed his mind that anyone would ever actually invoke it.

Shannon stood up as well, that fucking smile on her face getting on his last nerve. "Yes. It's been used before, and it will be used again. The *entire* elder council is unanimous in this, Gideon. You have no way out."

Gideon shot a look at Xavier, who looked torn but didn't say anything. Fucking elders. Fuck all of them. The Mating Clause was an old ritual whereby, if the Alpha needed a mate to help provide a future for his people, then the Pack would find him one. They would form a marriage, and then, over time, the bond would be formed. It wouldn't be true mating, but with enough power and with a touch of witch magic, they could procreate and provide the next generation of power for the Pack.

It had never been used in his lifetime, and he'd be damned if it would be used now.

He fisted his hands and his side, reining in his control. If he shifted right then and spilled blood, he'd only prove to them he was too weak to hold his own wolf. They were basing their actions on the fact they thought he was too weak to lead alone, and he wasn't about to give them any more ammunition.

Something else clicked and his wolf howled.

"That's why you have Iona here. You want me to mate with her so you can have your precious power. By forcing me to mate, you tell the Pack that you're just as strong, if not stronger, than I am."

Shannon angled her head in the way of the wolf. "Does it?"

He knew he had a way out. Fate had provided him with the answer after all, but it was the wrong choice. He *knew* it. Brie was too submissive. She wasn't a Talon. She was way too fucking young.

And he'd yet to even speak with her on the matter.

But if he didn't tell the elders now, his entire Pack would be fucked. Letting them know of her existence wouldn't force her into a mating and wouldn't do anything other than give him time.

Time was the only thing he needed, and he prayed that Brie and the Redwoods would forgive him.

"You can't force me to mate with Iona."

"That's where you are wrong," Shannon purred. "We can, and we will."

Gideon shook his head and took a deep breath. "You can't because I've already found my potential mate."

Iona sucked in a deep breath, and he felt his family stiffen beside him. He ignored them for now. There would be time later to explain his actions and why he'd hidden her. They'd understand as soon as he told them exactly *who* his potential mate was.

"Lies!" Shannon spat.

"No. Not a lie. It's new, and we haven't had time to fully come to terms with it." Or even speak of it. "But you *will* give us time to find our path. I will *not* be forced into mating with her early." Or at all.

Shannon narrowed her eyes. "You have two days. Provide this sudden *mate* of yours, or you *will* mate

Iona." She smiled. "For the good of the Pack of course."

Gideon growled low and watched the others stomp away. He could feel his family behind him, but he didn't speak.

He couldn't.

There was no way this was going to work. He'd dug himself into a hole and buried Brie with him.

What the hell was he going to do?

CHAPTER FOUR

B rie ran her hands through her hair and tried to calm herself down. Her wolf pushed at her, and she pushed back, knowing that if she didn't start taking deeper breaths, she was going to shift and scare anyone who happened to walk by. Sure, she was in her home, and her roommate, Finn, wasn't even there, but people would be able to feel the pull of her wolf when she shifted.

It wasn't like people, including her, didn't shift all the time within the den, but her wolf was so on edge that it would be like sending out a beacon of distress. And since she was a submissive, all the other more dominant wolves would rush to her because they *needed* to make sure she was okay.

She didn't have a problem normally controlling her wolf. In fact, since she didn't have the extra aggression that some wolves possessed considering their dominant wolves, she had more control than most. Shifting for her—while painful like the others— was also a soothing release where she and her wolf would become one, and she could relax once she was in wolf form.

Now, though, she needed to shift because her wolf wanted to run out of the den and find their mate.

That wasn't going to happen.

Gideon hadn't even *called* or asked how she was doing. He wasn't her mate. He was just another wolf in her life. Goddess, he wasn't even *in* her life. He was just...there.

For freak's sake. She was acting like a middle school kid who'd found out at recess a boy liked her. Instead, she was a thirty-something virgin who had finally come face to face with her mate and walked away before he could do it first.

She could still feel the heat of his hands on her arms, the firm hardness of his chest against her body as he caught her. Her face heated when she remembered *why* he'd held her. Of *course* she'd tripped like an idiot and had to have the big, bad Alpha hold her and save her from the evil floor.

She was surprised she hadn't swooned and clutched her pearls at the sight of him.

Goddess, she didn't like herself right then.

She might not be a fighter, but she wasn't some weak-spined young pup who'd never seen a man before. The only reason she was a virgin was because she was seventeen when she spotted Gideon for the first time, and her wolf had decided that was it. There would be no one else for her. Since then, she'd pushed other men away because she didn't feel what she should with them. She'd dated, and even gotten far with a couple of wolves and a male witch who lived in the den, but when the time came to get physical, she hadn't been able to. It had nothing to do with the men and everything to do with who they weren't.

That didn't bode well for the rest of her life considering how her wolf was acting right now.

She had a feeling her family had figured something was off with her, too. Sure, her dad was pleased with the fact that she'd never gotten serious with another wolf. Pleased because he'd never had to beat up a poor young pup for being near his precious, perfect daughter—his words, not hers. But even he'd remarked on her lack of a boyfriend recently. He loved her enough to let her go—only there was nowhere for her to go in the first place. Her mother was worried, as were her two younger sisters who were dating wolves and growing up.

Brie, it seemed, would be left behind because her wolf had already chosen, and while submissive, it was too strong for Brie to overrule.

The future seemed bleak at best, and she wasn't sure she wanted to listen to her wolf anymore. It might be best for her to gain the power she hadn't thought she had and find a wolf to be with. Even if she never mated, she could at least have fun. Her cousins were all growing up and enjoying life. Why couldn't she?

It wasn't like she had nothing in life. She had a home she loved and shared with Finn. It wasn't big, but it was just enough for the two of them. Eventually, when Finn mated, he'd move into a bigger place so he could raise a family. Then she'd be alone in the small place. It seemed like a bleak future, but she'd make the best of it. Maybe one day her wolf would let her mate someone else. It wasn't unheard of to find another potential mate...only extremely rare. And with the den on alert because of the humans, it was getting harder and harder to find others that could be just right for them.

She'd had her chance and fate had blown it.

Her wolf nudged at her again, and she cursed. "Stop it," she growled. "Just stop it. He's not ours. He will never be ours. He's a freaking Alpha, and mooning about it will just make things worse. I am not some bright-eyed little girl who can't live without a man. I am a member of the Redwood Pack. I'm stronger than this."

"Damn it. It's true then."

She sucked in a breath then turned to see Finn and Quinn, a member of the Pack and the Alpha's enforcer, standing in the doorway.

Tears filled her eyes, and she blinked them back. She hadn't heard either of them come in the house, hadn't scented them. Damn it. She'd been so focused on herself and her wolf that she'd let her guard down.

Now they *knew*.

"What are you talking about?" she snapped, trying to put as much force as she could into it.

Quinn sighed and shook his head. "I'm sorry, Brie," he whispered. The big man with dark hair and chocolate brown eyes sighed, yet looked genuinely worried for her. Why would he feel like that? He'd mated her cousin Gina so he was now family and acted like a big brother, but he'd never looked at her like *that*.

She frowned. "What? What do you have to be sorry about? What's going on?"

Finn held out his hand and took hers. She pulled back, worried. His eyes glowed gold for a moment before going back to their normal Jamenson jade. A lock of dark brown hair fell over his face, and he brushed it out of the way, the tension in his shoulders visible.

He leveled her a look then ran his hands over his jeans. "Brie, you're going to have to sit down, okay? We need to be fast and form a plan before the parents find out."

Now she was really confused. What on earth was he talking about? It had sounded like they knew something about what had happened, yet she was sure she was missing something important. Why were they hiding everything from their parents? And why the hell was Quinn here? Nothing made any sense.

"Tell me what's going on, Finn. You're starting to scare me."

He let out a breath. "Well, you have a reason be scared it seems."

"What the hell are you talking about? And why are you here with him, Quinn?"

Quinn grimaced then started to pace. "You know that I used to be a Talon, right?"

Brie blinked. "Yeah, before you mated Gina." Gina was Finn's sister, as well as the new Enforcer of the Redwoods. The two of them had met when the Talons and Redwoods formed a council fifteen years ago. Quinn, along with his son, Jesse, had become Redwoods when he and Gina mated.

"Well, because I grew up with the Talons, and some still consider me an honorary Talon, I hear things from the Pack before the other Redwoods do."

"Okay..."

"First, Brie, I need you to be honest with me, okay?" Finn asked before Quinn could finish his thought.

She turned to her cousin and frowned. "I'm always honest with you," she whispered, knowing that wasn't quite the truth. She'd hidden her discovery for years and hadn't mentioned the pull she'd felt. That, however, was her business. It wasn't as though she'd outright lied about the fact that she'd found her mate and subsequently let nothing come of it.

Finn's mouth pressed into a thin line, and she sucked in a breath. "Is Gideon your potential mate?"

She blinked. She knew he'd ask something along those lines. He said as much when he walked through the door, but it was still a shock to hear it clearly stated. She'd never really spoken aloud about it except for tonight. And now look where it left her.

She couldn't lie though. It didn't feel right. "Yes. He's my potential." Both men cursed, and she waved her hands, her eyes burning. She didn't let the tears fall though. It hurt like hell, but she wasn't weak. And maybe if she kept telling herself that, she'd believe it.

"I'm not going to mate with him, Finn. I'm not stupid. He's the freaking Alpha of the Talons. I'm a submissive. Those two don't mesh. The moon goddess got it wrong. I get that. So don't worry. I'll stay away from him, and then, eventually, our wolves will find a way to move on." Hopefully. "And one day, maybe I'll find another mate. Or I can find a wolf I want to spend the rest of my life with, and then one day the bond might form. This isn't the end of the world."

Only...it felt like it.

"Fuck," Quinn mumbled then started to pace again. She hadn't noticed he'd stopped, but again, she'd been in her own head.

"What's wrong?" she asked. "I don't get it. You guys sound like you knew that this was a possibility before you walked in." She froze. "Did Gideon say something? Hell, he shouldn't have. We haven't even spoken to one another about it. Or, really even spoken to each other beyond that one time in the meeting. He's not going to want to mate with me, guys. Everything will be fine. It won't disrupt the Packs. We'll both get over it. I'm sure he has already." Her heart ached at that last part, but she pushed it away. She'd deal with the pain later. She always did.

"Its not that easy anymore," Finn whispered.

Easy? How on earth was this easy? If this was easy, she didn't want to know what hard felt like. Her wolf nudged at other, a scrap of claws along her skin.

Finn looked at Quinn, and Brie wanted to scream at them to just tell her what the heck was going on.

"You remember that the elders of the Talon Pack keep trying to control Gideon, right?" Quinn asked.

She nodded, her wolf growling at the idea that Gideon had to deal with that. He might not actually be her mate in truth, but she still didn't want others to take advantage of him.

"They had issues with you and Gina mating," she said.

Quinn snorted. "That's one way of putting it. Well, they're back. Or, more precisely, Shannon is back." He swallowed hard. "She's apparently gotten the rest of the elders on her side."

Something cold crawled up her spine, and she froze. "What side is she on?"

Finn met her gaze. "She's invoking the Mating Clause."

Brie sucked in a breath. She knew that clause because she'd read the old files with her Uncle Reed when she was younger. She wanted to be part of the Pack and help any way she could. "No. They can't do that. Can they? Gideon's fine without a mate." Her wolf slammed into her, and she barely kept on her feet. Goddess, it *hurt*.

Quinn shook his head. "They have the entire elder council on his back, Brie. They even picked out a woman for him. Iona. I know Gideon used to sleep with her, but I know they aren't mates."

She jerked as though she'd been slapped, taking a step back.

"Fuck," Quinn said sharply, his eyes wide. "I'm sorry, Brie. I'm going about this all wrong."

Finn stepped toward her, but she took another step back, holding her hands up.

Her mind whirled, but she would force her words to come out clearly. She could do this. She was stronger than she thought—least she prayed she was. "If Iona isn't his mate, how can they invoke the Mating Clause?"

Quinn sighed. "They're going to force it. Between the Clause and magic from a witch, the two of them will be able to procreate."

A tear fell down her cheek, but she didn't brush it away. This wasn't supposed to be easy. The idea that the *one* wolf for her would be readily handed off to another woman hurt like hell. They could deal with her tears.

"Okay," she whispered. "Why are you telling me this?" she asked, her voice harsh. "If he's going to mate with this woman, why are you here? What do I have to do with it?"

She wanted them to leave. She wanted to crawl in a hole and let time pass just for a little bit so she could get over whatever fantasies she'd held about mating.

"Gideon bought some time," Quinn said carefully.

"And how did he do that?" she asked, her voice emotionless.

"He...he said he'd found his potential mate so they couldn't force him to mate with Iona."

She staggered back, gripping the back of the couch for support. "Did...did he say who?"

Finn shook his head. "No, not in front of the elders. They weren't pleased, but they gave him time to mate with the potential before they forced Iona on him."

She shook her head. "Then why are you here?"

Quinn let out a breath. "Because we know it's you, Brie. We knew before you told us. Gideon had to explain to his family what was going on as soon as they were in private. I don't know what his plan is, but he said your name, and then Walker called me. He wanted to warn me before the shit hit the fan. Because, Brie, the shit *will* hit the fan."

She forced herself to take two steps then sank down on the couch, her legs unable to hold her up anymore. Gideon had felt it then. Had said her name...but only to save himself.

Well, wasn't that fate being a bitch?

He wouldn't have her if he had been given the choice. In fact, she wasn't sure he'd chosen her at all. He hadn't exactly contacted her, had he? No. Instead, he was in his den forming a plan that would disrupt her life and change it forever, yet he hadn't bothered to let her in on the secret.

"Do you know what he's going to do?" she asked woodenly. *Did he know what* she *was going to do?*

"I have no clue, Brie," Quinn answered. "But there is a lot riding on this, and yet, I don't know what the best thing he *can* do is."

"He's not going to force her," Finn snapped, and Brie's head shot up.

"Excuse me?" she asked softly.

"You're my family, you're *our* Pack. You aren't a Talon. You didn't mention the fact that he was a potential, so something must have held you back. Come on, Brie, he's a fucking Alpha. His Pack isn't going to want a submissive as the Alpha Female. It's unheard of. I don't want you to get hurt just so Gideon can rule the way he wants. You're more important than that."

The tears fell freely now, but she refused to let either man closer to her. Finn's words might be true, but they hurt like hell.

"Don't you think I know I would never be accepted as Gideon's mate? I'm Jasper and Willow's daughter. I'm a Redwood. My place is here. I'm a submissive who doesn't like fighting. I'm not Alpha-mate material," she said, her voice rising with each word.

Finn winced. "Damn it. I didn't mean it like that, Brie."

She rolled her eyes then wiped up her tears. No use crying when it didn't accomplish anything. "Well, it came out that way. I know I'm not good enough to be the Alpha's mate. It's fine. I was getting over it. But now Gideon is using me without telling me. He might not have said my name to the elders, but he's on a deadline to show up with a potential mate or else he's forced to stick with this Iona."

She already hated Iona, and she hadn't even met the woman. It wasn't as though Brie had a reason for this jealousy, but she couldn't handle holding back *all* of her emotions.

Quinn blew out a breath then sat down on the couch next to her. Her wolf prickled at the closeness of two such dominant wolves near her, then calmed somewhat in their presence. Damn wolf. Finn rubbed the back of his neck then lowered himself to the coffee table.

"I don't know what Gideon is going to do, Brie, but there is no way he'll force you do to anything you don't want to do." Finn growled the last part, and she sighed.

"He's not like that, Finn," Quinn put in. "He might be an Alpha you don't know, but he's not a monster."

Finn growled again, and she closed her eyes for a moment before slowly opening them.

Put a bunch of testosterone-driven, dominant males in a room and things went to shit. Finn might be powerful and the Heir, but he wasn't an Alpha yet. She didn't want to see her cousin, or any of her family, get hurt because of something out of their control. She also didn't want to see Gideon get hurt despite the fact that she didn't know him, and he'd yet to even say he wanted her.

He *didn't* want her—he only needed her—and that was the problem.

She swallowed hard, knowing there was only one *right* thing to do. Gideon had put her existence out there for a reason. He didn't want to mate with Iona. He might not want to mate with Brie, but he might not have a choice.

Which meant she didn't either.

If he wanted to keep his Pack secure and keep the elders off his back, he needed a mating bond.

Lucky for him she could provide him one.

She'd deal with the consequences later.

Her wolf whimpered then nudged at her, secretly pleased.

Damn wolf.

She lifted her chin and met Finn's eyes. "Can you get me to the Talon den and to Gideon?" she asked, her voice steady.

Finn stood up so quickly he almost fell over the coffee table. "You're fucking kidding me, right? You can't just go to the Talons and offer yourself up like a sacrificial lamb."

She winced at the imagery. It might have been accurate, but that didn't mean she had to like it.

"Stop it, Finn. This is my choice."

"It's not your choice if you're forced into it. Gideon can get on without you."

But what if I can't get on without him?

She quickly pushed that thought out of her mind. No good would come of it. "Just get me there, Finn. I can fight and protect myself, but I'm not an idiot. Going off alone to another den isn't smart. I could use the help."

"I'll take you," Quinn said softly.

She turned to him, surprised. "You will?"

He nodded then stood. "Gideon is one of my best friends. He'd be damned lucky to have you as his mate. Is it going to be easy? Fuck no. But Gina gave up everything to be with me, and I was an idiot when I didn't see what I could give her at the same time. So, yeah, I'll go with you to make sure Gideon realizes what he's getting out of the situation. Plus that den used to be my home. I'll be by your side if you need it."

She swallowed hard, knowing Quinn was in a tight spot, but she was grateful he was going to help.

"Well, fuck," Finn muttered. "Fine. I'll take you, too. I won't have him hurting you." He met her gaze, his eyes cloudy. "You sure you know what you're doing?"

She shook her head. "I have no idea what I'm doing, but I know it's the right thing. He needs a mate, and well...I'm here." *And I want to mate him even if he doesn't want me and I'm all wrong for him.*

Not that she would ever say that last part.

"Well, let's get a move on then if we want to make it out of here before the parents find out and things officially go to shit."

Brie shook her head then stood, her hands trembling. "You have such a way with words, Finn."

He grinned at her, though it didn't reach his eyes. "I try."

She swallowed hard and looked down at her tattered jeans, boots, and top. It wasn't the best outfit to meet a future mate in and pledge herself, but it wasn't like it really mattered. For all she knew, he'd reject her as soon as she put herself out there. Even if he accepted her bond, she then had the entire Pack to deal with. It wasn't going to be easy, but hell, it had to be better than this loneliness that never seemed to ebb.

They made their way to the Talon den in silence. Quinn drove while Finn sat in the passenger seat, his wolf on alert from the way his shoulders never dropped. Brie took deep breaths, trying to calm herself once again. She knew she was doing the right thing, but it didn't make it any easier.

Once they made their way to the front gates, Quinn spoke quietly to the sentries. The other wolves looked into the car and nodded, frowns on their faces. She didn't know what they were thinking, but she'd deal with it later.

She'd have to deal with a lot of things later.

They got out of the car and followed the sentries into the wards. They couldn't bring their car into the den since they were outsiders, but since they were accepted inside on foot, that was at least a step in the right direction.

"The sentries alerted Gideon that we were here. That's why they let us in," Quinn whispered.

She nodded and focused on putting one foot in front of another. This wasn't a death march. She wasn't giving up her life. No, she was merely giving up her *way* of life. She could do this. She was a Jamenson, and she was strong as hell.

Just because her wolf wanted to lower its head and nuzzle into the nearest dominant for reassurance didn't make her weak. It just made her who she was.

"We can still go back," Finn said from behind her.

She shook her head. "I've made my decision. Just be by my side and step away when I need you to. If you do that, then you're doing all you can."

Finn growled but didn't say anything else.

She felt the gazes of others on her, but she didn't look at anyone. People had come out of their homes to see the Redwoods walking through the den, but as they didn't comment on it, she didn't either. They'd all know soon enough the reason for her visit. She just hoped it didn't end in bloodshed like many unwanted matings did.

Gideon stood at the door when they walked up, and she sucked in a breath.

Apparently they never had to worry if she'd be attracted to him. There was no mistaking the heat running through her veins at the sight of him leaning against the doorway, his arms crossed over his chest.

His piercing blue eyes bored into her, and then he turned to look at Quinn, dismissing her in that one movement.

The hurt shocked her, but she didn't back down. She was there for a reason, and he'd just have to get over whatever feelings he had. If he had another way to save his position without mating her, then she'd gladly hear it.

She might not like it, but she'd listen anyway.

"I see someone has a big mouth," Gideon said causally to Quinn. Though, really, there was nothing casual about Gideon, and they all knew it. Her wolf brushed up against her at their mate's presence. She fisted her hands by her side, forcing her wolf to back down at least for the moment. She needed to keep her wits about her if she was going to get through this whole...or at least sane.

"She deserved to know," Quinn answered. "She's here on her own. This is her choice."

Okay. That was enough. While she might be submissive, she didn't like the big bad men taking care of her and talking over her as if she wasn't there at all. That would not be how she started this mating.

"*She* is right here," she snapped, though it didn't come out as strong as she wanted. She met the Alpha's eyes. "Gideon. Can I come in? I'd like to talk. Finn and Quinn can wait outside."

"Brie—"

"I've got this, Finn." She cut him off. He growled behind her and Gideon let out a growl of his own.

This wasn't going to end well.

"I've got this," she repeated, her voice so low she was afraid only she heard it.

Gideon tilted his head and studied her. "Do you?" he whispered then stood straight. "Come on in, Brie Jamenson. It seems we have a lot to talk about."

Finn gripped her hand, and she squeezed it before pulling away. She left the two men standing on the walkway while others came closer. She didn't look to see who they were. There would be time for that later. Instead, she followed Gideon into the house. When he shut the door behind her, everything seemed to come into focus.

She was standing in the Alpha's home.

Her *mate*'s home.

Alone.

Her pulse quickened, but she didn't lower her head. She didn't feel the need like she did with so many other dominants, and that had to be due to who Gideon was to her...or at least who he could be.

Goddess she hoped she wasn't making the wrong choice.

"I take it you heard that the elders have forced my hand."

"They didn't give you a choice really," she answered, not liking the way he wouldn't look at her.

He snorted then lifted her chin with his knuckle. She sucked in a breath, the heat of his touch intoxicating. His gaze me hers, and her wolf howled.

Mate.

"It's either mate a woman who means nothing more to me than being a member of a Pack or a woman I don't know. Not much of a choice, anyway."

She didn't flinch, but damned if she wanted to. "You need a mate, and it seems fate has provided you one. I'm here so you don't have to go against your wolf."

There. That sounded better than *please, take me and never let me go.*

He brought up his other hand and brushed his thumb against her cheek. "Mating isn't for the faint of heart, little wolf."

She didn't pull back, nor did she move into his hold. "And you would know, how?"

His mouth twitched. "Touché. You're willing to give up everything you know to mate an Alpha, a man you've hardly spoken to. A man who is at least a hundred years older."

She swallowed hard but didn't move her gaze from his. "I'm willing to follow my fate and trust in the moon goddess." Again, she prayed that she wasn't making a mistake.

"You don't know me. You don't love me. I don't love you."

She didn't flinch, but it was close. "No, there's no love, and frankly, I don't even know if I like you. How can I when I've only seen you from afar? But in order for you to fully protect your Pack, you need a mate. Why hurt yourself and your Pack worse by mating someone you can't form a true bond with? Witch magic isn't the same as wolf magic. A bond formed from something outside the goddess won't help you the way a true bond will."

He nodded, his thumb still brushing her skin. Did he know how much his touch soothed her and made her ache all at the same time? Her body heated, yet she was scared to do anything more right then.

His voice lowered, and she pressed her lips together as he spoke. "You're a submissive, Brie. How are you going to be able to protect the Pack if you can't fight for it?"

Her hands once again fisted at her sides, but she didn't growl. "You, above all people, know the value of a submissive in a Pack. I don't need to make another bleed to show my worth. I can fight if I need to, but I can also show the compassion and soothing that are required to make a Pack healthy."

He nodded, this time his thumb brushing against her lip. It took everything in her not to lick the tip and suck it into her mouth.

"The Pack might not accept you. Are you ready to deal with that? I will never treat you like you aren't wanted because that's not the kind of man I am, but I cannot force the Pack to love you. If I do that, you lose all credibility."

"I get it. I'll have to fight—in any way I can—for my position."

He let out a breath then ran a hand down her arm. "Your family is going to kill me."

She shook her head, her heart warming again. She was already becoming addicted to his touch and it had only been a few short moments. It had to be the mating urge and hopefully this...ache would tone down eventually. "No, they won't. They've all been through their own issues with mating. Ours will just be a little different."

He closed his eyes and pulled away. Her heart ached, and she felt cold at the loss. "I can't let the elders think they have control over me. It's too dangerous out there for our Pack to be fighting within itself."

"Then mate with me and let me help you with that burden."

"I'm not good with sharing."

She took a step toward him and placed her hand on his chest. His heart beat against her palm, and she licked her lips. The fact that he didn't pull away spoke volumes. Or at least that's what she told herself.

"I'll be your mate, Gideon Brentwood. I'll do my best to be the mate you need, the mate the Pack needs."

"I hope you don't regret this, little wolf."

She shook her head. "I can't regret it. If I did, then it's not a choice worth making."

With that, she stood on her tiptoes and brought her lips to his. He stiffened for a moment then wrapped one arm around her waist and placed a hand on the back of her head.

She gasped then parted her lips, letting his tongue tangle with hers. He growled, nipping at her lips, taking control of the kiss. Her shoulders melted, her body sinking into his. He tasted of spice, power, and a future she couldn't see.

When he pulled back, they were both breathless, and she could feel the hard ridge of his cock against her belly.

At least his body wanted her.

His heart, though, would be another matter.

He cupped her face and studied her. "I suppose that sealed the deal," he said, his voice a deep rasp.

She swallowed hard, his taste burned forever on her tongue. "I suppose it did."

Her fate was locked with his, entwined around a promise and an uncertainty.

She only prayed she hadn't made the biggest mistake of her life. Because no matter how much the idea of a Pack despising her scared her, it wasn't the worst thing that could happen.

No, the fact that she didn't have Gideon's heart was the one thing that could break her.

And when he pulled away again to catch his breath, she had a feeling she'd be broken long before she could figure out the next step. Some things were out of her control, and those were the ones that hurt the worst.

Or at least that's what she feared.

CHAPTER FIVE

Gideon had been wrong. He wouldn't die by a betrayal or by something out of his control. No, today he was going to die at the hands of an Alpha and a former Beta who wanted his blood for daring to touch their precious little princess.

He ran a hand over his head and wondered how the hell he'd been put in this position. Was it really less than a week ago that he'd been worrying about lone wolves trying to attack his den and hiding his people from the humans? He was *still* worrying about all of that, but now, he had a whole new set of demands and problems tacked on to those.

Not that he wanted to call Brie a problem, but what else was he supposed to call her?

The elders had forced his hand, and she had offered herself up like a sacrificial virgin, not knowing she was tempting the beast that lurked beneath his skin.

He froze.

She wasn't a virgin, was she?

She had to be in her thirties if he was doing the math correctly. There was no way someone that

66

beautiful, someone with so much spirit, would be untouched. If she was, well, the wolves in her den were fucking idiots.

The thought of any of those wolves laying a hand on her made his fists clench, and he had to force himself to relax. Getting jealous over men he'd never met, picturing his future mate tumbling between the sheets with them, wasn't going to help his mood.

In fact, this was all so fucking crazy he felt as though he had no idea what he was doing. That was just par for the course these days.

He finished doing the buttons on his shirt then tugged on his sleeves. He didn't like wearing button-down shirts with long sleeves, but he'd wanted to at least try to look nice.

After all, today was his mating ceremony. These things didn't come around often.

He let out a sigh and tried to remember *why* he was doing this.

The elders had forced his hand, and rather than mate with Iona in a bond that would never be whole and could eventually hurt the Pack rather than better it, he'd been offered a choice. He knew he shouldn't have said he'd found a potential mate when he'd met with the elders, but he hadn't been able to help himself. In all reality, he'd thought he'd be able to find a way out, but that was only a small chance.

Infinitesimal really.

Then, of course, his family and Quinn had meddled, and Brie had come to him, rather than him finding a way to be a fucking Alpha and go to her. The bond they made would be a true one, real enough and blessed by the goddess, so his wolf would be appeased and so would the elders.

At least that's what he hoped.

The fact that his wolf craved her and the man wanted her beneath him didn't hurt.

"You look good," Brynn said from his bedroom door, and he looked over his shoulder.

"Yeah? Good enough for a mating ceremony?"

Brynn frowned, and he sighed. "You'll do, big brother. It's not about the clothes though. Are you sure you're doing the right thing?"

"I've been asking that question myself over and over, and I don't see a way out, Brynn."

His sister walked toward him and straightened his collar. He let out a breath and let her mother him. Their mother was long dead, and Brynn had done her best to fill that roll when needed—though she needn't have bothered. They'd done well without a mother for their entire lives since the woman who'd given birth to them had never treated them with an ounce of the love or affection the siblings had given each other. That, though, was far in the past, and he was over it. Really.

"Now you're frowning, Gideon. What's going on in that head of yours?"

He pulled away then sat on his bed to pull on his dress shoes. "I was thinking about Mom."

Brynn cursed under her breath, and he didn't blame her. "Don't bring that woman into your mating. She's not worth it."

"She won't be. It's my mating day. I don't need to think about our parents. They weren't the ideal mating to compare to anyway."

Brynn snorted then sat next to him. "Well, that was an understatement. Brie, however, was born into a loving family. Jasper and Willow are ideal parents from where I'm looking. And the rest of the Jamensons know how to take care of their kids. So, big brother, that girl is used to being loved and cared for. You sure you're up to the challenge?"

That was just one more thing he was afraid of. "Not even close. All of us might get along, but we're not the tight-knit family she grew up in. Yeah, she was born in the middle of a war, but she hasn't had to deal with the shit we have. Mating with me is just going to taint her."

Brynn shook her head. "She might not have had to fight in the war, but she grew up in a Pack learning to rebuild itself after that demon almost destroyed it all. She might have peace now, but she watched it rise from rubble. We've had peace since then too, big brother. At least she's coming into the Pack without dear old Dad."

His wolf growled at the thought of his dad or uncles anywhere near Brie. Those fucking wolves were the worst dregs of all things shifter, and he was glad they were gone. Even if killing his father had taken a piece of his soul, it had been worth it. He wouldn't let anything from his past touch his new mate though. She was too clean, too pure for it.

"Our past can't hurt her," he growled softly.

"Not if you don't let it," she answered cryptically.

"What do you mean by that?"

Brynn shrugged. "You're starting fresh, big brother. Yeah, this sucked with the fact that you're sort of forced into it, but hell, she's going to be your *mate*. You found the one person who could fit against you and be part of your soul, and she feels it too. I'm kind of jealous." Something passed over her eyes, and he frowned.

"What do you mean by that?" While he and Brynn were close, neither of them told the other everything. Some secrets were meant to be kept. However, he didn't like the shadow over her eyes and, if he could, he'd fix it. That's what big brothers did.

She shook her head then ran a hand over her face. "Nothing. Don't worry about it. You're about to be a mate and have someone to share the rest of your life with. It's a big deal. While I know you didn't get a real choice in the matter, you know you don't technically have to do this." She turned and met his gaze. "If you aren't sure about mating her, then don't. Don't hurt her because you feel you need to take a chance. And don't hurt our Pack because you're trying to do too many things at once."

He growled but didn't yell like he wanted to. "You're not making any sense."

"Yeah, I am, and you know it. She's a submissive, Gideon. Our Pack is going to eat her alive. There are still old-timers here who miss the way of life they had with Joseph as Alpha. We have to fight them daily to keep them from treating the women like shit and the submissives even worse. They aren't going to want to follow the lead of a submissive. A submissive who grew up in a different Pack."

"Don't you think I know that?" He ran a hand through his hair, cursed because he'd messed it up, and started to pace. "She's not meant to be an Alpha female. Her wolf is going to want to cower and be protected when she needs to fight for her standing. I have no idea what we're going to fucking do, but if I force the others to respect her, it's going to make things worse."

Brynn cursed. "Meaning you're going to hand her over to the wolves. Literally."

He let out a yell and punched the wall. The plaster broke, and he cursed at the hole he'd left in the wall and the cuts on his knuckles.

"Great. Now you're going to bleed all over your shirt."

"I'll be fine," he spit out then went to wash off his hands, careful to keep the blood from getting on his clothes. Now he'd have split knuckles for his mating ceremony. The worst of the cuts would heal in time, but unless he used Walker to Heal the rest, they were just going to have to make do. Well, she was going to mate with an Alpha. She'd just have to deal with what she got.

"Brie will have to learn to be part of our Pack. It's not going to be easy, but we'll find a way to make it work. I can't help her with everything, and I don't know if doing this is going to weaken the Pack further, but I don't have a choice. Fate gave her to me, so I'm going to have to deal with this."

"Such lovely words on your mating day."

"Fuck off, Brynn. I'm not in the mood." He turned to see Brynn frowning at him.

"Just don't hurt her, okay?" She came to him and once again straightened his collar. "And don't hurt yourself. You're one of my favorite people in the world. I know the weight on your shoulders sometimes feels insurmountable, but maybe with a mate, you can learn to lean on someone."

He shook his head. "I can't lean on her, Brynn. She'll break."

She tilted her head and studied his face. "For all of our sakes, I hope you're wrong about that."

Instead of answering, he let out a breath then led her out of his home. They would be meeting most of the Jamenson family inside his Pack circle where the mating would take place. If he hadn't been Alpha, he might have been able to have the ceremony on Redwood land, but that wasn't an option. When he and Brie completed the mating later that day, she would not only become his mate, but also a Talon.

She'd be leaving the Redwoods and the loyalty that came with that behind.

He just hoped she was ready.

Because he sure didn't feel ready.

Brynn put her hand on his back, but he didn't relax. They weren't in his home anymore where he could lean—to some small degree—on someone else. They were outside where the rest of his Pack, as well as the Jamensons, would be able to see him.

When they cleared the circle, his breath left his lungs.

Brie stood in the center, a white sundress flowing down her body, baring her arms and showcasing her curves. Her long, brown hair flew off her shoulders when the wind caught it just right, framing her pale face.

He knew she was beautiful.

He'd seen her, tasted her, held her.

Yet right then, he wasn't sure he'd ever seen anyone look as glorious as she did.

Yes, the paleness of her face and her wide-open eyes told him she wasn't as calm as she tried to look, but it did nothing to diminish her features.

When he stepped fully onto the grass in the center of the circle, the crowd that had gathered quieted, their attention on him.

It seemed he was the last to arrive.

Even the elders were in their places, Shannon's watchful eyes boring holes into him. Iona was also there, her place near the elders letting him know what side she stood on. She didn't look particularly sad that he was mating someone else, but she also didn't look happy about it. He couldn't blame her since none of this made sense, but honestly, he didn't know what her endgame was. He would have to watch out for her since he didn't want Brie hurt because of his past.

He looked at the others, for only a moment though, because his attention was on the woman about to bind her life to his.

Brie stood between her parents, Willow and Jasper, her chest rising and falling as she breathed. Willow stared at him, a mixture of hope and anger in her eyes. He could understand the anger, and he prayed he didn't fuck up the hope. Jasper, on the other hand, looked ready to commit murder.

Again, he didn't blame the man.

"Gideon," Kade said as he walked around Jasper, his hand out.

Gideon shook it, not even wincing as Kade squeezed. The two of them were past power plays, but today was a different day.

"Kade." He looked past the Redwood Alpha to the rest of the Jamensons who filled the circle.

And there were a lot of them.

It seemed that every single aunt, uncle, and cousin had made the trip. Even Gina and Quinn had come with their son, Jesse who was now in his twenties. He hated himself for pulling Brie away from this, but these were the cards they'd been dealt.

He swallowed hard then turned to walk toward Brie and her parents.

"This is pretty fast, Alpha," Jasper growled out.

"Jasper," Willow whispered then squeezed her mate's arm. "Gideon, welcome to our family," she said, her voice strong. "We'll move out of your way, but after the ceremony, we'd love to get to know you more."

Gideon swallowed hard and stood straight as Willow patted his arm before pulling her mate away.

"You hurt my baby girl, I'll kill you," Jasper growled, his voice so low that Gideon knew only the two of them could hear. "I don't care that you're the Alpha. You're the man taking my Brie."

Gideon nodded. "Understood," he whispered back. And he did. Jasper wasn't challenging the Alpha, but the man who would mate Brie. There was a fine line, but Jasper hadn't crossed it.

Yet.

Gideon finally took the last steps toward Brie and sucked in another breath. She tilted her head and stared at him, her wide green eyes blinking slowly.

"You ready for this?" he asked, his voice brisk.

"Of course," she said simply.

There was nothing simple about what they were about to do, but he nodded anyway.

Ryder, his brother and Heir, took a few steps closer to them. The other man would be preforming the ceremony that day since Gideon couldn't do it himself as Alpha and Kade couldn't do it on Talon land. Any one in his hierarchy could do it, but Gideon wanted Ryder. He was calmer than the others and would be able to make the words meaningful. Or at least try to.

Mitchell, as Gideon's Beta, had been through too much shit in his life to have to be forced into it. The other man might be in charge of the daily needs of the Pack, and had the bonds and scars to prove it, but he also needed his space. His Enforcer, Kameron, was too harsh, too used to fighting to protect the Pack from outside forces to perform the ceremony. Brandon would have been a good choice as the Omega since he could feel all of the emotions of the Pack, but it didn't feel right since Brie wasn't a Talon yet. If Gideon had been mating a Talon member, it would have been different, and Brandon's calming force would have been useful. Walker also would have been an okay choice as the Healer, but the man had his own reasons for staying away—reasons even Gideon wasn't entirely sure of.

Ryder would have to do, and Gideon trusted his brother to make it worth it.

Gideon shook off those thoughts and held out his hands, surprised to find them trembling. Brie slipped her hands into his before anyone else could notice his weakness and squeezed. His wolf calmed, soothed at her touch.

It was the first time in over thirty years he felt as though his wolf could take a breath. Was it Brie? The fact that she was about to be his mate? Or because she was a submissive wolf?

He didn't know, but he had a feeling she would constantly surprise him. Honestly, he didn't know how he felt about that, but now he had to take the next step.

"Since everyone is here, we can begin," Ryder said. He stood between them with Gideon's family on one side and Brie's on the other. The rest of the Pack sat on the stone benches surrounding them. Gideon felt their confusion, their anger, their...happiness at his mating. He didn't know exactly what would happen next, but he was about to find out.

Ryder spoke of the moon goddess and the story of how she made the first shifter. When the goddess had found a hunter who'd taken the life of a wolf for pleasure, and not for survival, she'd forced the human to share his body with the spirit of the wolf he'd killed. That hunter became the first shifter and made more over his lifetime. He'd also found another who could complete his human's *and* his wolf's souls and took her as his mate.

"Since that time, mating has been one of the most sacred of bonds, superseding all bonds within a Pack," Ryder continued. "We are here to witness the union and handfasting of our Alpha and his mate. May the goddess bless you and your future."

"Goddess bless us," Gideon whispered, his voice joining with Brie.

Ryder gave him a look, and Gideon swallowed hard. It wasn't unheard of for those in the ceremony to say those words, but Gideon had never been one to firmly place himself in those traditions. However, with Brie by his side, he couldn't help himself. He honestly didn't know what to make of that.

He swallowed hard, knowing it was his turn to speak next.

"As your mate, I, Gideon Brentwood, promise you, Brie Jamenson, that I will honor and cherish you until the end of our days. I will protect your body and soul and remain faithful with every ounce of my being."

He didn't speak the words that had been spoken for ages upon ages but, rather, something from his own heart. Something he could promise. The others had spoken of love, but he didn't love her. He didn't *know* her. Brie didn't love him either, and lying to one another during their mating ceremony would hurt more than leaving out a promise of love.

Brie's eyes brightened at his words, and he knew he'd done the right thing. He hadn't lied to her but, rather, told her what he *could* promise to do rather than what others might want to hear.

"As your mate, I, Brie Jamenson, promise, you, Gideon Brentwood, that I will honor and cherish you until the end of our days." She took a deep breath and squeezed his hands. "I will soothe your hurts and protect your heart and soul with every fiber of my being. I will stand by your side as your mate and honor your trust, as well as remain faithful until I take my last breath."

He blinked, and his wolf howled. She'd spoken of his heart and of the ways of a submissive wolf. While it might have stung for any other wolf, he reveled in it. She was letting him know that she wouldn't be as other alpha females wolves would try to be. She was going to be herself and hope that was enough.

Goddess, he hoped that was enough for his Pack.

Ryder said the rest of the words and then squeezed both of their shoulders. When Brie looked up at him expectedly, Gideon licked his lips. Everyone in the circle had quieted to the point that he could hear the wind rustle in the trees as well as the soft sounds of her breathing.

He let go of one of her hands and cupped her face. She leaned into his touch, and his wolf pushed at him, wanting more. Aware of the others watching him, he slowly lowered his head and gently pressed his lips to hers.

It was just a whisper of a promise, a bare caress of lips, but it sealed his fate.

When the wolves howled around them, he pulled back, moving his hand from her face but not releasing their clasped hands.

Ryder stood behind them then put his hands back on their shoulders. "I present to you, Gideon and Brie Brentwood!"

The howls grew louder, and Brie squeezed his hand yet again.

It was only the beginning, the first step, but he'd never been so fucking scared in his life.

"I think my mother likes you," Brie said calmly when they made their way back to his home. No, it was *their* home now.

Gideon grunted, trying not to think too hard about what they were about to do.

"No, really. She smiled and everything. Willow might seem nice and sweet, but if she doesn't like you, she can get mean."

He opened the front door and pulled her into the house, closing it firmly behind them. There might not be anyone outside now, but he knew they'd be watching the house at some point. What was about to happen inside was too important not to be curious. Fuck, he felt like one of those kings from the Middle Ages when people stood beside their bed to watch them consummate a marriage.

Instead, he had wolves all around him who knew that he and Brie would be cementing their bond with both the mating mark and sex.

Not the most romantic way to start their lives together.

Though, in retrospect, nothing about this was all that romantic.

Brie pulled at his hand, and he looked down to see her frowning. "I know you're having a weird day because—hello—so am I, but if you keep waiting for someone to put a glass on the door so they can hear what's going on, you're going to end up crazy."

He snorted at the visual then shook his head. "Sorry. I'm not usually so..."

"Awkward?" she supplied, and he let out a low laugh.

"Awkward is a good word for it." He closed his eyes and took a deep breath. "So, let's be honest, shall we? We're about to get into bed for the first time and pretty much two entire Packs' worth of people know what we're doing."

Brie blushed a pretty red and ducked her head. "Pretty much. But we don't need to let them in the house." She looked up again and rolled her shoulders back. "The thing is, we can ignore them right now. We have to. It's just the two of us, and since we *know* what's about to happen...we should try to enjoy it, I guess."

Gideon barked out a laugh, and Brie looked at him as though he was crazy. He shook his head then cupped her face. "Brie, you're gorgeous, caring, and my mate. I want you. Don't think I don't. When I make love to you, we're both going to enjoy it. Fuck, I've had a hard-on for you since I first saw you, but I just don't like others knowing what I'm doing. I also don't like the fact that we don't really know each other, and we're doing things backward." He wasn't usually so cautious about sex, but this was different than all those other times for more reasons than one.

Her eyes widened, and her gaze went to his dick. She blushed even more, and he snorted. His cock was so hard he was surprised he hadn't already burst the zipper.

"Well, at least I know you want me, right?" she asked, her voice a bit shaky. He could scent her arousal, and it only pushed him further. "Because I want you too."

She held out her hand, and he took it then pulled her close to his body. She gasped then melted into him.

"I'm an Alpha, little wolf. I like control. You okay giving it to me?"

She nodded, then licked her lips. "Take it. Take me."

He growled and crushed his mouth to hers. Her lips parted, and he thrust his tongue inside as he cupped the back of her head. She rocked and his wolf pushed at him, wanting more. If the wolf had his way, he'd slam Brie against the wall and fuck her hard right there. When she moaned under him, he wrapped her hair around his fist and forced her to stay put. He needed her taste sealed on his tongue, needed her to know that he was the one calling the shots.

When he pulled away, they were both gasping for air. "Bedroom," he growled out, and she nodded.

He put the thoughts of his Pack and everything else that would interrupt them out of his head. Right then, this would be just for them. They both deserved it even if he didn't know what would come next.

When they got to his room, her gaze went to the new hole in his wall, and he held back a curse. She just turned toward him and raised a brow.

"I'll fix it tomorrow."

"Okay." No questions. No accusations. Maybe he could get used to having a mate.

"You ready for this?"

"Stop asking and take me." She licked her lips, her wolf in her eyes, but still a shy smile on her face despite her words.

Damn, he wanted her. He kissed her again, this time letting his hands roam down her back to cup her ass. She rocked into him and let out a little moan. His little wolf liked his touch. Good.

He molded her ass in his hands then pulled back so he could strip off her dress. He swallowed at the sight of her in nothing but her panties.

Small. White. Lacy.

Her nipples, already pink, blushed a soft red as he stared. He couldn't wait to suck on them until they reddened a dark cherry. "I...I didn't have a bra that worked with this dress."

"Fuck, you look amazing." He reached out and cupped her breast. Her eyes widened, and he rolled her nipple between his fingers. "I like that you're already unwrapped for me. Makes it easy for me to taste every inch of you." He cupped both breasts and felt the weight of them in his palms. "I know you have to wear a bra every day since your tits will bounce without them, but I'm going to enjoy unwrapping you myself too."

She pressed her breasts into his hands, and he grinned. "Please..."

He pinched her nipples hard, and she let out a little gasp. "Please what, little wolf? Please lick your nipples? Please suck on them? Do you want me to fuck them? Stick my dick between the two of them and slide between them? Or maybe I'll do that and have you suck on my cock at the same time. What do you think?"

She squirmed, and he grinned. He didn't know she'd be like this, so open, so ready. He'd been afraid she'd be scared of what he wanted, but from the way she moved, he was wrong. He wouldn't do everything tonight, no use scaring her, but maybe they could make this mating work—at least in the bedroom.

"There...there's something you should know."

His hand was lower on her belly, playing with the edge of the scrap of lace between her thighs, and he froze. "Okay."

"I've never done this before."

He blinked. "You mean you've never mated before."

She shook her head, her eyes downcast. "I've never made love before."

He pulled away, shocked but, honestly, not that shocked. He'd had a feeling even if he hadn't wanted to admit it.

She looked up at him, her eyes wide. She crossed her arms over her breasts, her face pale.

"You can't be serious. You're in your thirties, Brie. You're a wolf. You might be submissive, but you have needs and heat just like the rest of the females in the Pack."

She raised her chin, her eyes filling with tears. "Yes, but I'm not like the other girls."

"What the hell do you mean by that?" Fuck. Tonight was not going right. He thought he was doing okay, but hell, it looked as though things fucked up before they could even start.

Her lower lip trembled, and he wanted to pull her into his arms and make everything better.

He didn't.

"I saw you when I was seventeen, Gideon. You were in the den talking to Kade, and I just saw the back of you. I knew who you were to me from that day forward."

He sucked in a breath. The ramifications of what she was saying hit him hard in the chest. "You've known all this time?"

She nodded, a single tear falling down her cheek. "Yes, and I didn't do anything about it. I was damn sure to make sure you never saw me until I had no other choice."

"Why?" His wolf slammed into him then whimpered, as if he was angry and hurt at the same time. He didn't blame it; Gideon was feeling pretty much the same.

"You know why. Don't think I did it because I enjoyed the pain of knowing you'd be with others, but I couldn't because my wolf had already chosen. I was never going to be the right mate for you. You know that too, or you would have come for me as soon as you found out. Instead, we're forced into this. So yes, I'm a virgin because I couldn't find a wolf that my wolf would accept, even if only for a night."

"I...I don't know what to say, Brie."

She shook her head. "Then don't say anything. We need to complete the bond, and I don't want to start this mating feeling like I did something wrong."

He took a step toward her and cupped her face in both hands. "You didn't, little wolf. You didn't do anything wrong."

She bit her lip and closed her eyes. "Please, can we just get this over with?"

He lowered his head, resting his forehead against hers. "I'm going to make this good for you. It might hurt, but I'll do my best to make it worth it."

"Okay," she whispered.

Damn it. He felt like a heel. Not only were they mating under the wrong circumstances, now he was going to take her virginity. He'd deal with the fact she'd known about him all this time later. It would hurt the both of them if he worried about it now.

Instead, he pulled her closer and kissed her again. She stood frozen until he licked the seam of her lips. Slowly, she melted against him. He slid his hands down her arms and forced her to lower them, baring her breasts. Her body shook, and he stood back, admiring her curves.

He traced her breasts then her sides, before slowly taking off her panties. He sucked in a breath at the sight of the dark triangle of hair between her thighs. He could scent her and knew she was wet, ready for him, but he wanted this to be as good for her as possible. He also knew that she would feel vulnerable standing naked in front of him while he kept his clothes on. Next time, he'd take more control, be rougher, but not this time.

Instead, he stood back and stripped out of his clothes. She'd seen naked bodies before, of course. She couldn't be a wolf on the hunt and *not* see them in passing, but he wanted to make sure he gave her enough time to study him. His wolf was on edge, forcing his body to shake, but he took control, knowing he had to...for her.

When her gaze rested on his cock, he took it in hand and stroked it, watching the way her eyes glowed gold.

Good.

He then took two steps toward her and slowly lowered her to the bed. He felt her tremble beneath him, so he kissed her softly, trying to soothe. He wasn't any good at this soothing and caring shit. He was an Alpha who took and made it good for his partner because they took what he gave and reveled in it. This was different for him, but then again, all of this was new.

"Scoot up," he whispered, and she made her way to the head of the bed.

He knelt between her legs, his hands on her knees. "I want to taste you, little wolf. Will you let me?"

She nodded, her breath coming in pants.

He slowly parted her legs, baring her for his gaze. He licked his lips then lowered himself so he could taste her. When he looked up at her, he saw her blush and knew she wasn't comfortable.

"You know what I see, Brie?"

She shook her head.

"I see a woman who wants me. Wants me to taste her then fill her. That's want I want too, little wolf."

Her throat worked as she swallowed hard.

He lowered his head then licked up her pussy, flicking at her clit. She bucked off the bed, moaning.

"Gideon."

He nipped at her inner thigh then slowly licked and sucked at her, wanting her to come before he took her.

"Touch your breasts, Brie. Pretend your hands are my hands. You remember what that felt like?"

She moaned again then tentatively cupped her breasts. He growled against her clit then worked her some more, using one finger to breach her entrance. Goddess, she was tight, and he knew he would hurt her, but he'd do his best to make it good for her.

When her panting grew faster and her clit swelled, he sucked on the little nub and worked her harder. Her pussy clamped around his finger, and she arched, coming against his face.

"Gideon!"

His name on her lips pushed him over the edge, and he pulled away, positioning himself at her entrance.

"You ready, little wolf?"

Her gaze met his, her eyes filled with tears. The sight broke him, and he cupped her face, wanting to know how to fix what he'd fucked up.

"I'm ready," she whispered.

He positioned himself and pressed forward. She winced, her body stiffening when he broke through her hymen. Slowly, oh so slowly, he filled her, his cock pulsing as he worked his way in and out of her. He'd never been with a virgin before, but he at least knew how to make her feel better.

He worked his hand between them and rubbed her clit, watching the way her eyes widened as she grew wetter. Finally, his cock was fully in, and he froze, waiting for her to stretch to accommodate him.

"You okay?"

"You're big," she rasped out.

Surprised, he chuckled, and she laughed softly with him. "I like the way you think." He kissed her softly then lifted his head again. "I'm going to move now, Brie. It might hurt, but then it'll feel better. I promise."

"I trust you."

His world tilted, and he nodded. Her words stunned him, and he prayed that he was enough of a wolf to be worthy of that trust. He kissed her again then worked his way in and out of her. Their gazes locked, never leaving one another as their bodies connected, their breaths synchronizing as he pushed a little harder. His wolf howled, his fangs elongating, ready to mark Brie as theirs. He could see her wolf in her eyes and knew she was close to the edge as well. He pumped in and out of her, his body shaking, sweating with exertion.

This was it. This was the end of the line yet the start of something scarier than anything he'd ever faced.

When she bowed beneath him, he thrust home once more, his lower back tingling and his balls tightening. He came deep inside her, his seed filling her. He gasped as their souls locked, entwining around one another like a solid band, much stronger than he'd ever thought possible.

She turned her head to the side, baring her throat, and he moved so he could cup the back of her head, bringing her mouth to his neck as well. With one last breath, he bit into the meaty part of her shoulder, marking her as his for all time. His wolf howled once more, and he arched against her, pumping again as his cock filled. She bit into his shoulder, and their wolves found one another, their mating complete as their human souls joined.

He lifted his head from her neck then licked the wound closed before taking her mouth in his. He didn't care that he could taste the blood of their mating, could taste the promise of the unknown, he knew only that he had to have her once more.

Her nails raked down his back, bringing them closer as he pumped in and out of her. With one last thrust, they both came again, their bodies sweat-slick and spent.

He could feel her soul, feel her against him, and knew this was only the beginning.

The beginning of what he didn't know, but he knew they'd find out.

Together.

CHAPTER SIX

Finn Jamenson stood in the center of the Talon den, his hands in his pockets and mind on everything and nothing. He'd watched his best friend and cousin mate a man she didn't know, a man who might break her because he wouldn't know how to do anything else.

It wouldn't be easy being mated to an Alpha. He knew it wasn't always easy for his mother, but her wolf was dominant enough to not only face his father's wolf but also deal with the Pack's politics. It wasn't that Kade treated Melanie badly—in fact it was the exact opposite. It was that sometimes the Alpha's wolf needed to let out aggression...

And that was enough of that line of thinking.

He ran a hand over his face then turned toward the festivities. Brie and Gideon had left to cement their mating, and most of the people in front of him were probably doing their best *not* to think about what that entailed. He wasn't sure how his Uncle Jasper was faring, but it couldn't have been easy for the very dominant wolf to let his daughter marry into another Pack.

That thought brought his wolf to the surface—not that his wolf was ever too far down anyway.

Brie wasn't one of them anymore. She was a Talon. A Brentwood. The Alpha female.

He wasn't sure how her submissive nature was going to play out in this case, but if she ever needed him, he'd be there. It didn't matter that he'd have to cross Pack lines to make sure she was cared for. He might be the Heir, but he was also a Jamenson. Family was important. They'd already lost so much in the wake of a war that had been brought to them.

Finn might have been only a young child at the time, but he still remembered flashes of what his family had lost, could still remember the screaming and burn of the fire as the demon had lashed out. He remembered the exact moment he'd become the Heir—the way the bonds had latched on to him, digging into his soul and spirit.

He also remembered the time before that when he'd lost something important to him. Though he could remember only flashes of the pain that had almost killed him, he knew the memories were still there, buried to shield him.

He swallowed hard then pushed that from his mind. Today was supposed to be a celebration, though no one truly believed that. Willow might have been doing her best to bring the Brentwoods closer so her daughter would be loved, but it wouldn't matter if things went to hell.

"Why are you frowning?"

Finn turned around at the woman's words then stuck his hands back in his pockets.

"Brynn, right?" he asked. The woman with dark hair and bright blue eyes nodded, a peculiar expression on her face. Damn, she was sexy, but his wolf didn't perk up beyond the normal way he did when a strong wolf of another Pack was near.

"Yes, and you're Finn. We haven't met formally yet, though we've been to a few things together." There was something off about her voice, but he couldn't place it. Whatever it was, it wasn't as though he could fix it. He'd done nothing wrong, and he honestly didn't understand women.

He was at least man enough to admit that.

"So, why were you frowning?"

He shrugged, but when she narrowed her eyes, he spoke with honesty. "We don't know your brother or how this mating will change Brie. She's ours, even if she has to be yours now because of the bonds."

She nodded, though she frowned harder. "I understand. Gideon is very important to my family—beyond being the Alpha. I don't know how this will work either, but I know I don't want your cousin being hurt because of it." She met his gaze, and he saw the wolf in her eyes. "I can't protect her, Finn. If I were to try, I'd cut off her legs before she had a chance to stand. She'll have to face the Pack on her own, though I will be there to try to catch her if she falls."

He blinked, stunned that she would admit such a thing. "You're the dominant female of the Pack at the moment, aren't you?"

She nodded. "Yes, and I will continue to be so, even with Brie here. I'll answer to her because she is the Alpha's mate and because I hope she will do good things for our Pack, but in terms of the strength of our wolves, I will always be stronger."

Finn cursed under his breath. "It's fucking confusing. I don't envy you."

Brynn shrugged, but he saw the anger rolling under her skin. "I'll do what I can, but Brie will have to find a way to earn their respect. I just hope she's strong enough."

"She's plenty strong. She only shows it in different ways."

Brynn met his gaze once again, this time a pain in her eyes that he didn't understand. "I hope so. I hope she does good for our Pack. We've been coasting for far too long. This might be good for us."

He didn't say anything but studied her face. Something was off about this conversation, an underlying importance he couldn't grasp.

"You don't know," she whispered. "How can you not know?"

He narrowed his eyes. "What are you talking about?"

She shook her head then backed up a step. "It's not important." She raised her chin. "Goodbye, Finn Jamenson."

"Goodbye, Brynn Brentwood." Oddly formal, but she'd started it.

She turned away and left quickly.

He honestly didn't understand women. And this Brynn was more confusing than most. It didn't matter though. He had work to do. A Pack to care for...and a cousin to try to keep safe, even though it was out of his hands.

CHAPTER SEVEN

B rie stretched gingerly, her body aching in all the right places. She'd be sore for a few more hours, but thanks to her wolf genetics, she would heal much faster than a human. While Gideon had been gentler once he knew about her experience—or lack thereof—he'd still been really...big.

She blushed at the reminder then scolded herself. She was a mated woman now. Blushing at the size of a penis wasn't the most mature thing to do. Though it wasn't that she was truly embarrassed. Hell no. She *loved* the feeling of him inside her. The intimacy was one thing—something she'd have to learn to understand—but it had been the feeling of heat and hunger that surprised her. She'd craved more even as she'd risen over the crests and peaks. It wasn't as if she'd ever felt something like that for a man before. No, thanks to seeing Gideon as a potential at such a young age, she'd grown up on a path unlike any other.

And now here she was, standing alone in Gideon's house—not hers, as she hadn't even moved anything in yet. But she wasn't sure when or *if* the house would ever feel like hers. Her mother had already made arrangements to send things over and Brie had done all of her packing already. Everything would be taken care of, and it was oddly easy to physically settle in as Gideon's wife. It was everything else that would be difficult. She ran a hand over her face then frowned.

Gideon was gone before she woke up, but she vaguely remembered him cupping her face and growling something at her as she slept. Honestly, for all she knew, it could have been a dream. A dream where she had a mate who truly cared about her, rather than a mate who saw her as a means to an end.

Yes, it wasn't fair to claim to know what he was thinking, but what else could she do? It wasn't as if he was here to tell her. Even if he was here, he probably wouldn't say anything along those lines. No, instead, he'd act like her uncles or cousins and grunt something that was supposed to make sense, and she'd end up as confused as ever.

Well, she needed to stop feeling sorry for herself and get on with the rest of her life. Whatever that life would be. They honestly hadn't talked last night—or even much before that—so now she had no idea what she was going to do. She couldn't scent anyone in the house, so she knew she was alone.

However, what her next step would be was beyond her. She probably should have thought beyond mating him and what that would entail other than the pain and loneliness, but she hadn't been able to get over her wolf's desires. That and Gideon's needs for his Pack.

Now she had to think of practical matters.

Such as if she should leave the house since she was the new Alpha female in a den full of wolves that had never met her. That wouldn't be awkward or anything.

"Brie?"

She stiffened at the familiar voice that she couldn't place and turned toward the front door.

"Brie? It's Ryder. I have breakfast. Can you let me in?"

She immediately relaxed and went to the door. Ryder had performed the ceremony with such a composed tone that she'd calmed a little more than she probably would have without him. She'd been so freaking scared, and yet excited at the same time, that she wasn't sure she'd remember what had actually happened for a long while.

When she opened the door, Ryder walked in, a small smile on his face and a bag in one hand and a set of coffees in the other. He looked so much like Gideon it surprised her. All of the Brentwoods looked similar and though Ryder was slightly more slender, she still thought her Gideon was the most attractive.

Her Gideon.

She supposed that was the case now, even though she wasn't sure she could truly feel that way and be honest.

"I brought doughnuts and coffee," Ryder said as he wiped off his shoes. "I figured you'd need some fuel before the rest of us show up."

Brie blinked then took a coffee from him, oddly relieved he was there even if she was confused. It was nice to not be alone. She'd grown up with dozens of cousins and more Pack members than she knew how to deal with, and now she found herself alone in a sea full of people.

"Thank you." She took a step back so he could move into the room. "And what do you mean the rest of you? Did I miss something?"

Ryder gave her a quick smile then motioned for her to sit down. Still confused, she sat at one end of the couch as he sat on the other.

"Gideon didn't mention that he called over the family to meet with you before the Pack hunt tonight?"

Brie blinked and set down her coffee, thankful she hadn't taken a sip when he'd spoken. "No. He didn't." She looked away from his knowing gaze and mumbled, "He didn't say a lot of things."

She winced at that last part, annoyed she'd let it slip. She wasn't this sad, little weakling, too afraid to voice her mind, but everything around her was new and stifling. She was in a home that wasn't her own, but now she was expected to live here. At least that's what she thought since she hadn't actually spoken to Gideon about it. She was expected to be the Alpha's mate and take on duties as such, but she hadn't a clue what those responsibilities were. Now she was going to be surrounded by a whole family of Brentwoods who, most likely, had been expecting a stronger mate for their brother and cousin.

Brie wouldn't be anything they expected.

Honestly, with the way she'd jumped in head-first without thinking, she wasn't who she was expecting either.

Ryder sighed then set his coffee down as well. "Gideon isn't a big talker." He snorted then shook his head. "Actually, *I'm* not the big talker. Gideon talks, but it's more of a bark as he orders people around. He can't help it. He's Alpha."

Well, wasn't that the understatement of the century? Though she couldn't get the image of him gently caressing her the night before out of her head. Her cheeks heated, and she ducked her eyes, embarrassed to be thinking about her mating while Ryder was in the room. Honestly, she needed to stop blushing at every dirty thought. It was getting annoying. Plus, with the family she'd grown up with, it wasn't as if she'd lived in pure innocence. They all were open about how they loved one another, and more than once, she'd walked in on her aunts, uncles, and parents 'enjoying their mating' as they put it.

She shook her head to clear her thoughts. There would be no use sharing her worries with a man she didn't know. Especially since that man was her new mate's brother.

"So, there's a Pack hunt tonight?" she asked, trying to get to know the man in front of her. She might as well get started learning to be a Talon. The hollowness in her chest that came from losing her Redwood bonds ached, but she knew that, one day, the Talon bonds would cement fully. As of now, they were mere whispers of a promise. They even felt different, as if they were a whole new entity rather than the Pack bonds that she'd grown up with.

Ryder gave her a strange look, as if he was reading her thoughts, then nodded. "Yes. Gideon wanted to do a hunt with you next to him to introduce you to the Pack outside the mating ceremony. It's not a full moon hunt, but since we don't actually need the moon to shift, we'll still go through all the same motions. And this time, you'll be with us. It'll be a good way for you to get to know the Pack."

She nodded, smiling slightly. "That was good of him to think of that." Though it would have been nice if he'd actually spoken to her about it first. She didn't like being kept in the dark, and if she was going to act as the Alpha's mate, she had to not look like an idiot.

Ryder smiled. "Gideon doesn't usually tell others what he's up to. He just does it." He leveled a look at her. "It will be something you'll have to work on with him. You might have a better shot than we ever did."

Nothing like having the weight of a family's worries on her shoulders before she even left the house.

They sat there in silence for a few moments, drinking coffee. It wasn't awkward since Ryder seemed to be a quiet wolf to begin with, but she wanted to ask more questions. Before she could open her mouth to start, the door opened, and the Brentwoods piled in.

She stood up, wiping her hands down her pants, trying not to feel out of place. It was almost impossible to do so considering she was the outsider, despite her new bonds.

These people would be her new family. It wasn't as if she was leaving her own family forever, but mating into a new Pack was different than just a normal mating. She'd lost the physical bonds she'd had before, and now she would have to make new ones. New ones with people she didn't know at all.

Why had she done this again?

Oh yes, because Gideon needed her.

His Pack needed her.

She needed to remember that.

The Brentwoods reminded her of her family in that all of them had a similar, distinctive look about them. Each of them had dark hair and bright blue eyes set in faces with chiseled features and full lips. Seriously, even the cousins looked as though they were all siblings with one another. Plus, they were some of the most beautiful people she'd seen.

Even though they were all attractive, she silently thought that Gideon was the best of the bunch. Not that she'd tell them that.

None of them spoke at first, but each sat down on the pieces of furniture filling the living room. Gideon came in last, and her wolf pushed at her, whimpering because they weren't close enough. Brie held back, barely. He stood in the doorway, his gaze raking her body before he turned away and moved past her to sit on the arm of the couch next to an open spot.

Without a word.

Well, heck. Now what was she supposed to do?

She went back to her seat and sat down, aware that every eye in the room was on her. Instead of cowering under the strength of their wolves, she straightened her spine and raised her chin without meeting any of their gazes. There was only so much her wolf could do in this situation. Maybe a more dominant wolf could have gotten away with more, but she was who she was, and despite what Gideon *might* have needed, there was no changing that.

Brynn tilted her head then sighed. "Well, it seems I'll be the first person to speak since my brother is being oddly quiet." She smiled softly, her face brightening a bit. "Welcome to the family, Brie. I know we've all met you over the years and even more of us last night, but big brother here thought it would be good to have all of us over so you can get to know us better without the rest of the Pack around."

Brie smiled back, relieved the other woman had broken the ice. The fact that it had been Gideon's idea in the first place warmed her. She didn't know him, yet she wanted to. She *needed* to. If she couldn't find out who he was directly from him—it was apparent he wasn't a big talker—then she'd find out through his actions and through others. It was going to have to be the best she could do.

And she could do this, she reminded herself.

Brie cleared her throat. "Well then, it's nice to meet all of you. Again." She let out a small laugh, grateful that a couple of them joined her. "This isn't awkward at all or anything."

Walker, the Healer she remembered, grinned. "Not at all, Brie. We're happy you're a Brentwood now. You know we've been friends with your family for a couple decades now, so we know some things about you. But it will be nice to find out more from having you in our presence."

Ryder sighed. "This *does* feel like an awkward date with the bunch of us seated like this. How about we all introduce ourselves and tell you our roles in the Pack. You might already know all of it, in fact, you *do* know it, but this way we can make it more formal in an informal setting since you are now our Alpha's mate, rather than Jasper's daughter."

"That sounds like a plan," she answered back, aware Gideon's gaze rested on her. Yet the man still hadn't spoken. She *really* wished she'd speak. They hadn't said a word to each other since they'd bonded. Considering they'd fallen asleep soon after in a tangle of limbs, the last thing she remembered of her mate was him pulling out of her.

Not the most helpful way to begin a mating in retrospect.

Ryder smiled softly. "Well then, Brie Brentwood, I'm Ryder Brentwood, Heir to the Pack. I'm the second oldest in our immediate family, hence why I'm the Heir and not Mitchell."

She stiffened for a moment at the sound of her new name coming from his lips, but tried not to show it too much. He'd said it before, of course, during the mating ceremony, but her mind had been on other things—namely trying not to pass out. She'd learn to live with the new name as many mates did, but it still didn't seem real, despite how she'd spent the night before.

Despite *who'd* she'd spent the night before with.

Mitchell, the one with the same blue eyes, though they held a touch more pain, gave her a curt nod. "Max and I are brothers," he said, pointing between him and another wolf with a very sweet smile. "We're also cousins to the rest of these guys."

"We were all raised together," Max said, a smile on his face. "Hence the reason why people confuse us as siblings."

Brie smiled at Max and held out her hand. This wolf she knew more than the rest because of his position in the Pack. "It's good to see you, Max. The council still going well?"

Max took her hand and kissed her inner wrist like he'd done so many times before then froze, pulling back quickly.

Brie froze as well, aware each person in the room hadn't moved or even dared to breathe. A low rumble came from Gideon, and she cursed at herself. Damn it, she was already ruining this mating thing, and she hadn't even started it yet. She quickly sat back and, without thinking, leaned into Gideon's thigh. Her wolf relaxed at the contact, and she felt her mate calm. He put his hand on her shoulder, and her wolf preened at the attention.

It would have been nice, however, if the man would speak.

Just one word would be nice at this point.

Max cleared his throat, his eyes downcast. "Uh yeah, the council is going well." He quickly shot everyone a look, his neck turning red. "Brie's not a council member, but since her cousin is, as are a few of her friends, she helps out. Hence the reason why we know each other." He looked at Gideon, his eyes still down. "I didn't mean anything by the kiss. I promise. It's just habit. It won't happen again."

"See that it doesn't," Gideon growled out.

Brie wanted to smack him for his rudeness just then, but instead, she warmed at the possessiveness. Maybe he *did* want her for more than just his position in the Pack. Though growling at his cousin probably wouldn't help matters when it came to her fitting in.

"We already have enough shit to deal with because of the elders," Gideon bit out. "We don't want them to think you and she had something going on in the past or on the side."

Brie deflated, shocked and hurt at his words. She blinked quickly, surprised she was starting to tear up. How quickly his words could change her emotions. She didn't like this roller coaster ride, nor did she like the insinuation that she would even *think* about stepping out of her mating bonds. Honestly, she wasn't even aware a mate could do that. The mating bonds were so strong with wolves that there was no reason to even *look* at another wolf, let alone act on it.

"You have nothing to worry about," she ground out. She refused to look at him, aware he *still* hadn't spoken to her. No, he'd only spoken once, and it had been to allude to her promiscuity. Or the rumor of such a trait. *Great* way to start a freaking mating.

Walker cleared his throat. "Well, after the cousins, there's the triplets." He tried to smile and failed. "We're the youngest of the bunch, but considering Kameron, Brandon, and I are all over a hundred and fifty, we're really not *that* young."

Brie's eyes widened. "I hadn't realized your ages." She blushed. "Sorry. Not that you're old or anything. I'm just hitting my thirties, so I guess I'm the baby in the room."

Brandon, the Omega of the Pack, smiled, and she cursed at herself. What had she been thinking with her emotions going all over the place? Now that she was a Talon member, Brandon would have been able to feel *every* emotion she felt. It would take time for him to learn her thread and be able to aid her pain or feel her true happiness, but he'd be able to feel her hurt and anxiety. The man hadn't spoken though. Like her uncle and cousin who were Omegas, they had enough going on in their own minds and hearts that they didn't speak much. She'd love to get to know Brandon more since her Uncle Maddox was one of her favorite people, but now wasn't the time. Especially since she could once again feel Gideon's gaze on her.

Frustrated, she turned to her mate, only to find that he'd shifted his attention elsewhere. It stung, but she pushed that away. It wasn't as if this was a normal mating. They'd never promised love, just protection and duty. She'd learn to deal with her new life.

Eventually.

The last of the Brentwoods, Kameron, scowled then gave her a nod. She knew he was the Enforcer, charged with protecting the Pack from outside enemies. He had to be one of the strongest wolves in the room because of the duties placed before him, but she didn't know him well enough to judge him. That would come though.

She'd learn each and every one of them and eventually find a way to make her place within the Pack. She knew who she was when she'd been a Redwood. Now she was a Talon. The Alpha female.

And so freaking lost.

"So, we're going on a Pack hunt tonight?" she asked, trying to break through the tension. Maybe if Gideon would actually speak *to* her, it wouldn't feel so awkward, but she didn't see anything changing soon. If this was how it was going to be for the rest of their mating, she'd have to change something. She might be a submissive, but she refused to lie down and bare her belly, letting others walk over her. Everyone would just have to learn that.

Gideon finally turned to her, and she held her breath. "Yes."

Oh, boy. One word. Watch out, world.

"Yes? Okay. Is there a special place you guys hunt? How long does it usually go on? Are you going to want me to run next to you?" She blushed at that but continued on. "I know Aunt Mel runs next to Uncle Kade every time she can. It's not only because it's tradition, but it's because she likes it." She added that last part so he would know she'd seen a true Alpha couple at work. She and Gideon weren't that couple, but maybe one day they could be friends who talked.

She wasn't looking for love. Not anymore. She'd given that up when she'd said yes to Gideon. Honestly, she'd given that hope up all those years ago when she'd seen him outside her window.

As long as she could live her life in something approaching happiness, she'd be okay.

She just had to get there first.

Gideon's mouth quirked in a smile for a moment, and she felt as though she'd won the lottery with that one gesture. There *was* a man under all that Alpha. She'd seen a glimpse of him last night. Now she just had to dig deeper to find the rest of him.

"Yes," Gideon repeated. "The Pack hunt is tonight. We will start in the clearing outside the circle. It's within the den and protected by the wards. Since it's not a full moon hunt, not everyone will be in attendance."

Ryder cleared his throat.

Gideon raised a brow but didn't move his gaze from hers. "What, Ryder?"

"Since it's Brie's first hunt, there might be more people there than usual."

She swallowed hard. Everyone who came would be there for her, wanting to get a peek at the new mate of the Alpha. She only hoped she lived up to their expectations.

Or surpassed them if they were too low.

Gideon sighed, and it sounded as though he had the weight of the whole world on his shoulders. He did, though, at least the weight of his Pack. Her job would be to help him carry that load if he ever let her. It was only day one though, and she had time to learn how to do her job. Hopefully.

"Fine. Then there might be a few more wolves than you're used to, but they'll watch us shift and start the hunt. It won't go on for too long, but we can go into the forest and let our wolves roam. We're going to do it during the day as well because this *is* different."

She nodded, understanding that this was only the first step of many include her.

"I understand. So when does it start?"

Gideon frowned then looked over her shoulder at the clock on the wall. "In less than an hour actually."

She blinked. That wasn't a lot of time to get prepared, though it wasn't as if she really needed anything *for* the hunt. It was more of preparing herself emotionally. Plus, she really wanted to talk to Gideon alone before they had to strip down in public and shift together.

Brynn stood up and stretched then gave Brie a smile. "We'll see you there then. That way you and Gideon can come in together and we're not all showing up en masse."

Brie stood as well, grateful the other woman seemed to be reading Brie's mind. Eventually, she wanted to get to know Brynn better, but right now, her mating was more important. It was the whole reason she was in this situation after all.

Soon, everyone left, either giving her a nod or a slight pat on the back on their way out. No one dared to hug or kiss her considering they didn't know her, plus Gideon's reaction to Max earlier hadn't been the most welcome. Wolves might be tactile creatures but there was only so much they could do in the face of a possessive Alpha.

When they were left alone, Brie turned around to ask Gideon a question, only to see his retreating back.

"Gideon?" she asked, wondering what he was up to. It would be nice to actually speak to him alone since they were mated. Maybe that was asking too much though.

"I'm going to go take a quick shower, and then we can head to the clearing," he answered without even looking back.

Well then.

She let out a sigh then went to her notepad and starting jotting down notes. She'd need to get the rest of her things and bring them to the house and do a few more chores so she'd feel as though she was home instead of being a guest at Gideon's place. Everything would eventually settle down, but it wouldn't be easy.

Nothing worth having ever was.

By the time Gideon finished showering and walked back into the room, she was at her wit's end. Of course, the fact that he came in with his beard and hair wet, his body filling out his clothes so well that she had to stop from swallowing her tongue didn't help much.

Gideon gave her a knowing glance then gestured toward the door. "Let's head on out. People will probably be getting there early to get a good look at you."

Nothing like feeling as though she was on display to get her ready for a hunt. She sighed and stared down at her linen pants and top. She hadn't brought over much, and it was really all she had left. It wasn't as though she was going to be in them for long, but she still didn't feel right in her own skin.

"Nothing like a bunch of wolves staring down at my every move to help my nerves."

Gideon sighed but took a step toward her. She froze as he cupped her cheek, his face drawn. "It's not going to be easy, Brie. We knew this going in. But I won't let anyone hurt you on the hunt."

Her eyes widened. Honestly, that thought hadn't even occurred to her. Yes, there *were* dominance battles on hunts since everyone would be in wolf form, but she'd never had to be part of one. She was a submissive who'd been happy with her standing in the Pack. Things were much different now.

And even though the thought of him wanting to protect her made her wolf feel all warm and fuzzy, she knew that wasn't the best way to go about things. Her wolf huffed at her, but some things Brie needed to do on her own.

"Well, hell. You might need to let me fight for myself then, Gideon. If they come at me, I will have to show I'm worthy enough to be your mate."

He shook his head, and her heart fell. "You're a submissive. You're not *supposed* to fight."

"But I might have to. You know that. Protecting and coddling me won't help matters in the long run."

"We'll deal with that when it comes to it. Let's just get this over with, shall we?"

She held back her sigh and followed him out of the house, aware that every eye in the Pack was on her. This wasn't going to be fun, and that was the understatement of the year.

If Gideon fought for her because he didn't think she was strong enough to be his mate, this wouldn't end well. However, she didn't know how to stop an Alpha from being...Alpha.

One step at a time, she reminded herself. She was the one who'd offered herself up. Now she had to be the one who dealt with the consequences.

Even if those consequences involved feeling as if she was alone in a sea of wolves.

Forever.

CHAPTER EIGHT

Gideon felt her staring at his back, but he didn't look around to see her. He couldn't. He didn't know what to say to her to make her feel better. He knew he was fucking up this mating thing, but he didn't know a way around it. He'd never felt so inept, and it was only day one of their mating.

This didn't bode well.

He wasn't used to answering to others when it came to his choices.

No, that was wrong.

All he did was answer to others these days. Whether it pertained to the elders or the rest of the Pack, each of his actions had consequences. The fact that he'd taken a mate would create its own ripple effect. He hoped only that the Pack wouldn't reject her outright. If he'd been a more ferocious Alpha, he might have held more sway in forcing others to think what he wanted to them to think. If he had been as his father, then he could have forced the others to accept Brie without blinking.

He hadn't been that kind of Alpha though.

He had never been cruel.

Brie would have to earn her place just like every wolf under his keeping.

If he had to bleed to protect her, though, he would. She hadn't asked for this, and he would not let her be hurt because of it. Despite the fact that he'd only just met her, she *was* his mate. He might not know how to care for her, but his wolf already claimed her as his— as *theirs*.

She wanted to fight for herself, but he wasn't sure she could survive it. Just thinking that made him a horrible wolf, but he'd worry about that later. Right now, all they had to do was shift, run around a bit, and then head back home. They had many other things to worry about, and she needed to officially move in.

The Pack hunt was just the first of many things they needed to accomplish to move on. There would be obstacle after obstacle, but if he tried hard enough, if she tried hard enough, maybe his pack wouldn't tear at the seams.

They were almost to the clearing when he felt Brie slip her smaller hand in his. He almost tripped over his feet but righted himself before he did something idiotic like fall.

He looked down at their joined hands then at her face.

"We're a team," she said simply, her voice much stronger than he'd given her credit for.

He nodded then continued moving. He needed to stop counting her out of the game before she'd even tried. He just wasn't used to anything like this.

When they reached the clearing, he held back a curse when he realized they were far from the first people there. No, in fact, he was pretty sure almost the entire Pack was already waiting. Some were even in wolf form, as if they couldn't wait any longer. Some of the maternal wolves, as well as those wolves with small children at home, weren't there of course. He made a mental note of any wolves that had no real excuse to *not* be there, just in case. He knew Ryder and Mitchell were probably doing the same. That's what made them so good in their roles. It wasn't that the wolves were required to be there, but he had to ensure they weren't there as some sort of statement.

He looked down at Brie quickly, only to see her studying the Pack as if she was trying to memorize each face, each nuance of body language. Again, he'd underestimated her. He shouldn't do it again.

When they reached their spot between Brynn and Ryder, his siblings gave him a nod, and he pulled Brie closer to his side.

"Thank you for coming on this Pack hunt with us," Gideon bellowed out. Every single wolf quieted, their gazes on him and the woman by his side. He felt the tension in Brie's body, but she kept her chin up and a small smile on her face. It was as if she wanted to show the others she wasn't afraid of them and, at the same time, showing who she was deep within.

A submissive at heart.

"As this is not a moon hunt, you do not need to hunt with the Pack. We want you to roam and be true to your wolves. There will be food at the den center for those who want it. For those of you I may not see later, may the goddess bless your hunts."

With that, he tugged Brie closer to him and turned so he could see her face fully. He leaned down so he could whisper and have only those closest to him—his family—overhear his words.

"We're on the edge of the circle, not the center, so you can shift at my side and no one will be able to see every inch of you as you shift." She'd be vulnerable while shifting in the Pack for the first time and he wanted to alleviate any pressure he could. Shifting wasn't easy. It was a painful process that took minutes, not seconds. Each bone broke and reformed, and muscles and tendons tore and shifted to create a new form. It wasn't the magic that people thought, but a process that took energy—enough energy that most couldn't shift more than once a day.

She tilted her head then reached up and kissed the bottom of his chin. He froze, unaccustomed to such public affection. The softness of her lips against the roughness of his beard made him want to shave so he wouldn't hurt her. His wolf pushed at him, already so on edge from the upcoming hunt that Gideon had to hold back hard so he wouldn't take Brie right then and there.

"Thank you," she whispered back. "Everything will be fine. Now let's let our wolves out and let their paws feel the ground." She put her hand over his chest, and he sucked in a breath. "I've never seen you as a wolf before. I'd like to now."

He'd never seen her as a wolf either, but as they'd just met, that made sense. He gave her a stiff nod then took a step back. He saw the disappointment on her face, but there wasn't anything he could do about it. His need for her surprised him, and this wasn't the place. Nor did he think she would welcome his attention considering she was still so fucking innocent.

He could still remember the feel of her under his body and against his skin, the feel of her clenching around him as she came, screaming his name.

He cursed again then stripped off his shirt, needing to shift.

Brie's eyes followed the movement, and she gave him a sly smile before stepping off to his side so the width of his body could shield her. Nudity didn't matter much to wolves, but shifting in front of over a hundred strangers while they were all staring at her probably wasn't the best way to start the hunt.

He knelt down on all fours and pulled on the bond between him and his wolf. Since he was Alpha, he could shift faster than any of the other wolves in his Pack. He wasn't sure how the bond between him and Brie would effect her change, but hopefully, it would make it easier on her. That was at least one thing he could provide in this whole mess.

The shift hurt like hell, but it was a welcome pain. His wolf rejoiced in his new form, their souls melding within their new body. He was a big man, and since he was also Alpha, he was a big wolf as well. His fur was black as pitch and made it easy to hunt at night. He stood out like a beacon in the snow, but there were other ways to get around that.

He shook off the last of his change and looked down at Brie. She was still shifting, but at least almost done. He studied the color of her fur, surprised to find it pure white. He shouldn't have been surprised though. It only made sense that fate would give him a pure white wolf as his mate to contrast his pure black coat. Opposite sides of the coin in all ways that mattered.

Once she finished shifting, she stood up, letting out a small whimper that only he could hear. He quickly licked her muzzle, showing her he was there. From the look of panic in her eyes, the shift must have come on much quicker than she was used to. He should have told her about the possibility before they'd started, but then again, he should have told her a lot of things before she'd become a Talon. There was no going back now.

He inhaled her scent, letting it flow over him. It somehow calmed and incensed his wolf at the same time, and he knew the mating urge was far from over.

If he wasn't careful, he'd have her against a tree and bury himself deep within her once they shifted back.

Of course, the idea held merit...and she *was* his mate.

From the look in her eyes, she knew where his mind had gone, and he let out a strangled cough before nudging her side. When she didn't move, he cursed himself then nuzzled her neck before gently biting down. He'd almost forgotten to claim her as his in front of the Pack in the way of their wolves. It wasn't that it didn't matter...it was just that he was so comfortable around her and with her by his side, as if she were meant to be there, that he almost skipped steps. Important steps.

Comfortable wasn't the right word though, considering he was always on edge around her. His need to protect her and *be* with her overrode all his good judgments. If he wasn't careful, he just might find himself falling for his mate.

An Alpha couldn't do that.

It would make her a liability.

He licked her muzzle then angled his head so he could study his Pack. No one had left since they would be waiting for him to make the first move. Some were still shifting, but most were done, watching him and Brie interact. Startled, he saw that the elders had come as well. They didn't participate in such events often, but since they were the reason he'd been forced to mate in the first place, it made sense. He also noticed Iona by their side, shifted and her head held high.

This would not end well if he let Iona anywhere near Brie.

With that sobering thought, he let out a howl, the sweet melody of Brie's howl blending with his own before the rest of the Pack joined in. He took off at a run, knowing the others would follow. He needed to burn off his energy as well as keep an eye on Brie. That meant he would not let his wolf go to the forefront of his mind. His wolf seemed to understand that, though, and made it easy for the both of them.

His paws pounded against the soil and grass at a steady rhythm. He sensed his family and Brie near him, running behind him but close. By the sounds around him, rabbits and other prey scurried away as they caught the scent of the Pack, but he ignored them. Unlike other hunts, he wasn't chasing animals. This was about the run and keeping an eye on Brie. He slowed down then, letting Brie come up by his side.

Just as he leaned down to nip playfully at her neck, the scent of other wolves reached them. He stopped completely and pressed his body against Brie's. She nudged back then took a step away, pushing at him with her nose. It seemed she wanted to say she had this, but he wasn't sure he could let her go.

Shannon jumped over a fallen log near them, and he twisted so he could watch her fully. The others would be able to care for Brie in case any one in his Pack came up with the idiotic notion to attack his mate as a sign of dominance.

She pawed at the ground, ready to pounce, so he slowly walked toward her, leaving Brie in the hands of his family. They would protect her at all costs.

He had promised it.

Shannon angled her head, her eyes full of bright anger. There was nothing he could do about that. He'd never been able to make the woman happy since he wasn't a vengeful psychopath like his father.

The woman wanted to rule like a tyrant, and he wouldn't let her.

Forcing him to mate because of age-old customs was only a small part of her arsenal. He was afraid to see what else she could come up with. The woman was up to something—he knew it. Or, if it wasn't her, something else was coming. The ache in his bones told him so. He wasn't an Alpha for nothing.

Brynn let out a yip behind him, and he growled. He turned, only to find a group of dominant juveniles come to Brie's side. Before he could growl, one of the wolves pounced on Brie, teeth bared and claws out.

Brie let out a growl as the other wolf clawed her. She moved, but not fast enough to escape another wolf latching on to her side.

The others weren't helping her. No. Instead, they were standing back with pain in their eyes, as if they wanted to help but couldn't.

What the ever-loving fuck.

Gideon growled then clawed at the wolves who'd dared touch his mate. He reached for another wolf but found him whimpering as Brie bit down on his neck. Surprised, he looked down at her, but she turned away, leaving the other wolf on the ground.

Hell.

He'd failed her.

He'd promised her she wouldn't get hurt, yet that's exactly what had happened. The scent of her blood on the ground beneath him enraged him, and he threw back his head and howled. There was no way he could complete the hunt now. Instead, he growled at every wolf nearby then went to Brie's side, nudging her so they were near a tree he knew would hold clothes that some of them left for emergencies.

With his gaze on hers, he started to shift back, needing to feel her and check her wounds.

She sighed as only a wolf could then shifted as well.

As soon as he stood, he looked down at Ryder who had come up to them. "Go back and finish the hunt.

I'll deal with all of you later. What the fuck were you thinking? She's hurt, and we all let it happen."

"Gideon."

He twisted around so fast he almost lost his footing. "Brie." He moved toward her, kneeling down so he could check her wounds.

She panted, her eyes bright with pain. "I'm fine. They were only doing what I asked them to do. Remember? I need to fight on my own." She sighed as he put his hands over the bite marks on her side. "You shouldn't have stood in the way. I could have handled the two of them. Now I'm going to have to start over to prove I'm worthy."

He growled out a curse then reached for a shirt in the pile at the base of the tree. "Put this on. I'm taking us home. We'll deal with what you were thinking there."

"Gideon."

"Not. Another. Word."

She raised a brow but didn't speak. Instead, she pulled a shirt over her head. He tugged on a pair of sweats and figured that would be enough to get them home. The others could deal with his and Brie's clothes at the clearing. He needed to see Brie home and check her wounds. His wolf growled, pushing at him and craving vengeance.

It shouldn't have surprised him that wolves would want a fight for dominance. None of the marks covering Brie's body were too deep, and they were all within the realm of reason. She *should* have to fight to prove herself. If she'd been any other wolf, he'd have applauded her. However, she wasn't.

She was *his*.

Only he didn't know what to do about that.

Without speaking, he picked her up and cradled her to his chest. They made their way to the house without uttering a word, his anger rising with each step. With one hand, he opened the door then slammed it behind him once they were inside. Instead of setting her down, he put her on the dining room table, his body shaking.

"Shirt off. Now."

"How about you use complete sentences? Hmm?"

"Fuck, Brie. Just take off your goddamn shirt so I can clean up your wounds. Then you can be all pissy about me doing my *job* and taking down that wolf who dared to touch you."

She raised an eyebrow then wiggled a bit so she could take off her shirt. That left her naked on his table, her nipples erect and begging for his mouth.

This was so not the time.

However, it seemed his dick didn't get the memo.

Her gaze traveled down his body to his cock tenting his sweats, and she licked her lips.

Dear. God.

"I'm not pissy, asshole."

He blinked. "Did you just call me an asshole?"

"Uh yeah. Because you're being one. I get it. You're an Alpha. You have dominant needs that require you to puff out your chest and growl and yell. I'm fine with that. I'm your submissive wolf, so I will make sure you're taking care of yourself. What you fail to realize is that because you're spending so much time worrying about others you're letting your own needs and wants go to the wayside. That's what I'm here for. Eventually the Pack will see that."

"It's not about sex," he said lamely.

She blushed but rolled her eyes. "Yeah, that sounded really dirty, but I was actually talking about things *other* than sex. If your wolf needs someone to care for, then I'm here. But standing in the way when I'm trying to fight for myself in a Pack battle won't help." She met his gaze and sighed. "You need to let me take care of myself. I know I can't win every fight, but I'm stronger than you think I am.

Gideon closed his eyes then leaned forward, pressing his forehead against hers. "You don't know my Pack, Brie."

"Then let me know them. Give me time." She put her hand on his arm, and he relaxed somewhat. "And they are *our* Pack now."

Gideon pulled away and opened his eyes. "You're right. But that doesn't make it okay that they would hurt you." He swallowed hard then went to get his medical supplies. Brie would heal fast, and if any of the wounds had been worse, he'd have called Walker to Heal her. He still wanted to clean the cuts and scratches just in case. He had to do *something,* and yelling at her wouldn't help anything.

When he came back, she had her legs up on the table, her arms wrapped around her knees. She eyed the box in his hands and sighed.

"I'm fine, Gideon. But if it will help you calm down by cleaning up my side, then by all means, go for it."

He narrowed his eyes. "Thank you for your permission."

He went to work, cleaning each cut and bite with precise care. She didn't wince, nor did she gasp when the sting probably should have made her do so. She was being strong for him, and that made him feel worse.

He had to do better than he was at this mating thing, but he had no idea what he was doing. There wasn't a manual for this thing.

"What the other wolves did wasn't wrong."

"I don't want to talk about it," he snapped then set everything down. He was done anyway. He moved so he stood between her legs, his hands on the table beside her hips.

She sucked in a breath, and he could scent her arousal. Damn. Not touching her was not going to be easy.

"Let me calm down, Brie. Then we can discuss what happened and how to fix it."

She reached out and cupped his face. Instinctively, he turned his head and kissed her palm. When her lips parted at the action, he couldn't help himself. He leaned down and took her mouth in a hungry kiss, forcing his palms to stay on the table and not move to his mate.

He pulled away, hungry. "Tell me no, Brie. Tell me no and I'll walk away right now. You need to heal. You need time to...well, you just need time." Time to be herself, time to be a Talon, time to not be in his clutches because he couldn't seem to hold himself back.

She wrapped her legs around his waist and pulled him closer. "I'm not saying no."

He swallowed hard then gripped her hips in his hands. "Good."

He slammed his mouth on hers, craving her more than he'd ever craved another. This wasn't only his wolf wanting a mate. No, this was him wanting the woman beneath him. He wanted to be inside her, claim her as his own over and over until they were both spent.

"I'm not going to go easy this time," he ground out, his chest heaving.

"Good. Take me as I am, and I'll do the same."

He searched her face, trying to understand her motives. He honestly didn't understand Brie. She was so strong in some respects yet seemed so scared in others. She was a puzzle his wolf demanded he figured out, but Gideon wasn't sure he'd ever be able to. She surprised him at every turn. She'd mated him for his Pack, not for herself. He understood that much. Didn't he? Why else would she throw herself into a situation that seemed impossible?

"Kiss me," she whispered, and he was lost.

He pressed his lips to hers once more, tasting her on his tongue, needing her more than he'd ever needed anyone before.

His hands roamed her sides, careful of the wounds that were already healing. They'd been superficial, although, in the heat of the fight, he'd feared they'd been so much worse.

She grasped his hand and placed it on her breast. His eyes widened, and then he grinned. It seemed his mate wanted him to keep his mind on the task at hand. That he could do. He plucked at her nipples, loving the way she gasped at each movement, her eyes glowing gold. He rolled her nipples between his fingers, pinching slightly to watch her eyes grow molten. She squirmed under him, the sweet scent of her arousal mixing with the heady scent of his own.

Her legs fell to the sides, spreading her wide. She seemed to be doing it subconsciously, but he didn't care if she'd meant to do it or not. He wanted her. Wanted her taste on his tongue.

He grinned then pulled away so he could kneel beside the table, which was the perfect height for what he wanted to do. Brie let out a squeal when he tugged her closer to the edge.

"Gideon."

"Yes, say my name. Remember it when you're coming on my tongue."

Her eyes widened then rolled back when he sucked on her clit. Goddess, she tasted magnificent. He licked and nibbled her pussy, wanting her to come on his face. He placed his hands on her hips, forcing her butt to stay on the table when she wanted to squirm. Each time he circled her clit, she let out a little mewling sound that was so fucking hot he was about to come in his sweats right then and there.

When he fucked her with his tongue, piercing her channel, her moans grew breathier, and he knew she was close. He let go of one hip so he could play with her clit with his free hand. As soon as he touched the swollen ball of nerves, she stiffened then arched her back, pushing her breasts up.

"Gideon!" she screamed as she came on his tongue. Fuck, she tasted exquisite. Like a heaven he knew he'd never get enough of.

He stood quickly, pulling his sweats down over his ass so he could free his cock. He was so hard he was afraid he'd blow in one go.

Her eyes widened, and she sat up, reaching for him. "I want to taste you to."

He shook his head, staying her hand. "Not now. I promise I want your sweet mouth around my cock." He groaned at the mental image. "But right now, if I don't get in you, I'm going to come all over your breasts and belly before I even fill you up."

She grinned then spread her legs wide. "Then get to it, Alpha mine."

He leaned down to kiss her, moaning into her mouth, as she wrapped her legs around his waist once again pulling him closer. This time he had one hand on the base of his cock so he could position himself at her entrance.

"Ready?" he asked, his voice a growl.

"Always," she panted.

It seemed his little mate wanted him just as much as he wanted her. Good to know.

He kept his eyes on hers as he pushed inside, loving the way she gasped, and his hips flexed. Her inner walls clenched around him, and his cock ached.

"Damn it, you feel so fucking good, Brie."

She grinned then moaned. "You feel fucking good, too, Gideon."

He leaned down and kissed her hard. "I like it when you say fuck. Makes me think of fucking you."

She rolled her eyes then shifted her hips, causing both of them to moan. "Stop merely thinking about fucking me and fuck me."

He growled, gripping her hips with bruising force, pulling out before slamming back in. Brie let out a gasp then threw her head back, her breasts bouncing with each thrust.

He pounded into her, aware their mating bond sparked with each movement, as if they were finding one another all over again. She raised her head, her gaze meeting his. He shifted so he had one hand on her hip to keep them steady and the other on the back of her neck. When he leaned forward, he pressed their foreheads together, their gazes never breaking.

"Come for me, Brie. Come around my cock."

She lifted her hips then parted her lips, shattering beneath him, around him.

He couldn't hold back any more, thrusting one last time until he burst, coming hard, deep inside her. His balls tightened even more, his dick pulsing as he filled her up with his cum. Just then, the image of his seed taking root and making her pregnant with his child flashed in his mind, and he sucked in a breath, shocked at how much that image appealed to him. He was, apparently, Alpha in every sense of the word.

He kissed her hard once more, pushing those thoughts from his mind. They had a hell of a lot more to worry about than getting her pregnant. He wanted to know her, and she damn well had a right to know him before carrying his child.

Nothing had been settled with the Pack nor with the woman beneath him, yet he couldn't care just then.

His chest warmed, and he knew he was feeling something he hadn't felt in a long while...if ever.

Contentment.

And that scared him more than he'd ever thought possible.

CHAPTER NINE

Leo Brentwood pumped his hips, finally near release with the woman on all fours in front of him. He let out a grunt then pulled out, spilling on her ass and lower back. He wasn't mated with the woman, so he didn't need to deal with children, but he liked showing his dominance by coming on her, rather than in her.

It was a mess she'd have to clean up herself.

Shannon, the Talon Pack elder, cursed when she looked over her shoulder. "Really? You can't just finish in me? I hate when my back gets sticky."

Leo shrugged then went to get a bottle of water while Shannon cleaned herself up. "Whatever. So, how was the Pack hunt with my dear nephew?"

Shannon rolled her eyes then pulled on her dress. "Boring, honestly. The wolves got close enough to her so she spilled some blood, but she's still breathing."

"We didn't want her dead now anyway. It's too early." Leo sat down naked on his piece-of-shit couch and sighed. One day he'd have the riches that were owed to him instead of hiding out in this rat hole.

Either that or his final plan would come to fruition, and it wouldn't matter anyway.

"I know, I know. But I don't like her." Shannon pouted then sat down next to him, rubbing his chest as if he liked when she did it. He didn't push her away though. She had her purpose.

"She's not Iona."

"No, she's not. Though Iona isn't in on the plan, so I don't know how much use she would have been. She's more easily controlled than Brie because of her thirst for ranking, but she still fights me over little things." She licked her lips then sighed. "One day you'll be Alpha like you should have been, and then we can rule the Pack in the way of the wolves, rather than the castrated humans Gideon is making us."

"I like the way you talk, Shannon." Though they both knew there was another layer to their plans if things went to shit. "When Gideon killed my brother Joseph, I thought I'd be next."

Shannon tut-tutted. "You *were* almost next. You're only alive because I got you out in time. The rest of your brothers are dead because they were moronic. They weren't smart enough to kill the little bastard when he was too young to defend himself."

Leo wrapped her hair around his fist and forced her gaze to his. The position forced her neck to be at an awkward angle, but he didn't care.

"Don't call my brothers moronic, little elder."

She rolled her eyes then reached down and squeezed his already filling cock. "Sorry, darling. Anyway, where were we?"

"We will wait until Brie is at her lowest. Gideon was foolish to bring in a submissive to be his mate. She doesn't suit. The other wolves will do most of the work for us. They will never accept her. And just when

Gideon is regretting his choice, we will make sure he fears her loyalties."

"Then we'll kill her."

He shrugged again, releasing Shannon. "Of course. She's worthless really, but her death by Talon hands will force the Redwoods to fight."

"And we can make it so they die as well, or at least get caught in the crossfire."

"That way we rise to the top. Once my sons and nephews, and Brynn too of course, are dead, I will have my rightful spot on the throne. They have no children between them, so I will be the new Alpha." And the rest of his plan can begin.

"And soon they will know they've been wrong all along."

He nodded, grinning. "Of course. We can't let them think they're too safe, can we?"

"I do like the way you think," she purred, running her hand up and down his length now. She licked her lips, her eyes glowing gold.

He grinned then moved her head down. She would know what to do. As soon as she opened her mouth, he kept her head in place and fucked her mouth, pumping his hips at a steady rhythm. She gagged then moaned. They suited each other in their views and proclivities.

For now.

"We will bring the Talons into the new dawn," he panted, holding her hair in a punishing grip.

Her nails raked his thighs, and he groaned, letting her go. She pulled up then straddled his waist. He lifted her skirt above her hips then thrust up, filling her in one stroke.

She rocked her hips, her hands on his shoulders. "We'll hurt him where it matters most," she panted.

"The lowest members of the Pack, his trust, his family, and now this new submissive bitch." He slammed into her with each word, knowing they were both close.

"Perfect," she said then screamed his name as she came.

He thrust one more time then came again, his wolf howling at the sensation of pleasure and need.

Yes, one day he would be Alpha. He would rule the Pack as it should have always been ruled. In blood and pain.

Gideon Brentwood would die full of shame and with nothing to his name.

Perfection.

CHAPTER TEN

Nothing was going right, but honestly, Brie shouldn't have been surprised. It had been a week since she'd mated Gideon, and she still felt as though she'd only seen a glimpse of the man beneath the power and title. They'd made love each night, learning each other's bodies and desires, but that was only a small part of what made a mating...a mating.

Entwining her soul with another person wasn't all about sex—despite the fact that all evidence so far indicated the contrary. At some point, she wanted to learn who he was, see him smile, make him laugh. She wanted to have inside jokes and cook dinner by his side. She wanted to be able to walk through the den with her head held high and smile back at the Pack members who truly wanted her there.

She didn't want her life to be only about hiding in her new home while she waited for Gideon to arrive so he could make love to her.

For all she knew, it was merely the mating urge riding the both of them through their bond that made Gideon want to be with her. Maybe he couldn't help himself because of an outside force, not because of who she was. She could have been any person at that point and he'd have gotten his rocks off because he could.

She closed her eyes and cursed herself. That was unfair of her to think that way since she hadn't actually asked him what he felt. There hadn't been time. She was also too scared to do so, but she wasn't going to think of that last part. The time thing was at least true. Gideon was almost never home. His duties as Alpha took him away from the house and her for hours every day. And since he didn't know her well enough to allow her to ease his burden, she was stuck at home.

Sure, she'd asked Ryder for the old texts that told the history of the Pack, but there was only so much reading and learning she could do without bashing her head against the wall. The Talons, like the Redwoods, had a rich history of survival. She'd been most interested in the *recent* history and Gideon's father, but unfortunately, that part wasn't in anything thing she'd read yet.

It seemed, to be able to understand the man she'd mated, she actually had to speak with him.

That would be a bit easier if he was actually home.

She ran a hand over her face then sank down into the cushions of Gideon's large couch. It wasn't hers, and she wasn't sure she'd ever feel like it *was*. This was Gideon's place, Gideon's things, Gideon's life. She was only a visitor that made it possible for him to remain Alpha without Iona latched on to him.

"Brie?"

She jumped up, claws out, and then sagged. "I didn't hear you." *Or scent you or notice you.* Some Alpha female was.

129

Gideon frowned at her, tilting his head like he did when he was in wolf form. "I didn't mean to scare you. I was just coming home for a quick shower before the Pack circle."

She held back a sigh. Oh yes, the Pack circle. Yet another thing she had yet to endure other than the one during their mating ceremony. She had a feeling this wasn't going to be fun. People would stare, judge, and wonder what the hell their Alpha had been thinking when he'd suddenly taken her as his mate.

Since the hunt, Gideon had practically locked her away in the castle, afraid of anyone hurting her. He didn't trust her to take care of herself. She didn't blame him since she'd done such a poor job of protecting herself on the hunt. She'd let those wolves make her bleed, though she'd been the one victorious until Gideon had stepped in and finished it for her.

The other Brentwoods had done their best to stand back and let her take care of herself as it was supposed to be. Gideon didn't seem to understand that. If she stood back and let others fight for her as if she was a cosseted princess, she'd never earn the respect she needed in order to stand by Gideon's side.

Considering how he hid her away though, maybe she wasn't supposed to be by his side. That thought hurt like a slice to the chest, and she quickly turned away so he couldn't see the pain in her eyes. Perhaps she was supposed to be the one hidden away, taken out only on special occasions. He'd been forced into this mating after all. Maybe he didn't want her except in the bedroom.

Her hands curled to fists, and she let out a breath. He'd have to think again if that's what he thought. There was no way she could hide out much more. Tonight was the Pack circle where the Pack would meet and discuss things they needed and events that had taken place. She would join in even if it killed her to do so. She would be *part* of the Pack. She was a Talon now. It was time she acted like it—whatever that meant.

She jumped again when Gideon touched her shoulder. "Sorry, I guess I'm a little jumpy today."

He cupped her face, his thumb brushing her cheek. She sucked in a breath, seeing the man who held her every night, not the man who ignored her during the day.

"Are you nervous about the circle?"

"Yes and no. Nervous only because it's my first Talon circle, but I'm excited too. I haven't been out of the house much." She hadn't meant to say the last part, but she couldn't help it.

The barb seemed to have stung because his face tightened before he relaxed again to that cool dominant air of his.

"I won't let anyone hurt you."

And they were back to that again. He was also going to just ignore the fact that she was locked away in the house for her own "protection".

"I can take care of myself, Gideon." She pulled away but gripped his hand so he would know that she was not walking away from him. She'd gone into this mating with her eyes wide open, and she'd work her ass off to make sure she didn't fail in what she had.

"You are mine to protect," he growled out, his words deep.

"I know. And you're mine to protect." She put up her other hand when he opened his mouth to speak. "Don't go into the whole weak submissive routine, okay? You're stuck with me for a long time, so let's get some things straight."

He raised a brow.

131

"I'm your mate. I'm the Alpha female. I need to *do* something. You need to not freak out if I leave the house and actually become a productive member of the Pack. I've only stayed in the house because your wolf is riding you hard, and I can see that. I hadn't wanted to push either of you too much when we were just getting to know one another, but I can see I was wrong."

"Wrong? You're leaving?"

She swallowed hard then shook her head. "No, you oaf. I'm not leaving. Thoughts like those are going to give you a heart attack. I'm your mate," she repeated. "I'm not going anywhere. But I'm also not going to be locked away because you're scared of what might happen to me. I'm not worth anything if I rely on others to live. I need to be my own person, too." She let out a breath. "I need to learn how to be Brie Brentwood. I can't do that if I never leave the house...if I don't get to know you."

She didn't like hiding the truth. She wanted to be as honest as possible, so if she had to bare her soul in order to be the person she wanted to be, then so be it.

Her mate leaned down, pressing his lips to her forehead, and her body softened. "I'm not doing this right."

She put her hand on his chest. "We did everything backward, Gideon."

He pulled away and nodded. "You're right. We met and then mated. I didn't...I didn't court you."

Her eyes widened, her mouth dropping open. "Courting?"

He smiled then, and she sucked in breath. He was handsome when he growled and looked intimidating. But when he smiled? She was lost. Those blue eyes pierced her, his lips full...tempting.

"Courting," he repeated. "And I'm going to try not to be an asshole, but it's not going to be easy."

She snorted then rolled her eyes. "You're not an asshole." He gave her a look. "Fine. You're not an asshole *all* the time. You're still learning how to deal with a woman in your life. I get it. I'm learning how to deal with living with a mate. So we'll work on it. Start fresh."

His eyes darkened, and she had a feeling she knew where his mind had gone. "Fresh."

She pushed playfully at his chest, and he caught her hands in his. She licked her lips, and his gaze went to her mouth. "Go shower so we can go to the Pack circle. Then after...well, after we get to play a game."

He growled softly, squeezing her hands. "A game?"

She smiled then, liking the way he reacted to her words. "Yes, a game. We'll play twenty questions."

"Huh?"

Poor guy, he seemed so forlorn. "We ask each other twenty questions and get to know one another. With each question, we get to find out not only another facet of who we are...but..." She leaned close so she could feel the heat of him. "I'll kiss you for each question and you can do the same."

He growled again. "Just a kiss?"

She went on her tiptoes and kissed the bottom of his chin. "I never said where I'd kiss you."

He took her lips, crushing his mouth to hers in a punishing kiss. She gasped, rocking her body into his. She felt the hard line of his cock against her belly, and she panted before she pulled away.

"Shower. Alone. Go. We can't be late."

He licked his lips when she spoke then nodded before moving past her toward the bedroom.

The image of him naked and wet and palming his cock while he finished what she'd started filled her mind, and she moaned. Gideon froze then turned around slowly.

"I won't finish what we started alone," he said, his voice low. "I'll wait for our...game for that."

Her eyes widened, and she smiled slowly. "Good."

With one last nod, he went back to the bedroom for presumably a *very* cold shower.

Goddess, she knew they were good in bed. That was one thing she never had to worry about. It was the soft moments like this, when he wanted to play with her, when she thought this could work.

Only things never worked out perfectly, she thought half an hour later when she found herself standing at the Pack circle on the raised platform next to Gideon. The Pack was in uproar.

And it was all because of her.

Words like *weak, submissive,* and *whore* were bandied about as if they had a right to judge her. Not everyone spoke, nor did they all yell. No, only a few shared their *opinions* of her as Gideon's mate.

They weren't doing it behind her back any longer.

No, this was directly to her face.

"She's not strong enough to be your mate!" one of the male wolves called out.

From the shape of his eyes, Brie thought he must have been one of the wolves who had attacked her on the hunt. While that hadn't been wise of him, it had been acceptable. She was new and hadn't fought for her position and respect yet.

However calling her a whore because Gideon had chosen her—because *fate* had chosen her—was stepping over the line.

"Are you going to stand there and just let them call your mate these things?" Brynn snapped from behind Brie. All of the Brentwoods were there, and she could feel the tension and anger rising from them as each minute passed.

Gideon looked the worst by far. It was as if it took every ounce of his strength as Alpha not to attack and kill everyone in his path. Only Brie didn't know if the anger was for her or the fact that they were also disrespecting him in the process.

"I want to hear what each bastard has to say. I want to see who speaks and who holds their tongues, even though it's clear they want to say something."

Brie's eyes widened, and she had to hold herself back from gripping Gideon's hand. He wasn't letting others hurt her. He was finding out who was stupid enough to call her out for being herself.

"They won't be allowed to do this again," he growled.

"Good. Because I'm about to kill them myself if you don't do anything about it," Ryder snapped, surprising Brie. He was the quiet one, the nonviolent Heir.

Little did she know, apparently.

"Are you done?" Gideon growled. While before he had been speaking softly so just the Brentwoods would hear, now he spoke to the entire Pack.

Everyone quieted, even those who seemed the most passionate against her.

"Good. Now listen to me and listen well. Brie Brentwood is my mate. My. Mate. Not yours. Not another's. Fate found her for me, and I am not giving her up because you don't seem to understand your place in the Pack."

Brie kept her chin up, gazing directly at those who had jeered and, most especially, on Iona, who had eyes for only Gideon. The other woman wanted the Alpha. Badly. It was clear on her face. Brie only knew that Iona used to warm Gideon's bed, but he had broken it off with her *before* the elders had put the mating game on display. Iona wasn't Gideon's mate, so in any other kind of mating, she wouldn't have been an issue. All wolves needed to find comfort and release—even though she herself had been quite different. Iona hadn't a leg to stand on other than the fact that Shannon had wanted her for the Alpha's mate.

Things hadn't worked out like the elder had hoped, and now things were going to shit. If they had been a truly healthy Pack, Gideon wouldn't have had to fight for what he wanted. Instead, it was as if he had to prove himself each time he wanted to act as Alpha. Brie figured that was because he'd had to kill his father to become Alpha. She had heard the stories, but she didn't know the entire truth. That was one thing she would have to speak to him about. She didn't like to be kept in the dark, and from the aggression she felt against her, it was dangerous not to know as well. From what she could tell, those who had followed Joseph, the previous Alpha, and remained Talons were not making Gideon's life easy.

Even though the moon goddess was the one who blessed those with the bonds of Alpha, Heir, Beta and so on, it took the strength of a healthy Pack to thrive. If there were diseased parts, thanks to their previous cloying loyalties, then that was something that needed to be fixed. It was a tricky situation, and Brie wanted to find out how she could help.

If she could help.

"You forget that all parts of the Pack help us remain who we are," Gideon continued. "We need not only the dominants, but the maternals *and* the submissives. It's not the nature of the wolf inside but how the wolf treats those around him that shows us how they can help the Pack. The fact that you are threatening my mate, because you're ignorant, shows me that some things need to change."

She sucked in a breath. This wasn't going to end well.

"I am Alpha. My word is law. For those of you who have forgotten that, you are welcome to challenge me. Let's see if your strength can help you survive. Let's see if you can be blessed by the moon goddess."

Not a single person came forward, and Brie held back a sigh of relief.

"I am Alpha," Gideon repeated. "I have bled for you. I have fought for you. What more must I do for you to trust my decisions? What more must I do for you to accept my mate as I have? She is your Alpha female. She is your Pack. Remember that."

Still, she didn't say anything. There wasn't anything for her to say. Words were nice. The fact that Gideon had put those out for her said something, but it would take her own actions and those of the Pack for her to gain acceptance.

That would come.

One day.

She hoped.

Gideon didn't look at her, and he didn't touch her in front of the Pack as they continued their business. For some reason, that hurt more than it should have. The elders had forced the mating because they'd said the Pack was growing weak because Gideon didn't have a mate. Yet his mating of her hadn't seemed to help. Instead, things were worse. What was the point of mating a man who didn't love her if everything they tried to build crumbled around them?

Gideon didn't trust her to protect herself, nor did the Pack trust her to act in her role.

She'd never truly felt like nothing before, but with every moment that passed, every look of condemnation sent her way, she was well on her way to nothingness.

"Are there any more matters for this circle?" Gideon asked some time later.

Brie almost sagged with relief. She wanted to go home and figure out what she was going to do. There had to be *something*.

"I have one, dear nephew."

The entire circle went so   quiet Brie was sure she could have heard a pin drop.

Nephew?

She'd thought all of Gideon's uncles were dead. Could the man have been speaking of another person?

From the way her mate stiffened, she had a feeling things were about to get way worse. Her new family around her growled softly, suddenly moving so they surrounded her in protection. Whoever this man was, whatever he had to say wouldn't be good.

Not knowing what else to do, she moved forward, putting her hand in Gideon's. She still stayed off to the side in case he needed to move quickly. He might have to fight if this other wolf, this supposedly *dead* wolf, provoked him. Brie did not want to get in the way of that, but from the way no one moved to stop this man or answer him, she thought her mate might need to know she was there.

Just in case.

The bond between them flared bright, shocking her. She'd always felt it there, a thin, translucent thread that merely told her that they were mates. Yet, right then, it burned, cementing them in a way she hadn't thought possible. Gideon's shoulders didn't relax, but something about him changed...as if he knew he wasn't alone.

Silly, she knew, but she'd take whatever she could get at this point.

"What, boy, surprised to see me?" the other man asked as he strolled into the Pack circle.

"Mitchell. Kameron." Gideon growled under his breath.

"Already gone," Mitchell whispered back.

"Checking it out," Kameron growled, and the Enforcer and Beta were gone, to ensure the wards were still working and to check for other threats.

Brie understood why Gideon wasn't moving, waiting to understand what was in front of him. The man would protect his Pack at all costs.

Brie's gaze moved from the man who looked much like her new mate to the crowd around them. This man wasn't Pack anymore, at least that's what she thought. That meant, unless the wards were down—and she didn't think that was the case—*someone* had let him inside the den.

Someone was in on it.

The loyalties of the den should have been to the Pack...but what if they weren't to the Alpha?

That thought shook her, but she didn't let her attention waver. The members either looked stunned or angry, but no one looked truly pleased to see him there. Iona looked as if someone had punched her while Shannon...well, the elder looked appropriately alarmed, but there was something *off* about it. It could have been Brie's own prejudices where the other woman was concerned, but she wasn't too sure. That was something she'd have to tell Gideon later.

"Still not speaking, son? I'm not here to hurt you."

Brie squeezed Gideon's hand as she turned back toward the man who'd spoken. Rage, confusion, and pain slid through the bond, and Brie sucked in another breath. She could *feel* him. That had never

139

happened before. He'd been so closed off for their mating. Yet something had changed. She pushed that to the side knowing now was not the time to worry about her own feelings and their mating. She quickly pushed back her own sense of purpose and soothed along the bond as she had done in a different sense all her life. That was why she was a submissive. She could assuage even the smallest of hurts of a dominant if they'd only let her.

Gideon squeezed her hand back then let out a low growl.

The hairs on the back of her neck stood on end, and her body shook. Gideon let out the power of his Alpha, the immense strength of the bonds with this Pack pushing down on each and every member.

The weakest of the Pack fell to their knees immediately while some were able to remain on their feet. She didn't fall. No, Gideon kept her up. Sill, the face of his power was awe-inspiring. He had no choice but to release the show of his strength to this man who had no business there, but the gravity of it still surprised her.

"Leo. You were supposed to be dead."

The other man grinned, his arms out from his body. "No, not dead. Just not...Pack."

"It's been thirty years. Where have you been all this time?"

"So many questions, boy, but don't worry. There will be answers soon enough. I'm not here to hurt you. I'm your uncle. I'm family." He grinned again, and she wanted to kill this Leo for the shudder rolling down her back. "I'm blood."

"You are not Pack. You are not welcome here. In fact you were supposed to die for your crimes against the Pack all those years ago." Gideon's voice held a sense of calm that scared her, but she knew through the bond that there was nothing calm about him. He would kill this man in an instant if he could. The fact that they had no idea what tricks the wolf had up his sleeves was the only thing that held him back.

Leo tilted his head in much the same fashion that Gideon did. She didn't have time to think of the parallels and family traits, however, because the man set his attention on her.

"I see you've mated, nephew. Let me offer my felicitations."

It wasn't lost on her that Leo kept saying the words boy and nephew. As if he was reminding Gideon and the rest of the circle that Leo was family and much older than Gideon. It sounded as if he was trying to be intimidating. However, all she felt was the urge to kill him where he stood. Something was wrong with this wolf, and she had a feeling, if he continued speaking, nothing good could come from what was said.

"Look at my mate one more time, and I will gut you where you stand."

Oddly enough, that was one of the more romantic things he'd ever said about her.

Leo narrowed his eyes but didn't move his attention from her. "You've grown cynical in your position of...power."

"Your crimes against your Pack proved you were nothing to us. You should be dead, Leo."

"What about your crimes, dear nephew? Shall we see what happens to those who are not held accountable?"

Out of the corner of her eye, she saw Kameron return, giving them a slight shake of his head. Gideon let out a growl, but before anyone could move forward, Leo gave a little wave then disappeared. A swirl of black smoke remained, stinking of dark magic and sacrifice.

Everyone moved then, either away and to safety or to where Leo had stood. She was afraid Gideon would push her away, but instead, he held on to her hand, keeping her close.

"You're not leaving my sight," he growled out then tucked her to his side as they moved forward.

She growled, her claws sliding through her fingertips, ready to protect herself as well as the Pack she'd been mated into. Whatever Leo had done in the past, and whatever purpose he held now, scared her to the point that she knew she had to be strong enough for the both of them. Secrets slid through the den as if they were commonplace, and there was only so much she could take.

Leo had been the signal of change...of something coming that she had a feeling none of them were ready for.

She hoped that they could prepare.

Because, if they couldn't, she was afraid all would be lost.

CHAPTER ELEVEN

"How the hell did he get through the wards?" Gideon yelled once more, knowing he wouldn't like the answer.

Kameron cursed, continuing his pacing through Gideon's living room. "I don't know. Someone had to have helped him. He didn't come through any of the sentry stations, meaning that a Pack member pulled him through willingly."

Gideon cursed then slammed his fist into the wall, breaking through the plaster.

"Gideon," Brie whispered then put her hand on his arm. He looked down at the small hand on his large muscles and sighed. His wolf was right at the edge, but with her single touch, he calmed. Not fully, but at least enough to be able to breathe for a moment.

"You're going to hurt yourself." She smiled softly, but it didn't reach her eyes. "We already fixed one wall in this house this week, do you really want to make it a weekly thing?"

He sighed then pulled Brie to his side. She wrapped her arms around his waist, and he let out a breath, his wolf calming at the feel of her. She soothed him like no other. At any other time, he'd rage and growl and would probably need to fight to let off his aggression, with Brie near him, he didn't need to.

It was...pleasant.

"Better?" she asked, patting his chest.

He nuzzled the top of his head, aware that his family was staring at him as though he was a lunatic. They'd never seen him react like this, and while it was a personal moment, he liked the fact that they were there witnessing it as well. Brie was part of his life now, and he was trying to figure out where she fit. This was just one step of many.

"For now," he whispered then kissed her temple. "Thank you."

"You're welcome. Now, what are we going to do about this Leo?"

He let out a breath then tugged her toward the sofa. She didn't complain when he pulled her into his lap. He needed her touch to settle down, but he wasn't about to admit it. If she really wanted her space, she'd have pulled away. That much he knew.

As soon as they figured out Leo had used witch magic to disappear, they'd searched for him before heading back to Gideon's. He had the largest home of all his family, and it was their unofficial meeting place—even if now he wanted to be alone with Brie when he could find the time.

"I'm going to kill him," Mitchell vowed, his voice low. Dangerous. Considering Leo was the man's father, he didn't blame him.

"I can't believe he's alive," Max breathed. "I...I don't know what to think." Max sounded so lost...yet the underlying thread of anger hit Gideon's wolf hard.

"Leo couldn't have just gone poof and disappeared through the wards," Brynn said once he and Brie were settled. "That's the whole point of the wards. You can't move through them without being Pack or without help from the Pack.

"True, but he could have used dark magic to move to another place *within* the den." Ryder ran a hand over his face. "Meaning our favorite uncle probably moved to a place near the wards and then moved through them to get out. Most times, it doesn't take the help of a Pack member to leave the wards. Only to get through them."

Brie let out a curse, and Gideon raised his brows. Interesting.

"I'd forgotten that," she said. "It takes extra magic from the witches you have on hand to make that layer of protection available. When my Pack—" She cut herself off then shook her head. "My apologies. Force of habit. When my *old* Pack needed that layer, it took a couple of days, but the extra layer held." She turned to meet Gideon's eyes. "I will say though that my Aunt Hannah was pivotal in that. She's a very strong witch, and the fact that she was also the Redwood Healer at the time helped. I don't know the strength of the witches you have mated in the Pack."

"We don't have many," Gideon answered honestly. "We had a period of time when the Talons didn't mate at all if you remember."

Brie nodded. "Yes, and it was my cousin Gina and one of our lieutenants, Quinn, who broke that streak."

"And then Quinn went on to be a Redwood anyway," Brynn teased.

"Well, Gina *is* the Enforcer of the Redwood Pack," Brie teased back. "It only made sense."

"Anyway," Gideon interrupted, though he liked the way Brie interacted with his family. "Like I was saying, we didn't have any matings for awhile. And in the times of my father's rule, those who mated with witches...didn't stay."

Brie sighed. "Probably for the same reasons my Aunt Lexi and Uncle Logan left the Pack."

Gideon closed his eyes and nodded. That time within the Pack hadn't been the easiest. Far from it. In fact, it was a time he wished he could forget. However, back then, he'd found the man he was today and became the Alpha in spite of it. Lexi and Logan were siblings within the Pack, their bloodlines pure, descendants of the original hunter. And when Lexi almost died, finding herself with child from a man who had been an enemy to not only the Talons but the Redwoods as well, she had been kicked out. Logan followed, and Gideon never forgave himself for not being able to help.

Loyalties were mended now, and Lexi and Logan were mated into the Redwoods, but the scars remained.

Brie ran her hand up and down his arm, and his wolf calmed yet again. She was good for him; he knew that much. Now he just had to figure out what the next step would be, not only with their mating, but also with her position in the Pack and his Uncle Leo. The other man showing up might have taken center stage, but the reaction to Brie's presence at the Pack circle was not lost on him. There were others out there who needed to learn the true meaning of Gideon being the Alpha. He was not a vengeful man, but he was not a man at all.

He was a wolf.

The Alpha.

This was not a democracy, and he had a feeling that many had forgotten that.

He'd shaken things up when he'd brought Brie in, but he had to believe that one day it would be for the better. Fate had chosen her for him, so it couldn't have been for the worse.

At least that's what he hoped.

The others were speaking around him, trying to guess Leo's intentions. He honestly didn't know what the other man planned, but he had a feeling it had to do with Gideon's position as Alpha. Leo had never been one of the blessed wolves. He'd been the Alpha's younger brother—as well as Max and Mitchell's father. The man had craved power yet had never been given any. He hadn't done much to earn it either.

Instead, he'd tortured and killed those lesser than him—what few there were—because he could.

When the explosion had taken out part of the den, Leo was said to have died. They'd apparently been wrong about that.

"Gideon?" Brie asked, her voice penetrating his senses.

"Huh?" he asked, aware everyone was staring at him.

"I was just asking if you were listening," she said softly.

"Apparently not," he growled out then regretted his tone. Her eyes widened, but she didn't lower her chin or look away. He liked when she stood up to him and his wolf. It made him feel as though she could handle all of him, not just the pieces he'd let her see.

"How about we head out and meet again tomorrow?" Kameron put in. "I need to set up more patrols anyway."

Gideon pulled his gaze from Brie and looked at his brother, the Enforcer. "Good. Keep an eye out. I don't want anyone in or out of the den right now."

Kameron's eyes widened fractionally, but he nodded anyway. "Done."

"You sure that's wise?" Ryder put in, ever the thinker. "Won't people feel caged?"

"They should," Gideon snapped. "Our Pack isn't safe, and it's rotting from within. We need to find a way to fix it. We know the danger is coming from the outside as well. This is only one step."

Ryder's gaze moved to Brie before coming back to Gideon. "And the other matter that occurred during the circle?"

Hell, his usually quiet brother was sure talkative tonight.

"We'll keep my lieutenants on watch," he ground out. His inner circle of wolves that not only protected him, but his mate, was made up of the most trusted of men and women. They were usually hidden outside so others couldn't sense their presence, but Gideon always knew they were there.

Brie did as well.

The fact that someone would be there to protect her if he couldn't aided his wolf. Yes, he could see now that she could fight for herself if needed, but she couldn't fight everyone.

No one could.

"Good," Brynn said softly then stood up. "Come on, boys, we need to give these two some privacy." She looked at Brie then lowered her gaze. "I'm with you, Brie. No matter what the idiots of the Pack think."

With that, his little sister left the house. Then the rest of his family surprised him by lowering their heads before leaving behind her.

Brie stiffened in his arms, and he felt the bond between them pulse. "Did they just do what I think they did?"

He pulled her close and moved her hair so he could kiss her neck. He loved to taste her neck. It tasted of sweetness and wolf. "Yes. They wanted to show you that you matter, that you are their Alpha, just as I am."

She wiggled away, and he let her go so she could stand and face him. "They could just do that? I mean I know they vowed to protect me and even showed me that they honored my requests during the hunt, but this was different. They haven't seen me do anything Alpha-like." She closed her eyes and pinched the bridge of her nose. "Mostly because I haven't *done* anything."

He sighed then gripped her thighs, bringing her closer to him. She staggered and fell. He caught her as he'd planned, and made her straddle his lap. Not only did he get to feel the heat of her above his dick, but he also got to see her face clearly when he spoke to her.

"That is my fault," he said softly, and she licked her lips. Maybe putting her on his lap wasn't the smartest thing to do since all he wanted to do now was pull off her jeans and sink into her cunt.

First things first though.

"I thought we were going to play a game," he said, not changing the subject but focusing it.

She blinked then sat back on his lap. "You confuse me so much."

"I know," he said honestly. "That's why we're going to play the game. Now, where do you want to start?"

She shook her head. "You start."

He nodded then cupped her face. "Okay. I can do that. What is it, Brie, that you want to do within the Pack?"

Her eyes widened, and he heard her pulse pick up. "Tell me, little wolf."

"I...I want to stand by your side and ease your burden," she said quickly.

He smiled then and watched the way she relaxed when he did so. He needed to smile more often if it relaxed her. "I know, Brie. You said as such during our mating ceremony. But what is it you want to *do?*"

She frowned then narrowed her eyes. "I want to come with you to meetings and talk with the wolves when you do. If I can help you make decisions or help the Pack members, maybe they can see me as a person, rather than a submissive wolf too weak to breathe on her own."

He growled at that, and she leaned forward to kiss his nose. It was such a playful movement that he froze.

"I also want to speak with the other submissives and make sure they're being treated okay."

"We don't torture them like my father used to," he blurted out and could have cut out his tongue. He hadn't meant to let that last part slip out. What his father and his followers had done was barbaric. Brie didn't need to know the pain his blood had caused. Yet, she *needed* to know everything eventually. She couldn't fight an enemy without knowing the path they'd walked. It would be too dangerous for his mate.

"He *tortured* them?" she asked, her face losing all color.

He gripped her hips, forcing her to stay on his lap. If she left him then, he had a feeling she would never come back.

"I...I can't talk about what he did right now," he said, his voice breaking. "Soon I will tell you everything that happened under my father's rule and how I became Alpha, but I...I don't think I can speak of it right now." He didn't want her to hate him for what he'd had to do. He'd pushed her away because he'd been afraid his Pack would reject her, yet now that he had her, he didn't want to lose her.

She cupped his face, tears filling her eyes. "That's why it's so important for me to speak to the submissives and even the maternals right now. If you're afraid to speak of it, what must they be feeling? I don't know what went on before my time, but I will need to know eventually, Gideon. Too many secrets only hurt those involved. I don't like being kept in the dark. And now with Leo out there, I really need to know."

He knew she was right, but he couldn't tell her everything. Not yet. He wanted her to know *him* before she knew of his past. Once she knew what he'd done to protect his Pack, she might never trust him again.

That was something he didn't know if he could survive.

"I will tell you everything. Soon." He met her gaze and pleaded with his eyes.

"I'll wait a bit longer, Gideon. Only because I want to know everything from *you*, not from anyone else."

He let out a breath. "Thank you. As for you speaking with the submissives and maternals, I think that's a great idea."

She smiled then, and he wanted her to do that forever. Her whole face lit up, and she looked...happy. He didn't know if he could ever make her truly happy since she'd mated with him knowing that things wouldn't be easy, but he could at least try.

"Really?"

"Really. I could use some help in that area, honestly."

"You're *really* dominant, Gideon."

He lifted his hips and grinned. "I know that, little wolf."

She rolled her eyes, even as her breath hitched. "I wasn't talking about *that*. I meant that some wolves might need to talk to someone not so dominant if they have issues. That's what your mate is for. Well, your mate and your Beta and your family. We might not be a democracy, but you have others around you for a reason." She cupped his face and kissed him. He froze, not wanting to break the moment. When she pulled away, she smiled again. "Let me help you."

"Okay," he whispered, and she relaxed into him. She could have had no idea how hard it was to even say that one word. He didn't ask for help. He took it from his family if he needed it, but he'd rather do it all on his own. There was less of a chance for others to be hurt. The fact that he was about to give Brie responsibilities that should be his, scared him, but he knew if she didn't do what she could, things would end up worse. The Pack needed to see her in a role of power, and Brie herself needed something to do so she wouldn't feel useless.

There was no way he'd ever think of her as useless, but getting Brie to see beyond the barriers of others' opinions was another matter altogether.

She wiggled on his lap, and he let out a growl. "About that game..."

He leaned forward and bit down on her lip. "I asked a question. Does that mean I get to kiss you, or you kiss me?"

She licked the spot he'd bitten and shuddered out a breath. "I think we should finish the game later."

"Oh?" he asked, his hands roaming up and down her back. "What should we do in the meantime? Because I want to taste you, little wolf. Every inch of you."

"Okay, fine. We can play the game, but I want to taste you too."

He groaned and lifted his hips one more time. "Little wolf?"

"You never let me go down on you," she said, her voice low. "You always say 'next time', but that never happens." She looked up at him, confusion in her gaze. "Do you not want me to?"

He cursed then gripped her hips harder. "Fuck, Brie. I want your mouth on my cock so much I almost blow just thinking about it. I just wanted to go easy on you while you're getting to know me."

She rolled her eyes. "I'm not a weakling, Gideon. Just show me what you like, and I will do everything in my power to make sure you come. Hard."

His balls tightened, and he counted to ten so he didn't come in his jeans like a teenage pup. Goddess his mate made him crazy in the best ways possible.

"What's your favorite color?" he blurted out, and she smiled.

"I thought it was my turn to ask the question," she teased as she slid off his lap.

"Just answer," he ground out, hoping he could last long enough. Though since he was a wolf, he'd rebound quickly and make it good for her. Still, it was the principle of the matter.

"Blue," she whispered. "I love blue."

She looked into his eyes, and he knew she meant the color of his eyes. Ironic because, "Mine is green."

She smiled then, and he knew she understood. She knelt between his legs and put her hands on his thighs. "Are you going to help me?" she asked, her tone innocent.

He might have believed that if she hadn't had the look of a siren in her eyes.

He nodded then undid his jeans. He loved to watch her face when he took his cock out. Her eyes always widened at the sight, and he prayed to the goddess that never changed.

She helped him take off his pants when he lifted his hips. When she settled herself between his legs, he licked his lips. This was his mate, his future, yet it scared the hell out of him.

He would think only of the here and now, and he'd be okay.

He sat up again and stripped off his shirt so he was completely naked. "There's something about you being fully clothed while I'm naked that makes me hard," he teased.

She grinned and raked her nails down his thighs. He hissed out a breath. "You said something similar to me when I was the one naked," she said, her voice husky.

"True. I like you naked." He grinned. "Stand up and strip for me, little wolf. I want to see those pretty tits and the wet cunt before you go down on me."

Her eyes widened at his words, but she did as she was told. Goddess, he loved when she moved like that, all sweet and sexy at the same time. She was really the perfect wolf for him.

When she was naked, she kicked her clothes away and went back to kneeling between his legs.

"Can I start now?" she asked, her breath hot on his cock.

He nodded then gripped the base. "Start at the tip and lick around the crown." He slid his finger over the top and licked his lips again. "You see this slit? If you tease it with your tongue, it feels really fucking good. Okay?"

"Okay," she whispered, her eyes on his cock.

When she tentatively lapped at the head of his dick, his hips bucked, and she swallowed the head instinctively. He pulled back and cursed, patting her cheek with his free hand. "Sorry, baby, I didn't mean to go so fast. You just surprised me."

She grinned, seeming to like the power she held over him. If she only knew...

"Now, when you're ready, you can swallow the head like you did. You can either run your hands up and down my length or roll my balls. I like both. You get me?"

"Uh huh," she said then went back to licking him.

Fire swept up his spine, and he ground his teeth. She wasn't the most skilled, but she took her time, tasting every inch of him. She pressed small kisses down the sides of his cock, then along his balls and his inner thighs. She licked up his length then swallowed the head again, this time using both hands to squeeze his dick.

He wrapped his hand in her hair, holding her in place for a moment before letting her go. She wasn't ready to deep throat him, but that would come another time. Right then, he loved her explorations and the way she studied him as she went down on him.

He sat up slowly, giving her time to move with him so he wouldn't choke her. "Keep licking, little wolf. I fucking love it."

She hummed against him, and he groaned.

With his free hand, he reached down and palmed her breast. She gasped and moved into his touch.

"Good girl." Her nipple pebbled against his palm, hard and ready for his mouth. Soon.

Her head bobbed up and down, her speed increasing, so he pinched her nipple, loving the way her throat contracted around his dick.

"Keep going, little wolf. I'm going to come down that pretty throat. You ready for me?"

She nodded even as she sucked him, and he grinned before shouting her name. His balls contracted, and he came down her throat, his dick pulsing with each burst. Before she could pull away, he tugged on her hair then lifted her to his lap.

He slid into her with one thrust and took her lips at the same time. He swallowed her gasp, but he could feel her surprise. He'd scented her arousal as she'd gone down on him, and he knew she was wet for him. He slid in so easily, he knew she was drenched.

Good.

He tangled his fingers in her hair and forced his gaze to hers. "Lift up on your knees, Brie."

Her eyes widened, but she did as she was told. He lifted his hips quickly, pumping in and out of her. Her mouth widened, and he gave her a feral grin.

"I'm fucking you because you're mine, little wolf. Just as I'm yours. I'm going to fill you up, and then you're going to come around my cock because...You. Are. Mine."

He slammed into her with each word, loving the way she moaned.

"Gideon, I'm so close."

"Give me your tits. One at a time, little wolf. I want to suck on those nipples."

She nodded then lifted her breasts, pressing them into his face. He kept up his pace, fucking her even as he sucked her nipples into his mouth. She tasted so goddamn good.

He pulled back then kissed her. She wrapped her arms around his neck, her hips meeting him thrust for thrust.

"You feel so good, little wolf. Can you come for me? Can you come for your Alpha?"

"For you? Always."

She ground her hips against him and screamed his name, her body shaking. Her cunt gripped him like a vise, and he couldn't last any longer. He came again, this time filling her up until he didn't have anything left in him. He felt her pulsating around him a second time and knew she'd come again. He fucking loved how responsive she was.

When he could speak again, he let out a laugh. "So that was your favorite color, what should I ask next, your favorite food? Favorite movie?"

She chuckled roughly then squeezed her inner muscles.

His eyes crossed, and he cursed.

"I don't think we'll survive that many more questions," she answered back, breathless.

He slapped her ass, and she gasped. "You want to find out?"

"Sounds like a plan to me."

Four questions in, they found themselves spent and boneless in the bedroom. Brie lay on his chest, passed out while he couldn't sleep. His mate had become close to his heart, and he wasn't sure what he was going to do.

He'd told himself if he fell in love with her she'd be vulnerable, but she might already be in danger as it was. Time would tell, and he prayed he hadn't made a mistake.

More was at stake than the woman in his arms, yet right then, she was the only person he could think about.

And that was beyond dangerous.

CHAPTER TWELVE

B rie wasn't the best baker in the world—in her opinion, that title went to her mother. However, since she was nervous about the upcoming meeting and *still* not allowed to venture out in the den without a guard, she decided that baking cookies would be just the thing. Hopefully, after today, she would feel a little more secure in her own skin when it came to her new Pack, but she didn't put much into that.

Actually, it wasn't her as much as the males in her life. Gideon and his brothers were *not* good with letting others have control. That meant that unless someone was watching her to keep her safe, they wouldn't be able to focus on the task at hand. That burden was on them, but since she was trying to find her place, she let them act overprotective.

For now.

That would change.

Soon.

The problem with mating someone so much more dominant than she—other than the Pack issues—was that Gideon could run right over her without meaning to. He was just so...strong that he wouldn't be able to help it if he did something out of protection that ended up hurting her wolf. It was in his nature to care for her in ways that sometimes put boundaries up where she needed to roam. Maybe she was wrong to let him have the control at first, but she hadn't seen another choice. He wasn't the usual dominant wolf, bringing with him a huge gap between them in terms of strength. He was also the Alpha, and she had to take into account his Pack needs as well. That, after all, was why they'd mated in the first place.

The Pack had needed a mate for the Alpha, and she'd stepped up.

Now, though, she needed to *actually* step up and be the mate. Their bond was there—she could feel it—but that was only one part of it. The Pack would eventually be able to feel the bond as well, not like she could feel Gideon, but in a different way. They would be able to feel an extra layer of protection and foundation because they now had two wolves on the top tier. She had felt it with Kade and Melanie, and one day, she hoped her new Pack would be able to feel it with her and Gideon.

In order to do that, though, they needed to accept her as their Alpha female.

Gideon, she thought, was just now beginning to see the need for her to be her own person within the Pack. He'd been so caught up making sure no one hurt her when he brought her in that he hadn't thought about the emotional toll. Today he would take her to the maternals' part of the den where she'd be able to talk to them privately. She couldn't wait to get to know the women who helped raise the Pack's future. She especially couldn't wait to see the pups. It had been far too long since she'd had an adorable baby wolf in her arms.

She blushed, thinking about what her and Gideon's pups would look like. Would they be dark and strong like their father or submissive and pale like their mother?

Okay, Brie, one step at a time.

She pushed those thoughts to the side and folded the chocolate chips into her batter. She'd already made a few batches of peanut butter cookies, and now she was making oatmeal chocolate chip. She didn't know Gideon's favorite—that hadn't been one of the questions they'd played with a few nights before—but she hoped he'd like one of these. She was making enough to bring with her to the maternals and also keep some around the house for the Brentwoods. The brothers seemed to eat her out of house and home.

She called them brothers, rather than brothers and cousins, considering Mitchell and Max were so ingrained into the family they weren't treated any differently than the others. She liked the closeness they had and the inside jokes she hoped one day to be fully part of. It reminded her of her uncles and cousins.

Tears pricked at the backs of her eyes, and she blinked them away. Though she video conferenced with her family daily, it was still hard not to be able to be with them physically every day. She especially missed Finn since she'd lived with him for over a decade. Her cousin was her best friend, and she hoped that one day soon he'd be able to come for a visit. She wasn't sure that it would be easy, though, because he was the Heir. It didn't matter that the Talons and Redwoods were friends. Sometimes wolves needed to keep that space so their aggression didn't get out of hand. They weren't human after all.

"What's wrong?" Gideon asked.

She jumped a foot and dropped the bowl. Gideon managed to catch it before it hit the floor, his quick reflexes oddly making her hot. Everything about this man apparently turned her on. He set the bowl on the counter then put a bouquet of wild flowers next to it before cupping her face.

His thumbs brushed under her eyes, wiping up the tears she hadn't meant to let fall.

"Why are you crying, little wolf? What happened? Who do I need to hurt?"

She closed her eyes and let out a watery laugh. There was so much wrong with what he'd just said, yet the woman in her relished it. He was just so damn *protective*.

"Nothing is wrong," she said when she opened her eyes. His bright blue gaze studied her without blinking, and she put her hands on his chest. "I'm fine. Just a little homesick."

Something flashed in his eyes, and he gave her a tight nod. "I know this has been hard for you. I'm sorry that you're missing your home."

She cursed herself then wrapped her arms around his waist. "I didn't mean I missed my home, I meant my family. Familysick just doesn't have the same ring to it as homesick. Plus, I don't even think that's a word. Gideon, my mate, I *am* home."

He let out a breath, and her wolf relaxed. He didn't let go of his tension often, and never around others, but the fact that he seemed to do it around her meant the world. One day soon, she hoped he'd be able to fully let his guard down in her presence. Then again, one day soon, she hoped to do the same.

"I don't know when we can plan a visit with your family, little wolf. Not with the Pack in jeopardy such as it is."

She leaned forward, though his hands were still on her face, and nipped at his chin. He growled, softly, but didn't kiss her.

"I know, Gideon. It's okay, really. Things happened fast, and we're in a different situation than most. Technology lets me speak to them regularly, so that's not a worry. I know I'll see them again soon." She smiled and leaned into his touch. "You know, I'm in a new family now. Right?" She held her breath, knowing she was being an idiot waiting for him to say something.

New matings were not for the weak. Mating an Alpha was even more unnerving.

He tilted his head then leaned down and brushed his lips against her own. "True. You have a new family now. Once we take care of Leo and those who spoke out against you at the circle, we might be able to actually feel like one fully."

She pulled away, even as she smiled. If she stayed in his arms, she'd never finish her cookies, and she wanted to bring something with her to the meeting. "Even with all of that going on, I'm slowly starting to feel like I'm part of you all. Walker, Brynn, and Ryder are very open and welcoming."

Gideon nodded then picked up the wildflowers. Her heart leapt, and she smiled at him. "I said I would court you, Brie Brentwood." Her heart beat faster, and she blushed. She reached out and brought the blooms to her nose.

"I love wildflowers. How did you know?"

He shrugged, his gaze lowering. She held back a gasp at the action. He *never* lowered his gaze to another. That this man would do so...she honestly didn't know what to think.

"You seem like you'd enjoy these more than a hothouse flower."

"You're right," she said, taking another sniff. She could pick up the spicy scent of her mate blended around the flowers, telling her he'd picked these by hand.

She fell just a little more in love.

Dangerous, but inevitable with a man like him.

"They're beautiful, thank you." She stood on her toes and kissed his chin. He lowered his head to hers, taking her in an achingly sweet kiss. Their touches were always so explosive, their lovemaking the one thing they always seemed to get right even if the first time had been somewhat awkward.

This kiss, though...this kiss seemed different.

She wasn't sure how she felt about that.

She put the flowers in a vase Gideon got down for her then let out a breath. "I need to finish baking for the meeting. What are your plans?"

Her mate ran a hand down her hair, the sensation of his touch intoxicating. He was starting to touch her more and more, as if it was ingrained and he was finally allowing himself that small pleasure. She prayed he never stopped.

"I took the afternoon off to take you to the meeting," he answered.

She opened her mouth to speak, and he shook his head. "I'm not staying for your meeting, little wolf. That's something you must do on your own. I will be close by with Walker because he needs me for a procedure, but I won't take over your duties."

She relaxed, her hands busy with baking. "Thank you. I know it's not easy, but I can't have you over my shoulder all the time and still be my own wolf."

He nodded then started putting the just-baked cookies on a cookie rack. She enjoyed the simple act of him baking with her. Who would have thought the big, bad Alpha of the Talon Pack would help her bake cookies? Of course, she should have thought he'd like it. Her Grandpa Edward had enjoyed baking when

Grandma Pat had let him. She and Grandpa had loved cookies, especially the sugar ones. He hadn't cared that she was a tomboy, roughhousing with Finn and the other boys. He hadn't cared that her pigtails were never even. He'd loved her because she was his granddaughter—submissive wolf and all.

Gideon gave her an odd look then went back to helping her bake. She licked her lips but didn't mention it. There was no use embarrassing him when things were going so well. "Why does Walker need you?"

"One of the wolves has a genetic condition that's rare amongst wolves. It's not a huge thing, but it affects their blood. Walker can Heal it, but it takes a tremendous amount of energy."

She nodded, filling up another cookie sheet. "So he'll use the bond between Healer and Alpha to help?"

"Yes, I'm there as backup in case Walker needs me. Ryder or Mitchell could do it as well, but since Walker's place is near where you'll be, it makes sense that I should do it. It won't weaken me since we're using the excess power, and it will help a Pack member."

She smiled at that. "You're a good Alpha, Gideon."

He didn't speak for so long she was sure he'd never answer, but when he did, it was a low growl. "I'm not yet, little wolf. But I will be. One day."

What must he have gone through to think he wasn't good enough? Now that she was part of the Pack, she'd help him fix it, but she wasn't sure how to go about it. Being kept in the dark didn't aid matters. That would have to change soon if she ever had any hope of helping her mate.

Instead of saying something he'd brush off as a platitude, she kept her tone light, asking questions about his family. She didn't want to dig too deep—

by the dominants, but she hoped she'd have a chance with the maternals.

Right then, it looked as if that avenue might be lost as well.

She wouldn't be going down without a fight though.

Brie set the cookies on the counter then looked out the window. The pups were playing a game in wolf form, bouncing around and wrestling with their claws sheathed. They had to be between six and seven years old and were so freaking adorable. She took a step toward the window then paused when Gwen put her hand on Brie's arm. She looked down then up at Brie, her wolf brushing along Brie's skin.

"Is something that matter?" she asked, her tone calm. Far calmer than she felt.

Gwen looked as though she wanted to say something then let go, clamping her mouth shut.

Oh no, that would not do.

"What is it, Gwen?"

The other woman let out a breath then raised her chin. "I can tell you're a good girl, Brie."

This was not going to end well.

"I'm a woman, not a girl, Gwen. I'm also the Alpha's mate." She frowned. "But that's the problem isn't it?"

Gwen sighed. "I'm sure you're a wonderful wolf. A pleasant submissive who, in the right setting, can help many a dominant settle their wolves so they can protect the Pack. You are *not,* however, good enough to be the Alpha's mate."

Shocked, Brie staggered back, her eyes wide. "Excuse me?" Her voice shook. She was astonished this woman would speak so bluntly. She did her best to keep her emotions in check. If Gideon felt something wrong across the bond, he'd be there in an

169

instant, and she couldn't afford that. If he didn't let her fight for herself, then it would only prove harder for her to find her place.

"You heard me, Brie," she said then sighed again. "I know I will probably get my throat slit for even saying it, but it's the truth."

Brie shook her head. "You are underestimating your Alpha if you think he'll kill you, if you think *I* will kill you for having poor judgment."

The other woman's eyes flashed, and Brie saw the truth of the other woman's nature. She was not a bad woman; she was a maternal. That meant she'd do all within her strength to protect the youngest of the Pack. Too bad she was going about it all wrong.

"You are a *submissive*, Brie."

"I know that," Brie snapped then reined herself back. "I've known that since I could first form thoughts."

"The Alpha can't have a submissive for a mate. Especially not an Alpha such as Gideon. He needs someone who can protect that Pack with him. You are too weak to do it." Tears filled Gwen's eyes, but Brie felt no sympathy. "Fate can be cruel. I know this more than most, but fate is wrong this time, Brie. You're going to die protecting the Pack because you're not strong enough. Gideon will die trying to save you because he can't do anything else. No matter what, you're not what this Pack needs."

Brie growled, her wolf rising to the forefront. She was *not* weak, despite what this woman thought—despite what others in the Pack thought.

"You cannot know the future, Gwen. You only know what others whisper in your ears and what you fear. You are *wrong*. I might not be a fighter, but that doesn't mean I won't fight. There are reasons submissives are part of the Pack, and you should know that better than anyone. I will not back down because people are scared I might whimper if someone growls too loudly."

Gwen shook her head. "You're only using the Alpha's bonds to act strong."

"Am I? Or are you underestimating me? You're underestimating the strength of your Alpha as well. I...I know that I'm not what any of you expected, but cutting my legs out from under me before I even begin won't help anyone."

Gwen let out a breath. "I cannot let you near the pups. You will confuse them."

Pain sliced across her heart, but she didn't let it show. Instead, she stalked toward Gwen. The other wolf's eyes glowed gold, and she backed up a step.

"I won't claw you. I won't even make you bleed," Brie said softly. "As you know, it's not in my nature. But I *will* hurt you if you don't move away. You might think you are more dominant, but you are not *my* dominant. You are a maternal wolf with too much power."

Gwen's eyes flared, and for a moment, Brie saw her true nature. "Iona would have been a better mate than you."

Brie slapped the other woman, keeping her claws sheathed. "Iona wouldn't have been his mate at all. You might have gotten me for a moment with the care-for-the-Pack bit, but you are just a jealous friend who wanted more."

"You're out, Gwen," Gideon said from behind her, and Brie cursed inwardly.

Damn it. Why did he have to be there? She was handling this on her own. Now whatever she did, it would be tainted because he was there. She might be grateful that he would always be there, but some things she needed to do on her own. When would he understand that?

Gwen's eyes filled with tears, and she sucked in a breath. "My Alpha, you can't do that. I've been the head maternal since your father was alive."

Brie reached back and gripped Gideon's hand, knowing he'd need the support even if he didn't.

"Yes, you have been. My mistake was letting you stay because I thought you were on the side of change. Go to the kitchens, Gwen. You're demoted until I can find a better use for you. Olivia will take your place. She cares for the children's welfare more than her standing in the Pack."

Sobbing, Gwen shot Brie a deadly look then stomped off.

Brie refused to look back at her mate, angry beyond all reason.

"You didn't call me," Gideon snapped, angry as well.

"I didn't need you to handle it for me," she said right back, her tone biting. "You just undermined everything I was working for by coming in and taking over."

Gideon stalked around her then gripped her chin. "I am Alpha. That's what I do."

She pulled away, cold at the loss. "Then what am I?" she asked, her voice hollow.

Aware they were starting to gain an audience, she turned around and headed toward the door. "I'll come back tomorrow and begin again. This is not over, Gideon."

"Little wolf."

She ignored him, instead walking back toward her home, her chin held high. She felt the stares of others around her and even the brush of a wolf against her as the lieutenants circled her as protection. She would never be without guards, she knew that, yet right then, she'd never felt so alone.

Gideon didn't understand, and Brie wasn't sure she did either.

Her place in the Pack was in flux, and each time he came to rescue her it made her life just that much harder. She needed to find a way to be her own wolf, submissive and caring, and also be the Alpha's mate, strong and protective.

Only, she wasn't sure that balance existed.

And if she could never find it, there wasn't hope for much else.

With that aching thought, she pushed out her pain, knowing she needed to be stronger than she as acting. Because if she wasn't careful, she'd lose herself, and without that, what did she have left?

CHAPTER THIRTEEN

T he warm body pressed to his shifted slightly, and Gideon held back a groan. It was too early to be awake, but he hadn't slept well. In fact, he hadn't slept well in weeks. Not since Leo revealed himself then seemingly vanished off the face of the earth. No matter the hunters he had on the situation and the technology at his fingertips, Gideon could not find his uncle.

Not only did that enrage his wolf, it made him feel fucking helpless as well.

Brie shifted again, this time her bottom pressing against his already rigid cock. He sucked in a breath, forcing his hips to stay put and not rock against her softness. She needed her sleep, not his grabby hands.

He held his breath, but she didn't move again. When he let it out, he forced himself to relax. Things were rocky as fuck when it came to his mate, but at least she still let him hold her. He tried not to think too hard about the fact that it could only be her wolf wanting the closeness, but he also knew she'd been practically touch-starved before their mating. She'd not only been a virgin, but she'd also held herself back from others just enough that her wolf had leapt into their mating, no holds barred. He knew she'd done that because she hadn't been able to stomach the touch of others once she'd caught the glimpse of him, and it killed him.

It wasn't supposed to be like this.

His mating wasn't supposed to be a point of tension within his Pack and within his heart.

No, that wasn't quite right. She wasn't a tension in his heart, as much as she was an unknown. He hadn't allowed himself to think of her beyond the need for her to be part of his Pack. He'd forced himself not to know the true Brie, the one who smiled at him, made cookies, and soothed his wolf. He hadn't wanted to get too close, only to lose her because he wasn't strong enough to protect her.

He sure hadn't been strong enough to keep her from being hurt by Gwen.

He let out a soft growl then froze. Brie merely pressed closer to him, as if she needed to calm his wolf even in sleep. Immediately, his wolf brushed against his skin, knowing their mate would be there.

Gwen had been part of his father's group and had followed the old man's views on submissives, humans, and those weaker than them. Only Gideon hadn't known the full extent of her feelings until he saw her with Brie. He kept her as the leader of the maternals because he hadn't wanted to strip the Pack of every leader in one fell swoop. Gwen had proven herself to him in her caring of the young, and he'd let her stay.

That had been the wrong decision, and now Gideon was left wondering what else he'd fucked up.

Taking over a Pack wasn't supposed to be a clean move. However, he knew it shouldn't have gone for him the way it did. The Redwood Alpha became the leader when Edward was killed, yet the transition, though heartbreaking, had been smooth. Kade's Pack trusted him and had grieved with him.

Gideon's Pack had formed two camps—those who praised him and those who wanted him beheaded for his actions. After thirty years, those two groups had blended somewhat, but clearly not enough.

Now Brie was facing the consequences of his actions.

She also wasn't truly speaking to him.

Oh sure, she would answer his questions politely, but a light had gone out of her eyes. She snuggled with him in bed, but he didn't touch her intimately as he had all the other nights before. He'd broken her trust when he came into the maternal ward and took over. He couldn't help it. His mate had been in pain, and he needed to fix it. Because of that, Brie had pulled away ever so slightly.

If only he'd stepped back for a moment and let her finish taking care of Gwen, Brie wouldn't have looked at him the way she did. He didn't think he'd taken away everything she'd gained with the maternals with her show of force, but he'd made it harder.

Stepping back and allowing her to do things on her own wasn't easy.

The fact that he'd even thought the word "allow" in the first place told him how far he needed to go when it came to not acting like an alpha asshole.

Today she would be going back to the maternals and working with Olivia. The other woman was kind and treated Brie with respect. It would be hard as hell to stand back and not do anything if she was hurt, but Brie could handle more than he'd given her credit for. He needed to remember that.

If anything happened to her...

No, he refused to think about that. He might not be able to keep her from every dirty look or judgment, but as she'd told him, the fact that she was out in the den and proving herself would eventually ease that distrust. It wasn't that she was a former Redwood that was the issue—no, his wolves valued that—it was that they were afraid she wouldn't be strong enough to protect them.

She'd prove them wrong.

She'd prove *him* wrong.

"You're thinking too hard," she whispered in his arms, her voice thick with sleep, and he let out a breath.

He'd known she was awake of course. His wolf had heard the change in her breathing, but he hoped she'd go back to sleep.

"Sorry for waking you," he grumbled then kissed her temple. It wasn't lost on him that she'd actually spoken to him. He just hoped she'd continue once she was fully awake.

She rolled over, her breasts pressing against his arm. It didn't matter that she wore a tank top and small shorts and he wore his boxer briefs—he just wanted her touch.

Her eyes glowed gold for a moment, and she smiled softly. "I see where your mind went."

He swore he could feel his cheeks heat, but he ignored it. "It's usually there when I'm around you," he said honestly.

Her eyes widened, and he wanted to curse. He wasn't good at this mating business. He didn't know what to say, even though it was his duty to *always* know what to say, what to do. He hadn't started off on the right foot with her, and every time he took a step forward, he messed up and fell back once more. One day he hoped he'd get the hang of this, but he had a feeling Brie would be the one leading him there. They might have mated for the wrong reasons, but now that she was his, he was going to make sure they had a true mating in all the ways that mattered. He refused to go about his life like his parents had. His mother had lost everything she was because of his father, even though what she became in the process was everything he'd feared.

Brie reached up and cupped his cheek. "Your face is so expressive sometimes. Where did you go just then?"

He sighed then turned his face to kiss her palm. "I was thinking of our mating and comparing it to my parents." He shut his mouth quickly, surprised he'd said that at all.

Her eyes widened yet again, but she didn't stop touching him. "You don't speak about them," she whispered.

"I don't," he agreed. The phone rang then, saving him from opening himself up for the hurt.

Frustration slid through Brie's eyes, but she masked it well. He rolled away and sat at the end of the bed, picking up his phone on the next ring.

"Yeah?" he said, not bothering to look at the readout.

"I know it's early, but can we meet soon to talk about the hunting runs?" Brynn asked, her voice brisk.

It sounded as though she'd been up for awhile, and he knew that was probably true. While Gideon's first priority was finding Leo, he had enough on his plate that he'd put Brynn in charge of the details. She was a strong wolf and hunter. He didn't know why the goddess hadn't blessed her with additional powers, but he had a feeling there was a reason for that...one that hadn't presented itself yet.

Gideon ran a hand through his hair, the strands going past his shoulders. He had to get a haircut soon, only he didn't know when that was going to happen with so much shit piling up.

"Sure. Give me an hour."

"Good enough."

"Get Ryder too. We could use his brain."

"Done."

She hung up quickly, not bothering to say goodbye. When Brynn was in hunting mode, she wasn't much for pleasantries.

Brie set her hand on his upper back between his shoulder blades, and he let out a breath. He hoped she wouldn't bring up what they'd been talking about. He still wasn't ready to lose her once he told her everything.

"No luck with Leo?" she asked. Good, they were moving on. For now. He knew it was only a small reprieve, but he'd take it.

"Not yet. I think we're going to have to put more men on it."

He stood up, not turning around. He wouldn't be able to hold himself back once he took a good look at her and her tumbled hair and sleepy expression.

"Do you have enough?" she asked. He heard the rustle of sheets and knew she was also getting out of bed. "You have people on the wards, the normal runs, and the tunnels between us and the Redwoods in case the humans find out about us. That's spreading ourselves a little thin, right?"

He nodded then turned around since she wasn't in bed anymore to tempt him. Goddess, she was breathtaking. Her chestnut hair was indeed in tumbles around her face but not as tangled as it was when he spent the night running his hands through it.

"We're not going to run out of wolves any time soon, but I don't necessarily enjoy having to face in so many directions at once." He liked this, their talking of such things as Pack matters as they got ready for the day. It was what he'd always thought of when he imagined finding a mate. He found himself wanting to know her opinions, thoughts, and needs. Maybe if he could step back and not take over like his wolf urged him to do, he could actually act like the mate she needed, rather than the mate she had.

"If you need more wolves, and your soldiers can't do it all, I know there are a few mid-ranking Pack members that could probably help."

He froze in the act of washing his face and turned to look at her. "Really? Who?"

She shrugged but didn't look at him.

"Brie, little wolf, you're my mate. I want to know what I'm missing. I'm bound to miss some things that look as if they're taken care of. I can't be everywhere at once." He grimaced. "As much as it pains me to say."

Her eyes met his. "You know, some wolves that used to live outside the den, blending with the human world, are moving back."

"Yes. It's too hard to hide their need to roam with the way the world is watching." Yet another matter he had his eye on. It was exhausting to think about.

"Well now that they're here, they're fitting in the den somewhat, but they don't have as clearly defined roles as they used to. They're not soldiers, maternals, or submissives."

"But they're just as important." He leaned down and brushed his lips over hers. "I'll talk to Ryder and Mitchell about it. Knowing my family, they already have their nose in that business since it's their job as Heir and Beta, but we all miss things."

She smiled then hugged his side. "I'm glad I could help. I'm going to take a quick shower then make breakfast. I know you have a few things to go over on your planner, so get that done, and then we can head to the center."

He kissed her again then left her to shower. If he stayed in there when she got naked, he wasn't sure he'd be able to hold himself back.

By the time they both were ready to go, the sun was peaking over the trees and people were out and about. He kept his focus on each of his Pack members, nodding and stopping to talk with them if they needed it. He also made sure that he gave special attention to those Brie had mentioned. He felt across the Pack bonds and knew she'd been right. Things were okay, pleasant even, but there was room for growth. He'd make sure Ryder and Mitchell were aware.

When they made it to the maternal area, he paused before the building, his wolf rising up. He didn't know why his wolf chose *now* to act like an overbearing ass, but he wasn't about to take it. Brie needed time to do her duties, and watching over her shoulder wouldn't help anyone. His wolf, however, didn't want to let her go.

Not surprising, but it was stronger today than usual for some reason.

Brie rolled her eyes when he growled then kissed his jaw. "I'll be fine, Alpha mine. Stop worrying. Olivia and I get on just fine. In fact, I'm helping her take the pups on a field trip to the circle so we can learn Pack history." Her eyes brightened, and he relaxed. "There's so much to learn. I feel like a pup myself."

He kissed her. Hard. "If you were a pup, I wouldn't be able to do that."

She blushed and rolled her eyes again. "Shush. The pups should be on their way now. Olivia wanted me to catch up so that the pups could learn what it felt like when another wolf was coming near them and they could scent ahead. Go off and do Alpha things. I'll be back tonight."

"I can pick you up and walk you home."

She shook her head. "You have two lieutenants on me at all times. At least. They can walk me home so I'm not alone in case Leo or someone else is around." She cupped his face and smiled. "You have things to do other than follow me around to make sure I'm safe."

He growled again then pressed a kiss to the corner of her mouth. "You can't expect the wolf to be rational about this."

"No, but I can expect the man to try his best. Now be off."

He sighed then stood back. "Fine. Go be the Alpha's mate."

She smiled, turned, and made her way to the building. She stepped inside, and his wolf relaxed somewhat since she wasn't out in the open. He turned and had made it about halfway to Brynn and Ryder when he heard it, a small whine like a spark being set.

He twisted and looked over his shoulder then took off at a run, his wolf on alert. The explosion blew him off his feet, the heat and fire scorching his skin. He was slammed to the ground, his thoughts on the woman he'd let walk into that building.

The building on fire.

"Brie!"

****

Brie's forced her eyes open then sucked in a breath, only to cough up smoke. What the hell had happened? One moment she was standing by the door, going inside to pick up a left-behind backpack, and the next she was on the ground, the sound of screams and fire all around her.

Half of the building was down and she saw the sunlight streaming in through the smoke. The roof was falling inward in some parts and shaky in the others. Beams and concrete littered the ground and stuck out at odd angles. The windows had blown in and glass was strewn everywhere. The door was off its hinges and the frame had bent in. Paint bubbled on the walls and the wallpaper was slowly peeling away.

It looked like a bomb had gone off.

And now that her brain stopped throbbing, she was pretty sure that was exactly what had happened.

She gingerly felt her limbs and figured she hadn't broken any bones. In fact, she had only a few cuts as far as she could tell, but she knew she didn't have much time to dwell on that fact. She had to get out of the building before the roof collapsed.

Her head still hurt, but she didn't know if that was from the smoke or her hitting her head when she'd hit the floor.

Thank god the babies had been out of the building.

Tears pricked at her eyes, but she pushed them away. Most of the pups and maternals had already started on the journey to the circle. There had only been a few children and adults outside when Brie had come back inside to get a child's bag.

No one else had been inside, but that didn't mean people weren't hurt. She *needed* to make sure they were okay. Those babies were so fragile. They didn't heal as quickly as adults.

"Brie!"

Gideon's voice reached her ears, and her wolf pushed at her, wanting their mate. Brie pushed herself up on shaky legs—her side ached something fierce—but she didn't fall back down. While she wanted to leave the building in case the roof came down, she needed to make sure no one else was in the building.

"Brie!"

"In here!" she yelled back. The panic in his voice mixed with rage, and she knew if she didn't find him soon, he'd go wolf and destroy anyone in his way.

The scents around her were too obliterated by smoke and fire so she couldn't scent if another wolf was nearby. But she *was* the Alpha female. She might be new, but she did have bonds with each and every wolf. She pushed out with her senses, trying to grasp for any bond that might be near. She felt Gideon coming and the others behind him, but she needed to focus on the others within—if there were any.

The threads were weak, ungrounded. She might have been mated in, but it would take time for those threads to strengthen.

There! There was one weak thread back in the kitchen area. Damn it. Someone must have come back.

"Brie, little wolf," Gideon growled, and she turned quickly to see him running at her. He picked her up in a gentle grip, surprising her. She'd have thought he'd almost crush her by the rage in his eyes, but instead he was caring...loving. He set her down then ran his hands over her body. "Are you hurt? What happened?"

"Big brother, feel up your mate at another time," Brynn barked, then coughed. "We need to get out of here. The roof that hasn't already fallen won't hold for long."

"There's someone in the kitchen," Brie shouted over the din. "I don't know who it is, but I can feel the thread."

Surprise lit Gideon's eyes, and he nodded. "Ryder."

"Got it," the Heir said then made his way carefully to the back. They were risking their lives for their people, but she wouldn't have expected anything else.

Gideon picked her up and cradled her to his chest. "We need to go."

"What about the others?" she asked, even as Gideon started moving. "The pups and maternals. Were we the only place that got hit?" Her heart raced. "I can walk, Gideon. Help the others. I'm fine."

He shook his head and kept silent. Before she knew it, they were outside, and Walker was there.

"Where are you hurt?" the Healer asked.

"Put me down," Brie growled. "I'm fine. Or I will be." She looked around at the carnage, and her heart raced. "Help the others. There might be more trapped."

"Got this one!" Ryder called, Olivia in his arms.

Olivia held her oddly bent arm to her chest and grimaced. "We needed more water for the trip. I don't think anyone else was in there, but I don't know."

"Help Olivia," Brie ordered Walker. "Gideon. Find everyone. Please. I'll help with the small cuts and bruises," she said, looking around at the others who were bleeding around her. The debris from the explosion must have gone far enough to injure some, but no one looked too bad off.

Gideon gave her a nod, an odd look in his eyes. "My brothers are searching for those who might be lost. I need to make sure they're safe as well."

Understanding filled her. He *needed* to ensure his Pack was safe, but he couldn't do that until he knew Brie was as well. Goddess, she totally got that. Gideon, even with as fragile a bond as they shared, was her priority as well.

"Go."

He nodded again then started barking more orders. Brie quickly got to work, helping Walker where she could. Her family had taught her some triage, but she wasn't an expert by any means.

Hours later, she was filthy, exhausted, and in need of her mate. However, from the looks of some of the wolves, she'd gained rank in their eyes. She felt so foolish for even thinking it. People had been *hurt*. The only thing she could do was help. At least people saw that now.

It was a step—she only wished she could have made it another way.

Warm arms wrapped around her, and she sank into Gideon's hold. "We're going home."

Not a question, but an order. One she'd gladly obey. She was exhausted anyway.

They made their way home in silence. It wasn't an uncomfortable one, more like they had nothing to say that couldn't wait until they were clean and sure the other one was safe.

He pulled her into the bathroom and stripped off her clothes then his. She let him care for her because they both needed it, but that didn't stop her from checking out his arms and hands. He had small cuts and scrapes from where he'd moved beams and other debris away. He'd heal by morning, but she didn't like seeing him hurt.

When he pulled her into the shower, he made sure the spray hit his back before it hit her. Her wolf, her mate, so caring.

He washed her hair, picking out the splinters and pieces of plaster, then he bent down so she could do the same to him. He had such soft, silky hair. The thick strands slid over her hands and arms when she rinsed the soap out. She loved the fact that it was so long. It wasn't as long as hers, but longer than most of the men in the Pack. It fit him.

They washed each other's bodies, slowly and carefully. It wasn't sexual, yet, at the same time, it was. They didn't linger, but her breasts ached, and his cock was hard against his belly. Still, they only rinsed off then dried each other before walking into the bedroom naked.

Gideon sat at the edge of the bed then pulled her onto his lap. His rigid cock pressed against her ass, but she didn't wiggle or move. They needed to talk first, if only to ensure they were okay—then she'd ensure he was *really* okay.

"Is everyone going to heal?" she asked.

Her mate nodded against the top of her head. "Yes. Only a few broken bones and one deep laceration. Walker took care of that." He let out a shaky breath. "None of the children had anything but small cuts and bruises. The adults threw themselves over the pups."

"I wouldn't expect anything else," she said, her voice hollow. "I just don't like the fact that it happened at all. Do we know what it was?"

"It will take us a while to go through the damage, and because of the accelerant used, we can't scent anyone other than those who were *supposed* to be there, so we don't know who was responsible."

She closed her eyes tight. "It was on purpose then? Not a faulty gas line or something electrical?"

"This was deliberate. Someone wanted to destroy the maternal area. Someone also waited until you were in the building to set it off."

Gideon's body grew tight as a bowstring, and she forced herself to relax. If she let out how scared she was, how angry, she'd set him off. Oh, he'd never hurt her, but he might hurt himself in his rage.

"We will find out who set it." She paused. "Have you searched for Leo's presence?"

He let out a small growl. "We didn't scent him. That doesn't mean it wasn't him or someone who is working with him. We still haven't found who let him into the den the first time."

"Do we want it to be him?" she asked.

"Yes. Because if it was him, we know the enemy. If it wasn't him? That means we have more enemies than we thought."

His body shook, and she curled her hand on his chest. Her mate had so much control, but sometimes control wasn't enough.

"Is there anything we can do about it tonight?"

He shook his head, his body moving under hers. "No. We have people out hunting and others studying the remains, but there's nothing you or I can do tonight."

"Then love me, Gideon." She looked up at him, and he swallowed hard. "Make love to me. Help me remember that it's okay to feel. Just be with me."

He blinked once, twice, and then lowered his lips to hers. She sighed into him, loving the taste of her mate. He wrapped his arms around her tighter, and she rocked.

He pulled away, breathless. "You're not too hurt?"

She shook her head. "I'm fine. Ready even." She smiled softly. "Please?"

"You never have to beg, little wolf." His eyes darkened. "Unless I want you to."

Her wolf whimpered, and she quickly wiggled off his lap.

"Brie..."

Before he could growl that she'd moved off his lap, she quickly got back on, this time straddling him. He grinned then cupped her butt, molding her cheeks with his large hands.

"I like the way you feel, little wolf. More than a handful." Squeeze. "Perfect for me."

With her knees on either side of him, she lifted up. His cock pressed along her pussy, and she moaned.

"You need more foreplay, little wolf," he growled softly. One hand let go of her ass, and he slid it between them, running his thumb over her clit.

She sucked in a breath then shook her head. "I'm always wet around you. Always ready." With that, she slowly, oh so slowly, slid down his length.

"Fuck. Me." Gideon growled, and she smiled.

"Trying to."

By the time she was fully seating on his lap, they were both sweaty, their bodies straining.

"I need to move, little wolf, but I don't want to hurt you."

She met his gaze then rocked into him. They both moaned. "Move, then. I won't break."

He *moved*.

She kept her gaze on his, never breaking eye contact. He squeezed her ass, pulling her up and down his cock, even as she rocked her body, increasing the friction. Her inner walls clamped down, and her mouth parted.

"Gideon..." she panted.

"Mine." He bit her lip, and she came. The possession in his tone, his growl sent her over the edge, and her pussy clenched around his cock, squeezing him. He went off with another growl, still pumping in and out of her as he came.

It was a quick, fast, hard fuck, but it was exactly what she needed—what *they* needed.

"Mine," she whispered back once she caught her breath.

Gideon cupped her face with one hand and brushed her hair back with the other. "Yours."

Her heart warmed, and she licked her lips. Yes, she could start to believe that, start to believe in the future. The darkness threatening them stalked her, but she set that aside for the moment. It would come, and she would fight, but right then, she was the Alpha's and he, hers.

Finally.

CHAPTER FOURTEEN

Gideon's body shook, and he forced himself not to punch through another wall. He had more control than that—though it didn't look like it lately. He quickly threw some cold water on his face, hoping it would calm down his wolf. Brie slept in the next room, exhausted after their lovemaking and the maternal house explosion.

Though he tried, he hadn't been able to fall asleep, his wolf too on edge for even a moment's peace. In fact, the only peace he'd felt in a long while was when he had Brie in his arms. He never thought he'd feel that way about another person. It hadn't crossed his mind he'd care for another being like he did.

He'd spent so long fighting for the good of the Pack, tarnishing his soul so others could breathe again, that the idea of a mate perfect for him seemed far-fetched. Then there were those long years without a single mating within the Pack. Some thought it was the moon goddess cursing the den because of what Joseph had done, but Gideon had another idea. What if the moon goddess was cursing him instead? He'd done the unthinkable and had the blood of so many others on his hands. He didn't deserve a mate, and he damn sure didn't deserve the woman in his bed.

She'd taken one hit and kept on coming, surprising him at every turn. Their mating wasn't a burden, wasn't something they were forced into anymore. It was something he wanted to cherish. In order to do that, though, he knew it was time to tell her the entire history of the Pack and how he'd become Alpha. In the times of war and strife, what he'd done might not look as bad as he felt it did, but it was dark enough that it hurt his wolf, his being.

It was time to face the truth and hope Brie and her wolf wanted him enough to stay. Oh, she'd always be his mate, but she didn't have to live with him, didn't have to keep him in her life. There were ways around that. He prayed she'd choose him once it was all over.

If she didn't...well, he didn't want to think about that outcome. He wasn't sure he could bear it.

He could still see the blood on her face, the soot and plaster covering her body when he'd first seen her in the rubble. His heart had leapt out of his chest, his mind going into panic mode. He'd been so close to losing her. If she'd been just a few seconds early or a few feet closer, he could have lost her. It didn't matter that she was a wolf and could heal faster and take more damage than humans; she could have been killed.

He didn't know what he would do if he lost her.

And that was the crux of it.

He'd found a mate who burrowed her way into his heart, and he had no idea how she'd gotten there. Now that she was there, though, he wasn't about to let her go. That meant he'd fight for her, even if she was the one who wanted to leave once he told her everything he'd done.

"Gideon?"

He turned toward the door between the bathroom and bedroom, and took a deep breath. Her sweet scent drifted toward him, and he found himself moving in her direction without a second thought. Her chestnut hair tumbled around her shoulders, and she'd put on one of his shirts, mixing his scent with her own. She was in his skin, just as he was in hers. While he wanted to rub along her body once more to make sure that scent lingered, he didn't. They needed to talk first.

"I thought you were sleeping," he murmured then cupped her face, unable to *not* touch.

She leaned into his palm and put her hand on his chest. "I couldn't. Not with you pacing in here. What's going on, Gideon? Are you worried about someone hurting the den again?"

He swallowed hard then shifted his hand so it was at the back of her neck, claiming her in a possessive manner. "We need to talk, Brie."

Her eyes widened for a moment, and then she bit her lip. "Whenever someone says that, it usually means something bad."

She met his gaze, her wolf in her eyes. She might not be aggressive, but her wolf *knew* his wolf would never hurt her. That trust was something he would do his best never to break.

"I need to tell you about my parents and how I became Alpha." The strength of his voice surprised him.

"Okay, we can do that." Her hand remained on his chest, and she petted him softly. "I know some of it, Gideon. Whatever you think you did that was so dark, so painful, it can't be as bad as you think. You wouldn't be the man you are today if that were the case."

He took her hand from his chest and kissed her fingertips, his wolf pacing. "I hope you feel that way once I'm done."

"Let's go sit on the couch then. I'll make coffee." She turned away, and he tugged at her, bringing her back to his chest. He nuzzled along her neck, inhaling her scent once more, ensuring he'd never forget it.

"You don't need to take care of me, little wolf."

She sighed but didn't pull away. "I thought we went over this already. I *do* need to take care of you. It makes my wolf happy."

He kissed her shoulder then pulled away. "Then, thank you."

She gave him a small smile over her shoulder and went to the kitchen. He took a deep breath and followed her. She wouldn't let him help, but he could carry the mugs back so she wouldn't have to. While her wolf wanted to care for him, his needed to care for her. It might have been a different kind of caring, but that's what made their relationship unique.

They settled on the couch near each enough to touch but not on top of one another like he usually preferred.

"My father was not a kind man," he began, then paused. "No, that's making it sound like he had bad moods. My father was a brute. A killer. He should never have been Alpha, but it was in his blood. He might have started out a better man than he became, but I never met that man. That wolf."

Brie put her hand on his knee, and he let her keep it there. Her touch settled him.

His submissive wolf, his mate.

"He and his brothers held all the positions of the hierarchy. Unlike our generation where Mitchell is Beta even though he's my cousin and not my brother, Joseph and his brothers held all the power." He met

194

her unwavering gaze and knew he could tell her anything. "They abused that power in all the ways possible."

She frowned. "If they did, how did the Redwoods never know?"

He let out a breath. "Because unlike the Centrals, who used their evil to call a demon to the world and show off their kills, the Talons, at the time, kept to themselves. You saw us as weaker than you but not evil because that's what Joseph wanted you to see."

She squeezed his knee. "I'm a Talon now, Gideon."

He blinked then nodded. "Yes. Yes you are. But you were born a Redwood, and that loyalty will never break. I will never fault you for being a Redwood in part of your heart as well, little wolf."

His mate blinked back tears but didn't say anything. There wasn't much *to* say at that point.

"Anyway, like I was saying, Joseph ruled with an iron fist. He wanted the power the Redwoods had, but he went about it the wrong way."

Brie nodded. "My grandfather knew his role as Alpha came with a responsibility of protection, not merely power. My Uncle Kade is the same way."

He brushed her hand with his fingertips, needing the touch of her skin to keep going. "Joseph had four brothers, Timothy, Reggie, Abraham, and Leo. Leo, as you know, didn't hold a place in the hierarchy. I think that's what shaped him into who he is today. He mated young and had Mitchell and Max, but Lina died giving birth to Max. I don't know if Leo was ever truly sane before that, but he broke after Lina died."

He sucked in a breath, knowing he, too, might break if he lost his mate, but that didn't excuse Leo for his crimes.

"Reggie was the Healer and Abraham the Enforcer, but they didn't do their duties. They were at Joseph's beck and call. We never had a true Omega to help us. No matter that we needed one desperately." Without someone to sense the true emotions of the Pack, to help siphon the good as well as the bad, they were lost. He met Brie's gaze. "Joseph and the others started with the submissives. You see, they didn't understand the true nature of wolves. They thought if they tortured those below them they could force the wolf to become aggressive."

He felt a flare of pain along the bond, the sense that her wolf was howling deep within. He squeezed her hand, and she did the same back but didn't speak.

"When they figured out they couldn't force a submissive wolf to become dominant, they killed him."

"That wasn't you, Gideon," she whispered. "You can't blame yourself."

He met her gaze, knowing he'd lose her. "I was the Heir, Brie. Before I grew strong enough to fight back..." He couldn't say it. Couldn't let her know...but he had to. "They made me watch, Brie. When I was too young to stop them, they made me watch. And I did *nothing*."

His wolf howled, clawing at him. Brie went sheet white but didn't pull away, didn't hit him, or run away.

"You were a *child*," she said, her voice like a whip. "You did *nothing* wrong, Gideon."

She didn't understand. She couldn't. She was good while he came from nothing but pain and evil.

"I watched them cut open men, women, and children because they couldn't understand how those different from themselves worked. I stood by and let it happen."

"Did you stand, Gideon? Did you really?" she asked, her voice soft.

He blinked. "They chained me to the chair until I was strong enough to break free."

"There. *That* is the man you are. Not the man who raised you. No, that's not an appropriate word. He didn't raise you. He tortured you just like he did them." She squeezed his hand. "He didn't have you in his image, so he tried to beat you into it."

He closed his eyes, letting out a breath. "When that didn't work, he let my uncles beat me, trying to make me become a man. Mitchell and Max had their own pain with Leo, and I don't know all that went on in their home until they came to live with us. My brothers, Brynn, and I though dealt with Joseph...and my mother."

"You don't speak of her." A statement, not a question.

"She was just as bad as him," he whispered. "She wanted the demons out of her sons. She blamed us for what her mate had become. I think...I think being mated to a man so evil for so long tainted her." He met her tearful gaze and sighed. "She killed herself because she couldn't handle it anymore. She abandoned us to a monster and his brothers."

"Oh baby," she whispered then moved to sit in his lap. She wrapped her arms around his neck, pressing her nose to his skin. His arms came around her, and he shuddered out a breath.

"Our Pack was dying," he continued. "Joseph kicked out your aunt and uncle because of what had happened to them and didn't think twice about the baby growing in her womb. Then the Centrals started their war, and we were losing people as well in the crossfire. Though I might be strong, I wasn't strong enough to take down an Alpha as well as the rest of the hierarchy. The rest of us could have done it, knowing we might die in the process, but with the Pack divided, we didn't know who to trust. It took too long, but I was finally able to kill my father."

She petted his chest, kissed his neck.

"We took out the rest of the poison, but we weren't able to get each member who followed my father. Not everyone participated in the tortures, the black magic. Some, like Shannon, hid behind their titles and had never truly sided with the others so they were able to live free. I've never been able to completely exorcise the demons from our Pack, but we're healthier now than we were." He paused. "Or maybe that was all a dream. Look at how they've treated you. It's been thirty years, and we haven't grown enough." He'd failed as an Alpha, and he knew it.

"Gideon, stop it," she snapped, her wolf in her voice.

He looked down at her and frowned.

"Your Pack dealt with death and pain for how long? Decades?"

He nodded. Joseph had been Alpha for far too long. "Over a century."

She gasped. "Dear goddess. And it's been only thirty years since you took over? In that time, you've forged a truce and treaty with the Redwoods, helped defeat a demon, and found a way to break the curse of mating on your people. The submissives, while not back to top form, are alive and breathing once again. The maternals are raising pups into beautiful wolves. Yes, there are some who need to have their minds changed or kicked out of the Pack, but *every* Pack has issues. Once we find out who blew up the building, you're one step closer. I know my mating you wasn't the easiest, but come on, I'm not exactly what people thought you needed." She gave him a wry smile. "I'm proving them wrong though. I feel the bonds within the Pack. They're growing stronger. You're a good Alpha, Gideon."

He let out a shaky breath and crushed her body to his. She wasn't leaving, wasn't looking at him as though he was a monster for what he'd seen and been forced to wait for so long to change.

She ran her hands up and down his back. "You are an Alpha we can all be proud of. We're still learning this whole mating thing, and we will continue to learn it for decades to come, but we're going to do it side by side. Okay?"

"You are too good for me, little wolf."

"No, I'm just right for you," she whispered.

He smiled then kissed her temple. "We will find the wolf that hurt our Pack. We will find Leo. I'm not letting my Pack crumble. Not after all we've been through."

She pulled back and grinned. "Now that's my Alpha."

Her Alpha. He liked the sound of that.

He framed her face, his wolf pressing hard against him. Tonight was the full moon hunt, and his wolf was too close to the surface. He might have had excellent control over his wolf, but with the stress of what was going on around him, his emotions riding high with Brie and the full moon, he knew he needed to run hard tonight.

"You need to forgive yourself, Gideon," she whispered, and his wolf howled. "You can't move on if you don't."

"Those who can never find their mates, see their children grow, or take another breath might beg to differ."

"Oh, baby," she whispered. He liked the way she called him baby under her breath. Not that he wanted her to do it in public. "You can't let what was forced on you to eat you up inside. You fought for them the moment you could. You might not feel it, but you are the Alpha you were born to be, not the Alpha they tried to force you to become."

He kissed her then, needing her more than he'd ever thought he'd crave someone. Her tongue tangled with his, and she gasped into his mouth when his hand moved down her back to cup her ass.

"Mine," he growled, nipping her lower lip."

"Yours," she whispered back then swallowed hard. "I..."

His wolf perked, waiting to hear what she had to say, hoping it was what he wanted to hear.

"Gideon?" A voice on the other side of the door. Brie pulled away, and he cursed.

"Come in, Brynn," he called. The hunt didn't start for another hour since their sleeping schedules were off, but if Brynn was here now, she needed something.

His sister ducked her head inside and blushed. "Sorry to interrupt. I...I can come back later. Or I'll just see you at the hunt."

He opened his mouth to tell her to get her ass over here, but Brie beat him to the punch. Though she was only dressed in his shirt, she stood up and took Brynn's hands in her own.

"Nonsense. You're here for a reason. Come on in. You want coffee?"

There was his mate, the submissive caretaker. There was something going on with Brynn, something he'd been aware of for a while, but he couldn't put his finger on it. He didn't want to corner her and force the issue since it looked as though she was handling it, but he liked the fact that his mate seemed to know something was wrong as well. This was what it meant to be Alpha. It wasn't all claws and growls. It was taking care of the Pack in every way possible. Yes, he had his family in their respective roles to handle duties as well, but some things only he could do—only he *and* Brie could do. The fact that her wolf *needed* to take care of others helped in this case. He'd never thought about that before, and now he was damn lucky to have her.

Brynn blinked at both of them and gave a sad smile. "Coffee sounds wonderful, thanks, Brie."

Brie cupped Brynn's face. "You're my sister now. Let me take care of you."

Brynn smiled a little more brightly that time. "Yeah, I guess I am. I'm not used to having other women around."

Brie laughed softly and went to get coffee. "Yeah, I guess the Brentwoods are a little testosterone-based."

"Hell, yeah," Gideon growled with a smile.

Brynn rolled her eyes then came to the couch to sit next to him. He wrapped his arm around her shoulders and tucked her close. She was so dominant that it was rare she'd let him hold her like this. The fact that she seemed to need it spoke volumes.

"You going to tell me what's wrong?" he asked.

"I can't," she whispered. "Not yet."

He nodded then rubbed his chin over her head. Brie came around to Brynn's other side and set the coffee mug on the table before wrapping her arms around his sister.

"We're here when you need us," Brie said softly. "You don't have to hold it all in."

Brynn pulled away to smile at both of them. "With Brie here, I don't think anyone can hold back their thoughts for long."

Gideon grinned at his sister then his mate. "Sounds about right."

He tucked his girls closer, his wolf content in their presence. He'd do anything for his Pack, for his family—even if it meant waiting for the right time to help.

This hunt was going to be different, Gideon thought, the feeling deep in his bones. This time it wasn't Brie's introduction to the Pack, but rather a moment where she was part of the Pack. The moon rode high in the sky, the tension in the air palpable. It was a different tension though, not unwelcome. His wolves needed their run to be able to let their animal side roam. No one was staring at Brie as though she was a newcomer this time.

There might still be some resentment, but he didn't feel it like he had before. He had a feeling Brie's insistence at taking over some of his duties had helped—plus the way she'd cared for the others when the explosion had hurt so many. She'd been cut and bruised but had stood by his side. There was a strength there that others hadn't seen because they hadn't been looking beneath the surface.

Because *he* hadn't been looking beneath the surface.

Thank the goddess for his stubborn mate. He wouldn't be making that mistake again.

He tucked Brie to his side and ran his chin over her head. "You ready to hunt?"

Brie scrunched up her face, and he laughed. "I want to run, but I've never been a fan of eating a bunny after it's hopped around in front of me."

He kissed her nose, and she batted at him. "We'll run together." He cupped her face, his tone serious. "If others fight you for dominance, I will do my best to let them live, but I can't promise anything."

She shook her head. "It's not the same this time. I'm truly your mate and not just the new member of the Pack, but thank you for trying." She lifted up on her toes and kissed him softly.

Truly his mate. Yes, he supposed that was the case. He wasn't as...angry as he'd been before, and Brie seemed stronger this time, more settled into her skin.

He kissed her soundly then pulled back, throwing his head back in a howl. The other wolves joined him, their songs a melodic harmony that soothed his wolf. There were dangerous times coming and many things left unsaid, but for this night, their Pack would run as one.

When the final howl faded, they shifted, each taking their time, their bodies twisting and reforming into their four-footed counterparts. Once Brie finished, he licked her muzzle, gently bit down on the back of her neck, and then started to run. She fell in place beside him, their pace not backbreaking but just what their wolves needed.

He sensed the other wolves around them, giving them space but not leaving his and Brie's presence. Brynn and the others followed them, on guard yet letting their wolves play as well. They made their way through the forest, jumping over fallen logs and through puddles left by the rain earlier in the day.

His wolf knew something was coming, only it didn't know when. It wouldn't be that night—they at least had that reprieve—but it meant that Gideon would do all in his power to cherish the time he had. It was the least he could do.

When the first howl hit the air he came to a halt, his wolf in awe. The man might not have known what the sound meant, but the wolf did through the bonds. Brie came to his side, her eyes wide.

The wolves' song wasn't for him, or the Pack as a whole...it was for *her*.

They were claiming her as their own.

She'd come out of a burning building alive and had cared for the innocent.

She'd stood up to the dominants around her and told them to care for the others, not her.

She'd become the Alpha's mate in truth.

He threw his head back and howled with them, pushing the emotion through the mating bond. He wasn't sure she understood, and when the last howl became an echo, he led her off to a small lake on their land where no one would come near. He could sense Kameron and Ryder close by but out of earshot. They would keep the others from dipping their toes in the lake and seeing too much.

While others would burn off the adrenaline from the hunt either by taking prey for a meal, play-fighting with others, or finding another wolf for intimate touch, he wanted only his Brie.

He shifted back, and she followed, her eyes still those of a wolf when she finished. Her breasts were high, her nipples hard pebbles. He scented her arousal mixing with his own. Unable to hold back any longer, he crushed his mouth to hers, tangling his fingers in her hair. His cock, hard as a rock, pressed against her belly.

"They were howling for you," he panted once he pulled away.

She gripped his dick, and he sucked in a breath.

"For me?" she asked, her hand sliding up and down then squeezing.

His eyes crossed, and he counted to ten. He would *not* come too soon. Just one touch and his mate had him ready to blow.

"They were welcoming you," he said, nipping at her lips, her neck, her tongue. His hands roamed her body, pinching and tugging at her nipples, loving the way she gasped with each motion.

"I...I don't know what to say," she whispered, her breath coming in pants as his hand moved down her body to the curls below.

"Say nothing," he growled then kissing her again. "We can talk about it later, little wolf. You're theirs as they are yours, but right now, you are *mine*."

The mating urge rode him hard, but he knew it was his mate as well that made him see stars, made him want to fuck and lick her until they were both breathless.

He kept his eyes on her and speared her with two fingers. Her mouth parted, a soundless gasp escaping her mouth. He worked in and out of her, her pussy so wet that he knew he could slide his dick right in and be welcome.

He wanted, no *needed*, to taste her first. He twisted his hand, running his thumb over her clit and fucked her with his fingers, wanting her to come on his hand. He kissed her again, keeping his eyes open so he could watch as she rose over the peak, her body shaking against his. When he pulled his hand away, he kept his eyes on hers, licking her juices from his fingers.

"So. Fucking. Sweet."

She growled then pounced. He hadn't been ready for her, and he fell back to the ground, the twigs and dirt digging into his skin.

"Want you. Now."

He grinned at her words and ran his hands over her back and ass. When he squeezed her cheeks, she let out a moan.

"Hop on, little wolf."

"No. I want you to come in my mouth first." She grinned, and he groaned. "You're Alpha, mate of mine, you can recover fast enough to fuck me hard after I have you."

He growled, rising up to his forearms so he could bite down on her bottom lip. Hard. "I like it when you talk dirty." He gripped her hair in an unforgiving hold. "I'm still in charge, little wolf. You get that?"

She nodded then wiggled her ass in the air since she was on all fours above him. "Please."

"Tease." He kissed her then pushed her toward his cock, wanting her mouth on him. "Suck me down. You know what to do."

Her mouth wrapped around him, and it took everything in his power not to close his eyes and come down her throat right then. He had one hand on her head, guiding her, and he leaned on the other arm so he could watch her move. Her mouth glided up and down his length, her tongue teasing his slit then doing wicked things down the rest of him. Her nails dug into his thighs, her body an arch of beauty as she went down on him.

Fuck, he loved watching her move, watching the way she worked him. He might have been the Alpha, but he was at her mercy—and they both knew it.

His balls tightened as she hollowed her cheeks, and he pulled on her hair. "I'm going to come, little wolf, pull back."

She dug her claws into his thighs, and he shouted, coming down her throat in one long rush. He pulled her away once he could see straight and kissed her. Hard.

"You are so fucking sexy, Brie."

She bit his lip and grinned. "You're pretty sexy yourself, Gideon."

They were on their knees, their bodies pressed against one another. He was still hard, and she'd only come once. His poor little wolf.

"On your hands and knees."

Her eyes widened, her mouth parting. He twisted out of the way, and she bent over, wiggling her bottom again. He got into position then slapped her ass. She gasped then moaned.

"You're teasing me," he growled. He leaned over her so he could bite down on her neck. She froze, her body warm and ready. He marked her as his once more then licked the wounds, his wolf eager to claim her again.

He positioned himself at her entrance, gripped her hips, and then slid into her in one thrust. They both shouted once he was buried in her to the hilt, but he didn't rest. He pumped in and out of her, feeling her need and passion through the bond mingling with his own. He bent over, rolling her nipples in his hand while keeping her steady.

"Gideon. Please. Make me come. I need to come."

He kissed her as she looked over her shoulder, slamming into her over and over. He felt her cunt slick and swollen. She was almost at the edge, but not quite close enough. He slid his hand down her belly and flicked his finger over her clit.

She came on a wave, her body bowing as her pussy clenched around his cock. He was so damn close to coming again, but he wanted her to ride it out once more before he followed her. Keeping up the pace, he pounded into her, loving the way she met his hips thrust for thrust, pushing back, allowing him to go deeper than he'd gone before.

He knew he needed to see her face when he came so he pulled out, flipped her on her back—careful to catch her with his hands so she wouldn't hurt herself on the rugged ground—and growled.

"Gideon," she panted, her eyes wide.

He gripped her knee and lifted her leg up and to the side as he slid inside. This way he could go even deeper. She moaned, her cunt still pulsing around him. He pistoned in and out of her, his wolf howling.

When she came again, this time he allowed himself to go with her, unable to hold himself back any longer. He filled her up, leaving them both sweat-slick and out of breath. He was still inside her as he brought her close to him and rolled so she lay sprawled over his chest.

There were no words needed, nothing left to say. She was his mate.

His.

CHAPTER FIFTEEN

"**A**re the Jamenson dinners always this loud?" Brandon asked as he leaned toward Brie. The Omega of the Talon Pack was one of the brothers that she didn't know well, but she was trying. He also happened to be sitting next to her during her first Brentwood family dinner.

"Louder," she answered back. "They used to be at my grandparents' house, and when everyone started having babies, they just added more room around the table." She paused, that familiar pain piercing her heart. "Then when Kade and Melanie became the Alpha pair, dinners began at their house. There are seven siblings plus their numerous children. And then of course the enforcers and others sometimes visit. It's never quiet."

Brandon's eyes narrowed for a moment, and that pain she'd felt before slowly leached away. She put her hand on his arm and shook her head.

"You don't need to take that away. I'm used to that pain by now. Its part of who I am."

"Sometimes I don't even realize I do it," he answered honestly. As the Omega, he wouldn't have been able to feel someone being in pain without helping, but she didn't want him to be overwhelmed either.

"You've only been at this for thirty years, right?" she asked. Only might have sounded sarcastic to a human, but it was different for wolves.

"Yeah," he answered. "All of us came into our powers at the same time and relatively late in life. The *others* didn't want to give up...duty."

That made sense. The hierarchy usually went over to the next generation—the Alpha's children and sometimes some outsiders—once both parties were ready. Unless, as in the Redwoods' case, death changed the game. In the Talons' case, the prior ones were too selfish to allow a healthy Pack to grow.

"Well, you all have experience now anyway," she said, trying to ease the awkwardness.

He gave her a small smile before it fell from his face. She'd grown up around an Omega who'd been through hell and back so she understood the pain of Brandon's burden made it hard for him to *want* to be around others. She wouldn't push him as long as he didn't look like he needed a reprieve.

Gideon's hand came around the back of her neck, and her wolf perked up. He kept his attention on Mitchell as the two of them spoke, but the mere fact that he couldn't keep from touching her made her heart swell.

Each of the Brentwoods had their secrets, and one day Brie hoped they felt comfortable enough with her to share them. Or at least some of them. After all, she didn't need to know everything. She only wanted to feel as though she was part of the family. She was getting there at least. Soon everyone was leaving, and she found herself standing outside on the doorstep talking to Walker. Gideon had gone to Mitchell's place with Brynn to discuss something about the ongoing hunt for Leo. She knew the lieutenants were around her, felt their presence, so she wasn't truly alone.

He might have been one of the youngest since he was one of the triplets, but as with Brandon, Walker's responsibilities made him seem far older. While there was an odd innocence around Brandon that she couldn't put her finger on, Walker seemed as though he kept his secrets close to his heart.

The Healer looked over his shoulder and lowered his voice. "I have been remiss in my duties, Brie."

She tilted her head. "How do you mean?"

"I never asked if you needed some form of birth control once you moved in." He didn't blush or sound embarrassed, but she could tell from her wolf that this wasn't a comfortable topic for him. Mostly likely because his brother, his Alpha, her mate was near.

She bit her lip and shook her head. "I...I'm not on anything, and we haven't talked about it." Stupid, she knew. It wasn't as though they could get diseases, and they hadn't used condoms because, at first, they needed the connection, and now...well, she hadn't wanted to. "Let me talk with Gideon about this. We've been stupid not to."

Walker gave her a small smile. "You're newly mated and the Alpha pair. Of course you're going to want children. The only matter is timing, and now that I've made you uncomfortable, I'll leave you to your mate."

She shook her head then gave the Healer a hug. "Thank you for looking out for us. Since we wolves can't have children outside of a mating, it's not something we think about." She cursed herself. "Though my mother raised me better than that."

Walker patted her cheek, and she smiled. "No worries. If you and Gideon didn't subconsciously want children, you both would have stopped it. It's the way of the wolves."

With that, he left her on the doorstep, confused as ever. In this day and age, accidental babies were a thing of the past usually, but she should have thought ahead. She put her hand on her stomach and shook her head. She'd talk with Gideon, but she had a feeling he'd feel the same way. Pregnancies, despite the size of the Jamensons and Brentwoods, were rare in their world. Each birth was a blessing from the goddess.

"Brie?"

She turned on her heel at the sound of an unfamiliar voice, her mouth dropping at its owner. "Iona?"

The other woman ducked her head, keeping her gaze below Brie's. "I didn't realize it was a family dinner night. I'll come by another time."

The fact that this woman who'd once shared Gideon's bed and had been slated to mate him had lowered her gaze puzzled Brie. She didn't know what to think of Iona and yet had never had a conversation with her. She shouldn't have let her emotions and whispers from others cloud her judgment, but she'd done just that.

"It's fine. Is there something you wanted? If you're here to talk to Gideon...well, I don't know if my wolf will allow you to do that right now." She might not be dominant, but she *was* this woman's Alpha female.

Iona raised her face but didn't meet Brie's eyes. "I understand, and if I was in your position, I would do the same thing. I'm actually here to apologize."

Brie blinked. "Huh?"

The other woman cracked a smile. "Yeah, I guess it's a surprise to me too. I just wanted to let you know that what the elders cooked up wasn't my idea.

They're my dominants, so I had to do what they said since they called it a Pack matter. I know Gideon isn't my mate. I was a little peeved when he shut down our relationship." She winced. "But it wasn't anything like what you and he have now. So I'm sorry if I caused you any pain."

"I...I don't know what to say. I suppose Shannon and the others would have just found another wolf to fill your spot."

"I think so. It's so stupid really. But in the end, he got his true mate, so I guess he wins."

Brie smiled at that. "Yeah. I guess he does."

Iona opened her mouth to speak then turned on her heel. The hair on the back of Brie's neck stood on end, and her claws came out.

"Run! Get in the house!" Iona shouted as two wolves came out of the dark and pounced.

Brie would not run.

Another wolf jumped toward her, and she slashed at its side. It would take too long for her to shift, but she could defend herself. She sent a shock through the mating bond, hoping Gideon would come. She wasn't stupid. There were way too many wolves for her to win on her own.

Iona sliced at another wolf who came at her and she fought them off. "Go, Brie! I'll hold them off."

Brie growled, kicking at another wolf, her own wolf not knowing what to do. She didn't want to fight, but she had to in order to survive. She felt more than saw the lieutenants come out of the darkness, blood covering their bodies. There must have been more fighting than she'd seen.

She'd turned to take down another wolf when someone came up from behind her. A pressure injector pressed against her neck, and she shouted, her mind going fuzzy.

The darkness swallowed her whole.

Brie woke to her own screams.

She blinked once. Twice. She tried to lift her body but found herself chained down to a table.

Her mother had once been in this position. It's how she'd become a werewolf.

"You're awake. Good."

That voice. She *knew* that voice.

"Leo?" she asked, her voice hoarse. She licked her lips, only to find them covered in blood. Oh goddess, how long had she been out, and where the hell was she? She needed to remain calm. That was the only way she could get out of this because, if she started to let the fear take over, there was no way she'd survive.

The man standing above her smiled, his eyes bright and wild. He looked so much like the other Brentwoods, but the taint of madness on his face changed everything. She'd known that this man was out in the wild...waiting.

How he'd gotten so many wolves on his side, *inside* the den wards, she didn't know.

Gideon was beyond enraged right now. She felt his pain, his anger through the bond, but it was faint, as if she was too far away to feel it fully. If only she knew more about their bond. Some wolves could speak to one another through it, and some could pinpoint their exact locations.

Hers and Gideon's bond was far too new.

And worrying about what she couldn't change wasn't going to help her today.

"I see Gideon has been filling your head with my past deeds." Leo licked his lips then ran a hand down her arm.

She flinched, trying to pull away, but he'd strapped her down too firmly. There was no way she could move. She might have the strength of a wolf, but these chains were reinforced with something magical. He'd have to release her, or someone would have to find a key in order for her to get lose.

Her heart beat loudly, and suddenly a wash of pain slid over her. It was as if her body was finally allowing her to feel *exactly* what the bastard had done to her. She could feel that all of her clothes were still on, so at least she'd been spared that agony, but there were slices all over her legs and stomach.

Leo grinned again and held up a bloody scalpel. Her eyes widened, and her wolf pushed, trying to get free. It was no use though. She was at his mercy until she came up with another plan.

"Yes, Gideon told you much of what we did. Did he tell you of our experiments on the submissives?" He sighed. "No matter how much we dug, we never could find their wolves. Damn shame but submissives were worthless anyway." He leaned closer, his putrid breath sliding over her. "I can't believe my nephew mated a submissive."

She growled, trying to bite at him, but he pulled away too quickly.

"I like your style, wolf," he bit back. "Maybe Gideon liked that too. That's why he stuck with you. Maybe he felt sorry for you because he watched all those little wolves being cut up into tiny pieces."

He threw his head back and laughed while bile rose in Brie's throat. If this was part of what Gideon had grown up with, she was surprised the others had grown up as sane as they were. Leo was a *monster*.

"Would you be as beautiful if you were cut into tiny pieces?" he murmured.

"Fuck. You."

He slapped her, and her head hit the back of the table hard. "Bitch has a spine. Good to know." Leo let out a sigh. "I can't kill you yet, you know. It's not in the plans. In fact, I have to keep you alive. I can mess you up some, let you bleed, but you're not going to die until I get what I want."

An eerie kind of hope slid through her. "What do you want?" she asked. If she wasn't going to die at that moment, then she'd get everything she could out of him. This man wanted to hurt her mate and Pack. He needed to die.

Leo sighed. "I want what I deserve." When he didn't elaborate, Brie asked again, not giving up that small amount of hope.

"You're a means to an end, Brie. Simple as that. Once Gideon finds you, then our plan will be in place. There are only a few more things that must be done, and then I will get everything I've wanted for decades."

He slapped her again, and she saw stars. "But before that, I get to have my fun."

The blade slid into her stomach, and she screamed. He laughed again, but his attention was on his work. He'd said he didn't want to kill her, but oh goddess, it hurt. A fiery pain on an edge of a blade.

He made two more cuts along her thighs, but she didn't scream this time. He seemed to enjoy it too much. Instead, she let the tears fall down her cheeks, her wolf silenced. She *would* get out of here, and then she'd find a way to kill the bastard.

"He's coming."

Brie looked to the right and growled; her wolf was back in the game.

Shannon, the fucking Talon Pack elder, shook her head. "He shouldn't have mated you," she said simply.

"You would have been safe with the Redwoods." She patted Brie's cheek, and Brie bit the bitch's hand.

When Shannon slapped her, she didn't even feel it, her wolf too enraged.

The elder cursed, shaking off the blood. "Stupid little bitch," she muttered. "You would have been *safe*. At least until we were ready to take down the Redwoods as well. Instead, you had to be so self-sacrificing." She rolled her eyes then narrowed them over Brie's head. "Stop looking at her like you want to cut her up some more. We need to leave now."

"Is everything prepared?" Leo drawled.

"Yes. Of course. I know what I'm doing." Shannon dug her claw into Brie's side, sending a blinding pain throughout Brie's body. "Now be a good girl and deliver a message. Tell your fucking mate that this isn't over. This is but one phase."

Brie sucked in a breath, gaining her strength. "He'll cut your bonds. You'll be a lone wolf." She swallowed hard, the pain pulling at her, draining her. "You won't be able to get any more of your wolves into the den to fight. You've shown your cards."

Shannon smiled then and dread slid down Brie's spine. "Have I?"

With that, the elder and Leo left the room. Brie pulled at her chains, trying to get free, but it was no use. Without the key, there was no way she could get out. Blinking away the agony, she searched the room for the key and shouted when she saw it in the corner along the wall. If someone came in and found her, they could get the key.

She just prayed that Gideon would get there soon. She didn't want to be saved like a damsel, but she knew when she was out of her depths. She'd fought back, but it hadn't been enough.

Next time she wouldn't make it that easy.

Her mating bond pulsed, and she let out a shout. "Gideon!" He was close; she knew that much. She pulled at the chains again, knowing it was futile, but she refused to lie back and wait to be rescued.

Her mate ran through the door, his body in human form, but the wolf in his eyes.

"Oh fuck, little wolf." He came to her side but didn't touch her, as if he was afraid to hurt her.

Tears slid down her cheeks, but she didn't care. "The key. Get the key." It hurt to speak now, the adrenaline fading away now that he was there.

"Where's the key, baby?" he asked, his voice a soft growl.

"The corner," she whispered, finding it hard to speak.

"Get the key, Brynn," he shouted behind him.

"On it. Oh sweet mercy," the other woman gasped. "Oh, Brie, honey, we'll get you out of there."

"I think they're magic-infused," Brie said, trying to keep speaking so she wouldn't freak out now that her mate was here.

Gideon ran hand over her cheek. She winced since they'd slapped her so many times, and he let out a growl.

"I don't know where to touch you that won't hurt."

"Just be here," she said simply.

"Got it!" Brynn said, and the chains fell away.

Brie tried to get up then gasped at the pain.

Gideon let out a growl. "Don't move. Walker! Get in here."

"You can pick me up," she said softly. "I just want to go home."

"Home," he whispered. "We can do that. If we move you right now though, we might hurt you more. Have Walker Heal you just a little bit so we can travel with you."

It made sense, but she honestly didn't want to be in the room any longer than she had to. Brynn seemed to understand and gripped Brie's hand. It was unhurt thankfully.

"We won't be that long." The other woman tapped the earpiece in her right ear and nodded. "Kameron said that whoever was here is long gone." She cursed.

"Leo said that this was just a warning," Brie put in.

Gideon pressed his lips softly to hers, and she whimpered, not in pain but in something much more agonizing—hope.

"Let Walker Heal you, and then you can tell us everything."

"I'm here," Walker said, sadness in his eyes. "This might hurt a bit, Brie, but then it will feel warm."

She sucked in a breath. "I know. I broke my arm once, and Hannah Healed it."

Walker gave her a soft smile. "Then just let me work and don't fight the Healing bond."

She gasped when he started working. He put his palms over the worst of her cuts, warmth spreading through her system. It was a tingling sensation that led into an odd knitting together of skin. She didn't look at exactly what he was doing because she knew herself better than that.

"Shannon!" she shouted. "Damn it. Shannon. She was in on this."

Gideon gave her a tight nod. "We know. I scented her outside the house as well as in here." He cupped her face softly, careful of the bruises. "I cut her bond to the Pack. She's shunned. She won't be able to hurt you anymore."

"Where am I?" she asked, her body aching.

"You're in an old abandoned building outside our territory. We didn't even know the place existed until they took you here. Come one, little wolf. Let's go."

Brie shook her head and winced. "She said it was only the beginning. She must have others working for her that are still part of the Pack."

"Then we'll find them," Kameron said from behind Gideon, rage in his eyes. "They won't be able to hurt our Pack again."

Gideon kissed her again then lifted her into his arms when Walker gave the okay. "We'll finish this discussion in the den, but know this, Shannon and Leo signed their death warrants. I'll have no mercy for them."

"They don't deserve it," Brie said simply. He caught her gaze, and she saw the relief there. She wouldn't think less of him because he would kill those who hurt the Pack—herself included. He was the Alpha for that reason, and she loved him—brutality and all.

And she wouldn't wait another day to tell him that either. Once they were alone, she'd tell him he was hers in all ways that were possible. She'd almost lost her chance once. She wouldn't be doing it again.

Leo and Shannon had pissed off the wrong submissive. It was time they learned about all kinds of strength.

For good.

CHAPTER SIXTEEN

B rynn found herself standing by one of the two entrances into the den, her body shaking. It might have been because of what she'd seen in the torture chamber they'd found Brie in, but Brynn knew better.

It was because of the wolf she was here to meet.

When they'd come upon Iona bleeding in the road, still gasping for breath, Brynn's mind had gone into overdrive. The other woman and the lieutenants had killed most of the wolves that had taken Brie, but they hadn't been able to stop Shannon from kidnapping the Alpha female. They knew the identities of the traitors, but they weren't sure who else was on the other side but hadn't fought. Iona would live from sheer will alone, and the fact that she'd fought to save Brie brought her up slightly in Brynn's book, but things had gone to hell soon after.

They'd rallied the troops and followed Brie's scent to Leo's torture chamber. Brynn had been able to think through the rage to contact the Redwoods about what happened once they got back. She should have done so *before* they'd run after Brie, but she was thinking only of her Packmate and the consequences *within* the Pack, not outside of it.

That wasn't a mistake she would make again.

Brie and Gideon were locked in their home, and Brynn knew they needed the privacy. They were not only newly mated, but Brie had almost *died*. Walker had Healed her so she might only be sore at the moment, but it had been a close call in the grand scheme of things. Once Gideon's wolf could breathe again, Brynn and the rest of them would meet to strategize, but what they didn't need was anyone freaking out even more.

And that just might happen when Finn showed up.

Finn.

That damn wolf.

While the rest of the Redwoods might have wanted to come to ensure Brie was safe and sound, Finn had somehow convinced everyone to allow him to come with only his cousin Charlotte. Finn was the Heir, and Charlotte was one of Brie's best friends and cousin. Plus, the woman had apparently been through hell on earth when she was a child, so she would be able to help Brie if she really needed it. Somehow the rest of the Pack was staying behind, relying on Finn and Charlotte to tell them everything. She wasn't sure how he'd done it since Brynn knew Jasper and Willow, and they wouldn't normally step aside when their daughter was in pain.

They must have trusted Finn a hell of a lot.

If only Brynn could do that.

It wasn't the fact that he was the Heir to another Pack. No, that was something she could deal with. It was the fact that she'd met him more than once now, and the damn wolf hadn't acknowledged her beyond the fact that she was a Talon.

He didn't stiffen around her, didn't breathe in her scent. He didn't reach out and need to touch her.

Instead he acted as if there was nothing between them.

Maybe there wasn't. Not to him.

Finn and Charlotte pulled up and she raised her chin. "Finn. Charlotte." She knew her voice held ice, but she couldn't hold it back. If she gave into what her wolf felt, she'd break and she refused to be that person.

Charlotte, a beautiful woman with long dark hair and dark eyes smiled at her, though Brynn saw the strain in them. "Thank you for allowing me to see my cousin, Brynn." She hugged Brynn quickly then pulled away so Finn could come up to them.

Brynn sucked in a breath at the rage in the man's eyes. She knew he was a strong wolf and Heir, but she'd never felt the wolf like she did now in his presence.

"Where is she?" Finn bit out, not bothering with pleasantries.

"Finn, stop being an ass," Charlotte snapped. "Brie is fine and we're going to go make sure of that fact so our wolves and the rest of the family don't go crazy. What happened isn't Brynn's fault."

From the accusatory look in Finn's eyes, Brynn wasn't sure the man believed Charlotte's words. Guilt threatened her, and she knew Charlotte was thinking the same thing. Brie had almost died on her watch, and Brynn would never forgive herself if it happened again. She'd find Leo and Shannon and gut them.

Not that she'd explain herself to Finn. She shouldn't have to. He was a Redwood wolf, not a Talon. He didn't mean anything to her.

Or at least he shouldn't.

"Let me take you to Brie so you can stop puffing out your chest and growling," Brynn snapped, pissed off that she'd let this wolf get to her.

Finn inhaled through his nose, his nostrils fairing then let out a deep breath. "I apologize for snapping. You don't deserve my wrath. I appreciate that you'll take me to Brie."

"Follow me."

So formal. As if there wasn't anything between them.

Brynn bit her lip hard, letting the pain wash over her so she wouldn't feel the pain inside.

Finn Jamenson was her mate.

Her wolf knew it.

Her human half knew it.

Yet, for some reason, Finn didn't seem to know it.

He was supposedly the one for her, but fate had never said she'd be the one for him.

She blinked away the lone tear and straightened her shoulders as Finn and Charlotte drove up.

She'd push those thoughts away for another day. Now was about Brie and what the next steps would be to ensure the Talons and Redwoods were safe. Something dark was on the horizon, something Brynn couldn't figure out. She'd need her wits about her.

Knowing she might never have the mate her wolf craved would have to be something she worried about later.

If at all.

CHAPTER SEVENTEEN

Gideon's hands shook once again, but he didn't let that stop him from letting them roam over Brie's body. Walker had Healed every cut, but it didn't seem as though it was enough. Gideon had to be *sure* his mate was okay. They sat in their bedroom, Brie on the end of the bed with Gideon kneeling in front of her. Finn and Charlotte had come and gone reassured that Brie was safe, yet Gideon wasn't fully ready to accept that.

Brie let him touch her and hold her. She didn't speak but rather kept her eyes on him, as if she was the one who needed to soothe him instead of the other way around.

That just enraged him further.

His wolf paced, needing blood rather than calm. They hadn't finished their hunt and hadn't caught Leo and made him pay for what he'd done to Brie. Shannon was out there as well. He might have cut the bond so she'd be in pain and alone without any help or care, but it wasn't enough. He needed to see her die for what she'd done.

The elder had ruined so many lives, and it was his fault. He'd been forced to keep her as part of the Pack because of her position. She'd never technically done anything that warranted being shunned or executed. Because of that, she'd been able to weave her web of deceit for far too long.

Never again.

Brie cupped his face, and he finally looked into her eyes rather than at the wounds that had been Healed away.

"Gideon, my wolf, please breathe."

He took a deep breath, his wolf more in control than it should have been. He let out a growl, but Brie didn't back down. Instead, she slid her hand down his chest and stomach to the edge of his shirt. When she touched skin, he sucked in a breath but calmed somewhat. Skin-to-skin, he could think again.

"You can't get hurt again," he growled out.

She shook her head. "I might get hurt again, Gideon." His chest rumbled, and her nails dug in, grounding him. "Our world is on the verge of something, we know this. Leo and Shannon aren't done yet. I'm not going to sit back and let people die for me."

He pinched her chin, forcing her gaze to his. "I cannot lose you. Don't you get that? You weren't supposed to be mine. I am, and will always be, too dangerous for you, but I'm selfish and want you anyway. Now that I have you, you cannot leave me. I'm not letting you go—and that includes you getting hurt because others want to take you away from me."

Tears filled her eyes, and she leaned forward, forcing him to release her chin, and pressed her lips gently to his chest. "I'm here. I'm not going anywhere."

He shuddered out a breath then tucked her close, needing her more than he'd ever thought he'd need anyone. He kissed the top of her head, running his hands down her body once more, just in case he'd missed something the first four times he'd done it.

His wolf pushed at him, wanting more skin. He slid his hands up her shirt, the warmth of her body calming him yet, at the same time, pushing him closer to the edge.

"You can't leave me," he rasped out.

"We don't let the others hurt our Pack, Gideon."

"The Pack is part of me," Gideon said honestly. "But they aren't you." He pulled away so she could see the truth in his eyes. "You weren't supposed to matter this much. You were supposed to calm the bonds within the Pack. You weren't supposed to be my heart."

Brie blinked up at him, tears in her eyes. "I stayed away for so long because I didn't think I was good enough, *strong* enough to be your mate."

He growled. "You were *wrong*. I was wrong. You are stronger than any wolf I've met."

She shook her head. "I wouldn't go that far."

"I would. It takes the strength of character, the strength of your heart to rule a Pack at my side without the urge to dominate. *That* is what makes you strong. That is what makes you mine, little wolf."

"I knew you'd come and find me. I tried to get away on my own, and when I couldn't, I did my best to keep calm and find another way out. No matter what, though, I knew you'd come." She swallowed hard. "When I mated you, I thought I'd always be on the outside looking in. I never thought I'd trust someone so completely. I trust you, Gideon. With everything I am."

He kissed her then, a sweet brush of lips as to not scare her away. "I love you so fucking much, little wolf. You're in my heart, my soul. You are my everything. If anything happened to you, I don't know what I'd do." He let out a shaky breath, baring his soul in a way he never thought he would. "I love you, Brie Brentwood. I love you with every ounce of my being and my wolf. Love me back and I promise you I'll do my best to see that you're cherished and loved until the end of my days."

Tears slid down his mate's cheeks, and he kissed every one away, not liking to see her cry.

"Don't cry, little wolf," he whispered.

"I'm going to cry, Gideon. I'm going to cry a lot. More than once. I can't help it. It's who I am. But right now? I'm crying because I'm so happy. I never thought I'd find my mate." She shook her head. "No, that's not right. I found you long before you found me. I just never thought I'd let myself be caught." She licked her lips, and his wolf brushed against his skin. "I love you, my mate, my Alpha, my Gideon."

He took her lips then, unable to hold himself back any longer. He nipped at her lower lip then along her chin, loving the way her breath came in little pants. His tongue tangled with hers once he came back to her mouth. She tasted of sweetness and his Brie, a uniqueness all her own. He'd crave her taste until the end of time and never have enough of her. When he told her so, she clamped her legs around him, bringing him closer.

He stripped off her shirt and groaned at the sight of her lace-covered breasts, perky and full—perfect for his hands. She reached around her back, a sly look on her face, and undid her bra. When the cups fell, she slowly slid them down to reveal her luscious pink-tipped breasts. Unable to hold back, he cupped one in his hand, loving the weight. He brushed the tip with his thumb, and she sucked in a breath.

"I love how soft you are, how full and round. I always have more than a handful, easy for me to grip when I pump in and out of you."

She blushed but raised a brow. "Most women— especially wolves—don't like to be called full, round, or soft, Alpha mine."

He pinched her nipple, and her head fell back. "You're not most women. You're sweet and mine. And I like every inch of you. I fucking *love* every inch of you. Never forget that." He leaned forward and sucked one nipple into his mouth, deftly playing with the other one with his fingers. She tangled her fingers in his hair, pressing him closer. He growled softly, biting down until she froze, her heart racing.

"I'm going to feast on your tits then lick my way down to your sweet cunt," Gideon rasped out, licking and kissing between each word. "I love the way you taste, little wolf. You're so sweet and juicy, like a ripe peach, delectable and swollen."

"You're getting good at that dirty talk." She giggled then gasped when he rubbed against the seam of her jeans between her legs.

"You haven't seen anything yet," he promised then did as he promised, feasting on her breasts.

She shuddered in his hold, her body bowing as she came by his touch on her breasts alone. "Holy hell. I've never come with you touching my breasts before."

He grinned. "You and I have only been together for a short time," he said, his fingers working on the button of her jeans. She lifted her bottom, helping him remove the rest of her clothes, leaving her bare to his gaze, his touch. "I'm going to enjoy finding out what spots taste the best and which spots make you shiver and come when I touch them."

She leaned back and put one foot on his shoulder. "Taste away," she teased, and he groaned.

"I love when you try to take control." He grinned when he kissed the back of her knee and she gasped. "Try is the right word here. Because I will always have control, Brie. I'm not the kind of man who can give it up."

"I wouldn't have you any other way."

He kissed up her leg to her inner thigh then stopped right before he came to her heat. She rocked forward, but he pulled back at her whimper, choosing instead to repeat the process on her other leg. He had both her legs over his shoulders and her pussy in front of his face, ready, wet, and his.

"Touch your breasts for me, Brie. Play with your nipples while I eat you out. I want you to feel every lick, every nibble, then come on my tongue before I slide into you."

Her body shuddered, her eyes dark and rimmed with a ring of gold. "I'm going to come at your words alone."

He kissed her inner thigh where it met her hip once more. "A challenge."

She leaned back on her elbows and started to roll her nipples between her fingers. He licked his lips, the sight of her touching herself almost more than he could bear. But he craved her taste like no other and held back the need to dive inside her in one thrust. Instead, he spread her for his gaze, his hunger riding him. Her clit was swollen, that little bundle of nerves peaking out from under its hood. She glistened, wet and pink from her orgasm, but he wouldn't allow her to stop at just one. No, instead he'd make her come at least two more times tonight, maybe more if his little wolf was ready.

He lowered his head and sucked her clit into his mouth. She bucked off the bed, and he put one hand on her hip, holding her in place. He flicked her clit over and over again with this tongue before teasing her entrance with his finger.

"Please! Gideon, I need more. I'm so close."

He growled, the vibrations forcing a gasp out of her. Good.

He fucked her with his finger then another, all the while keeping his mouth on her, loving the way she moaned and gasped with each movement.

When she came, his name shouted from her lips, and he lapped up each drop of her arousal, not wanting to miss even that much. His body primed, he stood up and stripped off his clothes, his wolf close to the surface but the man still in control.

He was on top of her in the next blink, slamming into her in one thrust. They both called out, their bodies freezing.

"I love you," he growled out, taking her lips. "I..." Thrust. "love..." Thrust. "you..." Thrust.

Her legs went around his waist, and her nails dug into his ass. "I love you, too. Now fuck me. Make love to me. Make me yours."

He kissed her again, his hips moving at a frantic pace. Her cunt gripped him as she came again, but he didn't stop. He'd take another out of her then release, but not before. He wanted her sated, full, and his for now and always.

When she came again, her arms falling to her sides, he pumped one more time then came on a roar, his body shaking. He filled her up, his hips pressed flat to hers. He wanted her marked as his, scented as his, and one day round with his child. The primal part of him shouted in triumph, and Gideon kissed his drowsy mate once more.

"Mine," he growled. A promise. A lifetime.

"Yours," she whispered.

"We don't know his full plan," Brie said the next morning, her hands clenched in front of her.

Gideon reached out and tugged one into his larger palm, not liking her so stressed. His wolf calmed when he felt her love through the bond. It was something he was still getting used to, but he didn't know what he'd do without it now.

"He wanted to test us," Brynn said as she paced the house. "He wanted to let us know that he could not only get to the Alpha's mate, but that he could get to *anyone* within the wards."

Kameron growled, his claws out. Gideon didn't blame his brother for the lack of control then. As the Enforcer, it had to be killing him as much as it was Gideon that there were leaks they couldn't plug.

"The witches should be done with the new layer of wards soon, but it's not soon enough," Kameron bit out.

"Shannon cannot enter Pack lands anymore without assistance, but that means nothing when we don't know *who* would aid her," Gideon put in. "Our patrols are stretched thin as it is." It grated on him, but they weren't as large of a Pack as the Redwoods. With traitors in their midst, they were fucked until they discovered the identities of those who would cause them harm.

"The tunnels are almost finished," Mitchell added. "Our treaty with the Redwoods and the connection we now have with them is secure. If we need to hide some of us because of technology, we can. But first, we need to take care of this problem."

"I don't know why I can't feel the dissent," Brandon bit out, the Omega looking far angrier than Gideon had seen him in years. "I should be able to help, but it's like I'm clouded."

Brie reached out and slid her free arm down Brandon's back. It didn't anger Gideon's wolf, not when Brandon needed the care, and it made Brie happy to do so.

"I think that Shannon, and whoever is with her, have been hiding what they've been doing for far longer than you've had your powers," Brie said calmly. "They've been shielding themselves somehow. We *will* defeat them, but it might take them coming at us for it to happen."

"And that's dangerous as hell," Brynn muttered.

"Everyone is on alert," Gideon said. "We have the sentries on duty as well as the soldiers on their lookouts. Each person in this Pack knows that it is someone from within. I didn't want the Pack to know it all for fear that our morale would crumble, but keeping them in hiding would only hurt us more."

Brie's hand squeezed his. "They are stronger than that. They won't crumble. We've all known there was poison within the Pack." She spoke as though she'd been a Talon all her life, and he couldn't have been prouder. "They won't go down without a fight. They're with you, Gideon. *We're* with you."

He brought her hand up to his lips and kissed her knuckles. Max let out a soft laugh next to him, but Gideon ignored it.

"We need to know what Leo and Shannon's plan is," Gideon continued. "They not only wanted Brie to die and for them to become the leaders of the Talons, but they had another plan."

Brie bit her lip. "They said they wanted to take over the Redwoods as well. It sounded like they were the Centrals all over again."

"And what did the Centrals want?" Gideon asked, though he knew the answer, dread in his belly.

"Once they got the Redwoods, they'd have been unstoppable," Brie answered. "They wanted to rule the humans, not only the wolves." Her eyes widened, and she shook her head. "In order to rule them, they'd have shown the world who they were. You don't think..."

Gideon cursed. "With all our plans of the tunnels and political maneuverings in case the wolves *were* revealed, someone on Shannon's side might have been in on that."

"What good would revealing who we are do?" Brynn asked, fear in her gaze. "We're not safe out in the human world. Humans try to silence what they don't understand."

"We're leaping to conclusions here," Ryder said, ever the voice of reason, but even he sounded skeptical.

"We need to be on alert for that as well," Gideon said. "We've been hiding for so long, becoming more and more insular as time passed because the humans were getting so close, that if Leo shows the world who we are, it could be disastrous."

"We don't know that's what he wants," Brie said. "That might have been what the Centrals wanted, but that doesn't mean he's on the same path. For all we know, he just wants to rule in secret until he dies."

Gideon let out a breath. "Leo has never been one to stop once he gets what he wants, no matter who he has to kill along the way."

He refused to look at Max and Mitchell when he said it, but he felt their tension. Leo was their father, the man who should have cared for them above all else. Instead, he was the man they would have to kill in order to keep their people safe. The brothers would do it, just as Gideon had done with Joseph, but it wouldn't be easy.

They were on the brink of war, the battlefield full of secrecy and pain.

Gideon's communicator beeped, and he looked down at it, answering at once. "What's going on?"

"Leo and Shannon are right outside the wards," the soldier began. "They have a pup, Alpha. They said if you and Brie don't come to meet them, they'll kill him and then others one by one until you do."

Gideon growled, low, deadly. "We're on our way."

The others had heard the conversation and were already on their way out the door. He kissed Brie hard and tugged her close.

"I'm going. You can't hold me back."

He sighed, pulling her with him as they ran toward the sentry post. "I can't hold you back, Brie. I also can't let that pup die."

"We'll fight for the Pack, Gideon."

He squeezed her hand, his wolf on the prowl. The war had come to them, and this time, there was no turning back. There was something off about this, and he knew they were running into a trap, only he didn't see a way out.

Lives were on the line, and he had one shot at saving them.

He hoped he hadn't made a mistake.

CHAPTER EIGHTEEN

Brie's wolf raged, wanting to kill the man in front of her and, at the same time, not wanting to fight. Her submissive nature had never been in such juxtaposition, but she didn't care. She'd fight to protect her mate, her family, and the pup in human form in Leo's hold. It didn't matter that it went against everything her wolf wanted deep beneath the surface. The only thing that mattered was her home.

Leo and Shannon had amassed at least eighty wolves to take down an entire Pack. Brie didn't understand how the two thought they would win, other than the fact that Gideon and the others wouldn't allow the pup to be hurt. So once they saved the little boy, they would be able to go all-out.

That was, unless, the other two didn't have something else up their sleeves. Brie had a feeling there was something far worse in store for her family, and she had no idea what it could be.

"It is simple, nephew," Leo called out. "Release the Pack to me, and I won't kill this pup."

"Jeremiah!" a woman, the pup's mother yelled behind Gideon and he cursed. Jeremiah's parents must have arrived. He wouldn't let them go through the pain of watching their son die.

The pup in question howled and whimpered, trying to wiggle away. Leo squeezed his arm, and the little boy quieted. Brie growled, her claws threatening to come out.

Gideon didn't even look at the child, and she knew this had to be killing him. There was no way he'd give up the safety of the Pack for one person, but he also wouldn't allow the pup to die.

They would fight.

Good, because Leo and Shannon needed to die.

As did the other wolves who fought with them.

Ryder came up behind her and leaned forward, his voice low enough for her ears only. "Only five of those wolves are ours." A pause. "Were ours. The rest are lone wolves. That would explain the fights Gideon has had to deal with in the past weeks."

She nodded, keeping her eye on Shannon. The woman looked too pleased at the turn of events. The Talons could rip these wolves to shreds, yet Leo and Shannon looked as though they were the ones with the upper hand.

There must be something she was missing.

"You cannot win this," Gideon called out, his voice pure Alpha. The power of her mate washed over her, giving her a strength she didn't know she could possess.

"So be it."

Leo threw the pup toward Shannon and clicked a receiver Brie hadn't seen in his other hand.

"Cameras," Kameron snapped. "He's going to film us fighting."

Brie sucked in a breath. She'd been right, though it was a far-fetched thought. What Leo was doing went against every boundary she could think of. "What are we going to do?" They couldn't shift on camera, nor could they technically fight. Damn it.

"We save our Pack," Gideon said softly. "Don't shift. Not even partially."

"If it's a live feed, we're fucked with the authorities," Ryder put in.

"I have contacts with the local law enforcement and others," Brynn said, not surprising Brie in the least. Every Pack had help from humans who knew about them and could be trusted. It was how they'd stayed in the shadows for so long. "As long as we don't kill or shift on camera, we will be fine."

"Then we get the pup and the cameras," Gideon growled, "and we take out the rest."

"Be safe," she whispered to her mate, wanting to hold him but knowing she couldn't. They might be inside the wards, but they wouldn't be for long.

"Always," he said back.

Leo shouted for his wolves to move forward. They couldn't go past the wards, not with Gideon there to cut the ties of those who had once been Talons. But with that pup out there, some of the Talons would have no choice but to go out there and fight.

Gideon stepped forward, and Brie wasn't surprised. Her mate would not let anyone fight when he could do it himself. He wouldn't be Alpha otherwise.

She followed her mate just as something exploded right outside the wards. The ground shook, and Gideon gripped her hand, keeping her steady.

"Go!" he shouted, and the rest of the wolves *moved*.

They kept their human shape, their hands not even going to claws, but they fought for the Pack. They needed to step outside the wards to do so, but in this case, it was more important to contain the threat than have relative safety inside a magical enclosure.

A small woman came at her, and Gideon let her go to fight a larger man. Brie blocked the kick to her face and punched the woman in the face. The other woman tried to bite her, her face elongating somewhat so her fangs came out. Goddess, Brie prayed that the cameras hadn't caught that. Brie knocked the other woman out but didn't kill her. She could still hear the cameras on them. Kameron and Mitchell had gone to find them and dismantle them, but until they did so, everyone had to be careful. There would be no telling what would happen if word got out about the things that went bump in the night.

"Got one!" Kameron yelled over the fighting, and Brie cheered inside even as she fought another wolf. She was trying to get to the pup and put him behind the wards—most of them were—but Shannon had circled herself with so many other wolves, it was difficult. The fucking elder looked like she was a cat that had finished the cream, holding the boy close while she dodged other wolves trying to attack her. The wolves on the elder's side of the battle were throwing their bodies in front of her, protecting her with their lives.

They all would die though.

It had to be that way.

Brie just hoped they didn't risk their future to make it happen.

Brie rolled to the ground as someone tried to jump on her then kicked the person's feet out from under them. They snarled at her, and she kicked them in the face. They passed out, and she moved on. She *hated* fighting, but she'd been taught by the best to protect herself in either form.

Shannon smiled at her again, and Brie wanted to claw the look off the bitch's face. "You can't win this, submissive trash."

"No, honey, you can't." Brie pounced on Shannon, having seen Brynn standing behind the other woman. Brynn twisted Shannon's arm, forcing the elder to drop the boy. Brynn caught the child in one arm as Brie snarled, bringing Shannon to the ground.

"I got you baby, I'm taking you to Mom and Dad," Brynn said to the pup and Brie kept fighting. The boy whimpered, but didn't cry. Strong little pup.

She punched Shannon in the face, her rage simmering, ready to blow. She couldn't yet. Not until she knew her people were safe from prying eyes.

Gideon growled beside her, his hand on Leo's neck. "Kameron?"

"I'm missing one! I can hear the damn camera, but I can't find it."

Brie kept Shannon pinned to the ground, squeezing tight. She could see the other wolves being pinned in the same fashion. As long as they didn't kill on camera, they'd be okay.

"You won't find it." Leo grinned. "It's time for a new beginning. The time for wolves. The humans have been living in gluttony and pride for far too long. They will die by our hands. They will scream for mercy from our sharp teeth and claws."

Dear goddess, the man was insane.

"Kameron!" Gideon yelled.

"Got it!" the Enforcer shouted back.

"Too late," Leo said then howled, his body shaking. Gideon snapped Leo's neck just as Shannon tried to lift up. Just like that, the man Gideon had once called uncle and had haunted his dreams was dead.

"Never again will you hurt my family." Brie snapped the other woman's neck quickly, not wanting

240

to prolong the fight. She wasn't cruel, but the death didn't weigh on her either.

Gideon pulled her into his arms, kissing her hard as the other wolves took care of the enemy.

"What did he mean by too late?" Brie asked, her voice shaky.

"I have no idea."

"I know," Mitchell said from their side, his eyes wolf. "They were filming far longer than we thought. They fucking shifted on camera, Gideon." He swallowed hard, and the bottom of Brie's stomach fell out. "It's a live feed, meaning that whoever watched it knows that we're real." He met Brie's eyes. "And knows where we are."

"Everyone behind the wards. Now!" Gideon shouted. "Bring the dead with you, leave no trace behind." Her Pack moved quickly, their fear tactile. "How much time do we have?"

Ryder sprinted toward them. "Kameron sent some of the soldiers out on reconnaissance, and Brynn is calling the Redwoods now."

"Fuck!" Gideon snapped. "We have resources for this. We aren't wholly without options, but Leo fucked us."

Brie licked her lips, rage and fear mixing into one emotion. "Leo never wanted to be Alpha. Neither did Shannon. They only wanted change." She met his eyes, fear warring within them as well. "This is one hell of a change."

Gideon cupped her face. "Kade and I have wolves all over the world ready for this, Brie. We won't be taken down easily. We have positions in politics and the military. We've been waiting for thirty years for something like this, since the last war. But having them shift for us? In a battle? We're going to be screwed for awhile now."

She pulled at his hand. "We need to get inside the wards."

"They won't protect us for long," Gideon murmured, his voice low. "But they can give us some protection while we see what the humans do. I don't know if we will be able to stop the onslaught this time."

She pulled him through the wards, the others joining them. She kept her gaze on the horizon, the fear within her sparking into a numbness she wasn't sure she could bear.

"We can handle this," she whispered. "We're not savages."

"No, and we have more power than we did when we fought the last war," Gideon said from behind her. He pulled her to face him, his eyes full of determination. "Whatever happens, little wolf, I'm by your side. I'm not leaving you. I'm not letting the humans destroy what we have."

She cupped his face, kissed his chin. "I love you, my Alpha. We'll fight if we have to and find the peace we all desire. Our secrets were never going to last forever, but maybe we can find a truce in the shadows."

The sound of a chopper's blades echoed in the distance, and Brie stiffened before throwing her arms around her mate's neck. He kissed her hard, his love and passion in every ounce of his being.

"I'm yours forever, Brie."

"We'll make it through this," she answered. "We don't have a choice."

The humans were coming. The time of the wolves was coming into the light. No longer would there be magic whispered under breaths. No longer would there be shifting in the forest with the goddess' blessing without a hint of danger.

Change had come to the Talon Pack on the trail of a past not quite forgotten.

Brie gripped her mate's hand. She had the loyalties and love of an Alpha.

They would survive.

They were wolves.

They were Redwoods.

They were Talons.

They were survivors.

The End

Coming Next in the Talon Pack World:

Finn and Brynn find their story in An Alpha's Choice

A Note from Carrie Ann

Thank you so much for reading **Tattered Loyalties**. I do hope if you liked this story, that you would please leave a review. Not only does a review spread the word to other readers, they let us authors know if you'd like to see more stories like this from us. I love hearing from readers and talking to them when I can. If you want to make sure you know what's coming next from me, you can sign up for my newsletter at www.CarrieAnnRyan.com; follow me on twitter at @CarrieAnnRyan, or like my Facebook page. I also have a Facebook Fan Club where we have trivia, chats, and other goodies. You guys are the reason I get to do what I do and I thank you.

Tattered Loyalties is the first book in the Talon Pack series! There will be more in this series with An Alpha's Choice coming next. However if you're new to the shifter world in my books, then make sure you check out the Redwood Pack series. The Talon Pack series is set in the same world and follows the Redwood Pack as well as the special novella, Wicked Wolf! Brie's parents as well as her aunts and uncles found their mates and set in motion the events of the Talon Pack series. You don't want to miss them in The Redwood Pack!

Make sure you're signed up for my MAILING LIST so you can know when the next releases are available as well as find giveaways and FREE READS.

If you enjoyed this story, take a look at my Montgomery Ink, Redwood Pack, Holiday Montana, and Dante's Circle series!!

Thank you so much for going on this journey with me and I do hope you enjoyed my Tempting Signs story. Without you readers, I wouldn't be where I am today.

Thank you again for reading and I do hope to see you again.

Carrie Ann

About this Author

New York Times and USA Today Bestselling Author Carrie Ann Ryan never thought she'd be a writer. Not really. No, she loved math and science and even went on to graduate school in chemistry. Yes, she read as a kid and devoured teen fiction and Harry Potter, but it wasn't until someone handed her a romance book in her late teens that she realized that there was something out there just for her. When another author suggested she use the voices in her head for good and not evil, The Redwood Pack and all her other stories were born.

Carrie Ann is a bestselling author of over twenty novels and novellas and has so much more on her mind (and on her spreadsheets *grins*) that she isn't planning on giving up her dream anytime soon.

www.CarrieAnnRyan.com

Also from this Author

Now Available:

Redwood Pack Series:
An Alpha's Path
A Taste for a Mate
Trinity Bound
A Night Away
Enforcer's Redemption
Blurred Expectations
Forgiveness
Shattered Emotions
Hidden Destiny
A Beta's Haven
Fighting Fate
Loving the Omega
The Hunted Heart
Wicked Wolf

The Talon Pack (Following the Redwood Pack Series):
Tattered Loyalties

The Redwood Pack Volumes:
Redwood Pack Vol 1
Redwood Pack Vol 2
Redwood Pack Vol 3
Redwood Pack Vol 4
Redwood Pack Vol 5
Redwood Pack Vol 6

Dante's Circle Series:
Dust of My Wings
Her Warriors' Three Wishes
An Unlucky Moon
His Choice
Tangled Innocence

Montgomery Ink:
Ink Inspired
Ink Reunited
Delicate Ink
Hot Ink
Tempting Boundaries

Holiday, Montana Series:
Charmed Spirits
Santa's Executive
Finding Abigail
Her Lucky Love
Dreams of Ivory

Coming Soon:

Talon Pack (Part of the Redwood Pack World)
An Alpha's Choice
Mated in Mist

Dante's Circle:
Fierce Enchantment
Fallen for Alphas

Montgomery Ink:
Forever Ink
Harder than Words
Written in Ink

The Branded Pack Series:
(Written with Alexandra Ivy)
Stolen and Forgiven
Abandoned and Unseen

Excerpt: Wicked Wolf

Did you enjoy this selection? Why not try another romance from Fated Desires?

From New York Times Bestselling Author Carrie Ann Ryan's Redwood Pack Series

There were times to drool over a sexy wolf.

Sitting in the middle of a war room disguised as a board meeting was not one of those times.

Gina Jamenson did her best not to stare at the dark-haired, dark-eyed man across the room. The hint of ink peeking out from under his shirt made her want to pant. She *loved* ink and this wolf clearly had a lot of it. Her own wolf within nudged at her, a soft brush beneath her skin, but she ignored her. When her wolf whimpered, Gina promised herself that she'd go on a long run in the forest later. She didn't understand why her wolf was acting like this, but she'd deal with it when she was in a better place. She just couldn't let her wolf have control right then—even for a man such as the gorgeous specimen a mere ten feet from her.

Today was more important than the wants and feelings of a half wolf, half witch hybrid.

Today was the start of a new beginning.

At least that's what her dad had told her.

Considering her father was also the Alpha of the Redwood Pack, he would be in the know. She'd been adopted into the family when she'd been a young girl. A rogue wolf during the war had killed her parents, setting off a long line of events that had changed her life.

As it was, Gina wasn't quite sure how she'd ended up in the meeting between the two Packs, the Redwoods and the Talons. Sure, the Packs had met before over the past fifteen years of their treaty, but this meeting seemed different.

This one seemed more important somehow.

And they'd invited—more like *demanded*—Gina to attend.

At twenty-six, she knew she was the youngest wolf in the room by far. Most of the wolves were around her father's age, somewhere in the hundreds. The dark-eyed wolf might have been slightly younger than that, but only slightly if the power radiating off of him was any indication.

Wolves lived a long, long time. She'd heard stories of her people living into their thousands, but she'd never met any of the wolves who had. The oldest wolf she'd met was a friend of the family, Emeline, who was over five hundred. That number boggled her mind even though she'd grown up knowing the things that went bump in the night were real.

Actually, she *was* one of the things that went bump in the night.

"Are we ready to begin?" Gideon, the Talon Alpha, asked, his voice low. It held that dangerous edge that spoke of power and authority.

Her wolf didn't react the way most wolves would, head and eyes down, shoulders dropped. Maybe if she'd been a weaker wolf, she'd have bowed to his power, but as it was, her wolf was firmly entrenched within the Redwoods. Plus, it wasn't as if Gideon was *trying* to make her bow just then. No, those words had simply been spoken in his own voice.

Commanding without even trying.

Then again, he *was* an Alpha.

Kade, her father, looked around the room at each of his wolves and nodded. "Yes. It is time."

Their formality intrigued her. Yes, they were two Alphas who held a treaty and worked together in times of war, but she had thought they were also friends.

Maybe today was even more important than she'd realized.

Gideon released a sigh that spoke of years of angst and worries. She didn't know the history of the Talons as well as she probably should have, so she didn't know exactly why there was always an air of sadness and pain around the Alpha.

Maybe after this meeting, she'd be able to find out more.

Of course, in doing so, she'd have to *not* look at a certain wolf in the corner. His gaze was so intense she was sure he was studying her. She felt it down in her bones, like a fiery caress that promised something more.

Or maybe she was just going crazy and needed to find a wolf to scratch the itch.

She might not be looking for a mate, but she wouldn't say no to something else. Wolves were tactile creatures after all.

"Gina?"

She blinked at the sound of Kade's voice and turned to him.

She was the only one standing other than the two wolves in charge of security—her uncle Adam, the Enforcer, and the dark-eyed wolf.

Well, *that* was embarrassing.

She kept her head down and forced herself not to blush. From the heat on her neck, she was pretty sure she'd failed in the latter.

"Sorry," she mumbled then sat down next to another uncle, Jasper, the Beta of the Pack.

Although the Alphas had called this meeting, she wasn't sure what it would entail. Each Alpha had come with their Beta, a wolf in charge of security...and her father had decided to bring her.

Her being there didn't make much sense in the grand scheme of things since it put the power on the Redwoods' side, but she wasn't about to question authority in front of another Pack. That at least had been ingrained in her training.

"Let's get started then," Kade said after he gave her a nod. "Gideon? Do you want to begin?"

Gina held back a frown. They *were* acting more formal than usual, so that hadn't been her imagination. The Talons and the Redwoods had formed a treaty during the latter days of the war between the Redwoods and the Centrals. It wasn't as though these were two newly acquainted Alphas meeting for the first time. Though maybe when it came to Pack matters, Alphas couldn't truly be friends.

What a lonely way to live.

"It's been fifteen years since the end of the Central War, yet there hasn't been a single mating between the two Packs," Gideon said, shocking her.

Gina blinked. Really? That couldn't be right. She was sure there had to have been *some* cross-Pack mating.

Right?

"That means that regardless of the treaties we signed, we don't believe the moon goddess has seen fit to fully accept us as a unit," Kade put in.

"What do you mean?" she asked, then shut her mouth. She was the youngest wolf here and wasn't formally titled or ranked. She should *not* be speaking right now.

She felt the gaze of the dark-eyed wolf on her, but she didn't turn to look. Instead, she kept her head down in a show of respect to the Alphas.

"You can ask questions, Gina. It's okay," Kade said, the tone of his voice not changing, but, as his daughter, she heard the softer edge. "And what I mean is, mating comes from the moon goddess. Yes, we can find our own versions of mates by not bonding fully, but a true bond, a true potential mate, is chosen by the moon goddess. That's how it's always been in the past."

Gideon nodded. "There haven't been many matings within the Talons in general."

Gina sucked in a breath, and the Beta of the Talons, Mitchell, turned her way. "Yes," Mitchell said softly. "It's that bad. It could be that in this period of change within our own pack hierarchy, our members just haven't found mates yet, but that doesn't seem likely. There's something else going on."

Gina knew Gideon—as well as the rest of his brothers and cousins—had come into power at some point throughout the end of the Central War during a period of the Talon's own unrest, but she didn't know the full history. She wasn't even sure Kade or the rest of the Pack royalty did.

There were some things that were intensely private within a Pack that could not—and should not—be shared.

Jasper tapped his fingers along the table. As the Redwood Beta, it was his job to care for their needs and recognize hidden threats that the Enforcer and Alpha might not see. The fact that he was here told Gina that the Pack could be in trouble from something *within* the Pack, rather than an outside force that Adam, the Enforcer, would be able to see through his own bonds and power.

"Since Finn became the Heir to the Pack at such a young age, it has changed a few things on our side," Jasper said softly. Finn was her brother, Melanie and Kade's oldest biological child. "The younger generation will be gaining their powers and bonds to the goddess earlier than would otherwise be expected." Her uncle looked at her, and she kept silent. "That means the current Pack leaders will one day not have the bonds we have to our Pack now. But like most healthy Packs, that doesn't mean we're set aside. It only means we will be there to aid the new hierarchy while they learn their powers. That's how it's always been in our Pack, and in others, but it's been a very long time since it's happened to us."

"Gina will one day be the Enforcer," Adam said from behind her. "I don't know when, but it will be soon. The other kids aren't old enough yet to tell who will take on which role, but since Gina is in her twenties, the shifts are happening."

The room grew silent, with an odd sense of change settling over her skin like an electric blanket turned on too high.

She didn't speak. She'd known about her path, had dreamed the dreams from the moon goddess herself. But that didn't mean she wanted the Talons to know all of this. It seemed...private somehow.

"What does this have to do with mating?" she asked, wanting to focus on something else.

Gideon gave her a look, and she lowered her eyes. He might not be her Alpha, but he was still a dominant wolf. Yes, she hadn't lowered her eyes before, but she'd been rocked a bit since Adam had told the others of her future. She didn't want to antagonize anyone when Gideon clearly wanted to show his power. Previously, everything had been casual; now it clearly was not.

Kade growled beside her. "Gideon."

The Talon Alpha snorted, not smiling, but moved his gaze. "It's fun to see how she reacts."

"She's my daughter and the future Enforcer."

"*She* is right here, so how about you answer my question?"

Jasper chuckled by her side, and Gina wondered how quickly she could reach the nearest window and jump. It couldn't be that far. She wouldn't die from the fall or anything, and she'd be able to run home.

Quickly.

"Mating," Kade put in, the laughter in his eyes fading, "is only a small part of the problem. When we sent Caym back to hell with the other demons, it changed the power structure within the Packs as well as outside them. The Centrals who fought against us died because they'd lost their souls to the demon. The Centrals that had hidden from the old Alphas ended up being lone wolves. They're not truly a Pack yet because the goddess hasn't made anyone an Alpha."

"Then you have the Redwoods, with a hierarchy shift within the younger generation," Gideon said. "And the Talons' new power dynamic is only fifteen years old, and we haven't had a mating in long enough that it's starting to worry us."

"Not that you'd say that to the rest of the Pack," Mitchell mumbled.

"It's best they don't know," Gideon said, the sounds of an old argument telling Gina there was more going on here than what they revealed.

Interesting.

"There aren't any matings between our two Packs, and I know the trust isn't fully there," Kade put in then sighed. "I don't know how to fix that myself. I don't think I can."

"You're the Alpha," Jasper said calmly. "If you *tell* them to get along with the other wolves, they will, and for the most part, they have. But it isn't as authentic as if they find that trust on their own. We've let them go this long on their own, but now, I think we need to find another way to have our Packs more entwined."

The dark-eyed wolf came forward then. "You've seen something," he growled.

Dear goddess. His voice.

Her wolf perked, and she shoved her down. This wasn't the time.

"We've seen...something, Quinn," Kade answered.

Quinn. That was his name.

Sexy.

And again, *so* not the time.

Find out more in Wicked Wolf. Out Now.

Excerpt: Find Me in Darkness

Love paranormal romance? Check out Julie Kenner!

I hope you enjoy this excerpt from Find Me in Darkness, A Dark Pleasures novella. This is the first part of Mal and Christina's story, and it continues Find Me in Pleasure and Find Me in Passion.

You can learn all about the Dark Pleasures series (and all my books!) at my website, http://www.juliekenner.com

And if you missed Callie and Raine's story, Caress of Darkness, a 1001 Dark Nights novella, be sure to grab a copy now!

--Julie

Chapter 1

Mal stood by the bed and looked down at the woman he'd just fucked.

She was drop-dead gorgeous, lithe and strong with alabaster skin and hair as dark as his own. She was smart and funny, had good taste in wine, and had sucked his cock with rare skill.

Not a bad resume, when you got right down to it, and if Mal had even an ounce of sense he'd slide back into bed, sink deep inside her, and try once more to forget how goddamn lonely he was.

Shit.

She didn't deserve that. Hell, none of the women he fucked deserved that. Which was why he had a strict one-time only policy. Shared lust and pounding sex to work out some of life's kinks was one thing. But Mal didn't do serious or personal. Not anymore.

He'd had serious. He'd had personal.

Hell, he'd had love. Epic, forever, everyone-else-can-just-melt-away love.

And not only love, but respect and humor and passion so intense that he felt alive only when he touched her.

He'd had all that.

Now, all he had was a nightmare.

On the bed, the woman shifted, then smiled up at him, soft and sultry. "Mal? What's wrong?"

He said nothing, and she sat up, letting the sheet fall to her waist to expose her bare breasts as she held out a hand to him. "Come back to bed and let me make it better."

If only it was that easy.

"I have to go."

"Go?" She glanced at the clock and then pulled up the sheet to cover her nakedness. "It's not even midnight." Her voice was indignant.

"It can't be helped."

"You son-of-a-bitch."

He didn't wince, didn't try to defend himself. What defense was there against the truth?

Instead, he moved to her side, then brushed his fingers lightly over her forehead. "Sleep," he said, then stepped away as the woman fell back against the pillows, lost once again to the world of dreams.

He pulled the sheet up to cover her, then glanced around the room in search of his clothes. He'd brought her to the penthouse suite at the stunning Gardiner Hotel, a relatively new Fifth Avenue boutique in which he held a significant financial position. Now he moved through the bedroom and parlor, gathering discarded garments as he walked.

He pulled on his jeans, then slipped his arms into the white button-down that he'd worn that evening before going out in search of a woman to take the edge off. He let it hang open as he stepped out onto the patio, then moved to the stone half-wall that separated him from the concrete and asphalt of Fifth Avenue twelve stories below.

It would be easy enough to jump. To end his pain, even if only for a few moments.

And a few moments were all that he would get before the phoenix fire would surround and gather him, reducing him to ashes before once again regenerating him.

Immortality.

Had he truly once believed it was a gift? To have an eternity in this body that could touch and feel and experience such profound pleasure?

Three thousand years ago, it *had* been a gift, but that was when she'd been beside him, and it was Christina he'd been touching. Caressing.

Christina he'd held in his arms. Whose lips brushed gently over his skin. Who whispered soft words so close to his ear that even her breath aroused him.

But then everything had gone to shit and he'd realized that immortality wasn't a gift. It was a curse.

He was immortal. He was alone. And every goddamn day was torture.

He closed his eyes and clutched the railing, his hands clenched so tight that the rough-hewn edges of the stone cut into his palms.

Christina...

He reached out with his mind, searching for her as he did every night with equal parts dread and longing.

Sometimes centuries would pass before he felt her presence resonate through him, sometimes only decades.

It had been two hundred and sixty years since the last time he'd found her, her energy reaching out to him even from across the Atlantic, even though she never had a conscious memory of him, or even of herself.

He'd gone to her—and once more, he'd done what he had to do.

Since then, he'd grown complacent, expecting—no, *hoping*—that he would not feel her. That he would not find her out there in the world.

That he would not have to go to her yet again.

Christina...

Nothing. Not even the slightest tingle of awareness.

Thank god.

He breathed deep, relieved, and slowly let his body relax. He turned to go back inside, but the moment he did, everything shifted. The force of her essence lashed out, catching him unaware.

It surrounded him. Burned through him.

Hot. Powerful. Desperate.

And close.

This time, she was close. So close that it wasn't just her essence that filled his mind, but *her*. The memory of her scent enveloped him, the sensation of her skin against his, the taste of her lips, of her flesh.

Oh, god. Oh, Christ.

He sank to his knees, wanting to run. Wanting to retch.

But he could do neither. And slowly—so painfully slowly—he stood.

He would do what he had to do, the same as he had done over and over again for millennia.

He would find her.

He would allow himself one moment to look at her.

And then, goddamn him, he would kill her.

Want to learn more? Visit the Dark Pleasures page at my website:
http://juliekenner.com/jks-books/dark-pleasures/

Delicate Ink

Did you enjoy this selection? Why not try another romance from Fated Desires?

From New York Times Bestselling Author Carrie Ann Ryan's Montgomery Ink Seires

On the wrong side of thirty, Austin Montgomery is ready to settle down. Unfortunately, his inked sleeves and scruffy beard isn't the suave business appearance some women crave. Only finding a woman who can deal with his job, as a tattoo artist and owner of Montgomery Ink, his seven meddling siblings, and his own gruff attitude won't be easy.

Finding a man is the last thing on Sierra Elder's mind. A recent transplant to Denver, her focus is on opening her own boutique. Wanting to cover up scars that run deeper than her flesh, she finds in Austin a man that truly gets to her—in more ways than one.

Although wary, they embark on a slow, tempestuous burn of a relationship. When blasts from both their pasts intrude on their present, however, it will take more than a promise of what could be to keep them together.

Find out more in Delicate Ink. Out Now.

Did you enjoy this selection? Why not try another romance from Fated Desires?

From New York Times Bestselling Author Carrie Ann Ryan's Dante's Circle Series

Humans aren't as alone as they choose to believe. Every human possesses a trait of supernatural that lays dormant within their genetic make-up. Centuries of diluting and breeding have allowed humans to think they are alone and untouched by magic. But what happens when something changes?

Neat freak lab tech, Lily Banner lives her life as any ordinary human. She's dedicated to her work and loves to hang out with her friends at Dante's Circle, their local bar. When she discovers a strange blue dust at work she meets a handsome stranger holding secrets – and maybe her heart. But after a close call with a thunderstorm, she may not be as ordinary as she thinks.

Shade Griffin is a warrior angel sent to Earth to protect the supernaturals' secrets. One problem, he can't stop leaving dust in odd places around town. Now he has to find every ounce of his dust and keep the presence of the supernatural a secret. But after a close encounter with a sexy lab tech and a lightning quick connection, his millennia old loyalties may shift and he could lose more than just his wings in the chaos.

Warning: Contains a sexy angel with a choice to make and a green-eyed lab tech who dreams of a dark-winged stranger. Oh yeah, and a shocking spark that's sure to leave them begging for more.

Find out more in Dust of My Wings. Out Now.

Charmed Spirits

Did you enjoy this selection? Why not try another romance from Fated Desires?

From New York Times Bestselling Author Carrie Ann Ryan's Holiday Montana Series

Jordan Cross has returned to Holiday, Montana after eleven long years to clear out her late aunt's house, put it on the market, and figure out what she wants to do with the rest of her life. Soon, she finds herself facing the town that turned its back on her because she was different. Because being labeled a witch in a small town didn't earn her many friends...especially when it wasn't a lie.

Matt Cooper has lived in Holiday his whole life. He's perfectly content being a bachelor alongside his four single brothers in a very small town. After all, the only woman he'd ever loved ran out on him without a goodbye. But now Jordan's back and just as bewitching as ever. Can they rekindle their romance with a town set against them?

Warning: Contains an intelligent, sexy witch with an attitude and drop-dead gorgeous man who likes to work with his hands, holds a secret that might scare someone, and really, *really*, likes table tops for certain activities. Enough said.

Find out more in Charmed Spirits. Out Now.

54705862R00173

Made in the USA
Lexington, KY
25 August 2016